Can I Give My Stepkids Back?

About the Author

Born in 1982 in the South of France, Aurélie Tramier is the author of a very successful debut novel and has recently published her second book. She has extensive international marketing experience and lives in Munich.

AURÉLIE TRAMIER

Can I Give My Stepkids Back?

Translated from the French by
Deniz Gulan

HODDER

First published in the French language as *Peindre la pluie en couleurs* by Editions Marabout in 2020

First published in Great Britain in 2020 by Hodder & Stoughton
An Hachette UK company

1

A CIP catalogue record for this title is available from the British Library

Paperback ISBN 9781529356861
eBook ISBN 9781529356854

Typeset in Plantin Light by Hewer Text UK Ltd, Edinburgh
Printed and bound in Great Britain by Clays Ltd, Elcograf S.p.A.

Hodder & Stoughton policy is to use papers that are natural, renewable
and recyclable products and made from wood grown in sustainable
forests. The logging and m
conform to the environme

Hodd
C
50 Vic
Lor

ww

FOREWORD

Morgan

Paris. January 2000

This is it. The nightmare is finally over. I shall leave my past behind in this room, like a snake shedding its skin. With any luck it'll be rolled up into a ball and thrown in the rubbish with that ghastly green gown they made me wear.

I get up, although I know I shouldn't. I'm unsteady on my feet yet I can't bear the thought of "waiting a while" as instructed. Every minute feels like an hour. I need to escape before my mother turns up. After all, it's my right. I signed all their papers, complied with their rules and now I'm out of here. I put on my baggy dress, leggings and backpack: standard camouflage for a student wallflower hoping not to be noticed. I open the door and slip out without glancing back.

I creep down the corridor. My old life is in that room, but I must look confident or I'll attract attention. This place is huge and there are countless people coming and going, so hopefully I won't stand out. Besides, they're in the middle of a shift change. I've just seen the evening staff arrive. Perfect timing. I know how things work here at the hospital; I used to visit my father in his office as a kid. Plus, I wasn't here for very long. The new shift doesn't even know I exist.

The door slides open. Free at last! It was easier than I thought. The wind and rain lash against my face as I pull up my hood. This is the new me: purified, unblemished, stripped of the past. I try to banish the memories but feel an overwhelming desire to look back at the vast white sarcophagus I left behind, to engrave its image in my mind forever. I can't locate my room amidst the hundreds of tiny squares. Somewhere up there is my seventeen-year-old self. Abandoned for good.

No! I need to forget and turn the page, a brand-new chapter, a clean slate. First, I shall get as far away from here as possible. I've already bought a ticket to Vietnam with my savings for after I turn eighteen. Then no one can tell me what to do or where to go. Yes, run away, so I no longer see my own reflection in my mother's sunglasses or have to contemplate my emptiness in my father's absent gaze. And most of all to avoid glimpsing my pitiful self in my sister Emily's hazel eyes. I'll miss her, but I can't tell her I'm leaving. With me in Paris and her in Marseille, she won't suspect a thing. I'll call her when I arrive; she'll forgive me. She knows how it is between Mum and me and she'll welcome me with open arms when I'm back. I would trust my dear sister with my life. She is just fifteen years old and incredibly pretty. In fact, she's just perfect. I sacrificed everything for you, Emily, and I pray you will never find out. Isn't that what a big sister does? Protect her little sis? You were always Mum's favourite, but I want you to know that from now on I no longer exist for Mum. The coast is clear, as it were.

I'm caught in the downpour. Too bad—a bit of rain won't kill me. And so what if it did, anyway . . . The wind and rain jolt me back to life. An accordion player loiters on the pavement singing. He smiles at me as if I'm a good person and treats me to a few notes of Edith Piaf.

> *The blue sky may fall in upon us*
> *And the earth can also crumble*
> *It matters little to me since you love me*
> *I don't give a damn about the rest of the world . . .*

That's funny, I don't give a damn about the rest of the world either. The difference being that no one loves *me* apart from my sister. Now I'm tearing up. I'm seventeen years old and my life is just beginning. Here's me, dropping out of university and going it alone with no one by my side. Except my little sis. I'll never let anyone control me again. I must get my act together; reach for the stars; follow my dreams. I'm running away now but, who knows, I might come back one day and become a vet or even a dog breeder. After rain comes shine. Isn't that what they say?

I hardly make it up the six floors to the box room that a uni friend has lent me while she's away. I deliberately planned it this way to avoid running into my mother. My legs wobble like jelly. I slam the door and flop onto the bed with a huge sigh of relief. I pull out a book from under me. It's *Electre*, the tragedy by Jean Giraudoux I read recently. I can't hold back my nervous laugh. This is a bad joke, right? My mother hasn't killed anyone ... nor have I for that matter. I flick through to the last page. I remember it well. The palace is burning, and a woman just stands there watching it burn. She even goes as far as philosophizing about it:

"What do you call it when the sun rises like today, and everything has been spoiled and decimated, and yet the air breathes, and all is lost, the city is burning, the innocent are slaughtering each other, and the perpetrators languish in a corner of the day that's breaking?"

And a beggar replies:

"It has a beautiful name; it is called the dawn."

To hell with beggars, wannabe philosophers, and accordion players and their love songs! I fling the book against the wall and collapse on the bed, sobbing quietly, as I tell myself, "Now I'm *really* going to start living."

17 YEARS LATER
JULY 2017

I

Elliot

I won a gold medal in athletics today at camp. Mum and Dad will be proud of me. Cesar was the fastest sprinter, but I was the best long-distance runner. I did ten laps! Juliette did very well too. She won the girls' medal and I won the boys'.

Poor Lea was eliminated right away but she didn't care. She was happy to stand on the sidelines with the little ones, cheering and clapping us on. One of the instructors gave them some fluorescent pompons to wave in the air. She did her big, sad puppy dog eyes to try to get some too and it worked! No one says no to Lea, not even the horrible dinner lady at school. She's the only one who gets second helpings of dessert! The little ones were great, waving the pompons around in the air, and Lea even got them to cheer me on, yelling, "Go Elliot go, you're the best!"

When I won, she flung her arms around my neck saying how proud she was of me! Lea's so much fun. Nothing gets her down, not even losing. When she's happy, I feel happy too.

"Bye Elliot, I'm off now," says Cesar. "Are you coming next week?"

"No, I'll be on holiday," I reply.

"Where are you going?"

"Bavaria. My dad's German. We go there every summer, to stay with my grandparents. Do you live in Maisons-Laffitte too or are you just here for camp?" I ask.

"We just moved here. I'll be starting at Jules Ferry when term starts."

"Me too! Year Five!"

"Cool!" he says.

I like Cesar, it'll be fun to see him again. I wave goodbye. It's three o'clock. Mum and Dad said they would be here early. We break up from school today for the summer holidays. They can leave work whatever time they like as they don't have a boss. They are solicitors and love their job. They spend their whole day shuffling files around and writing their names on pieces of paper.

When Mum signs my exercise book it's like she's doing artwork, a bit like Picasso, the famous painter who draws the mouth in the hair, the nose between the ears, and the eyes in the back of the head. We learnt about Picasso at school. With my mum it's the same. You can't see her name, but she insists it's there: *EMB: Emily Mercier Bauer.*

It's three thirty. They should be here soon. Mum hates packing. It takes her forever. As for me, I won't take much, just a sweatshirt and my Bayern Munich tee-shirt. Everything I need is at Oma Annett and Opa Georg's house. Lea insists on taking all her dresses with her, and Dad won't leave without his canoe. Our luggage will be full to bursting and Dad will say, "What on earth have you got in here?" It's the same every year.

Lea asks when Mum and Dad will be here. I tell her soon. She goes off to play with Louise a bit longer.

It's four o'clock and Benji's parents have arrived. He says bye and congratulates me on my win.

An ambulance whizzes by, then another. The noise is deafening. Lea puts her fingers in her ears. And there goes a police car, it must be serious. Mum always says how dangerous this road is: you can't see very well with all of the trees lining it.

Where on earth have they got to? I'm fed up with waiting. I fiddle with the medal around my neck, impatient to show it to Dad.

Sebastian, the instructor, calls over to me. "Elliot, can you give me a hand folding up the bibs please?"

"Okay," I shout.

He asks if I enjoyed my week at camp. I tell him yes but it went too quickly and I can't wait to come back next year.

"Your sister seemed to enjoy herself too," he says. "Weren't your parents supposed to get here early?"

"Yes," I reply. "They must have been held up at work or in the traffic. Mum will be in a bad mood if she doesn't have time to pack our cases. We're leaving tomorrow morning."

"Don't worry," he reassures me. "You're not the only ones left, and we won't be closing for a while."

It's five o'clock. Lea is getting bored: all her friends have gone home. She helps Sebastian stack the chairs. The ambulance whizzes past in the other direction. Then another, followed by the police. Lea puts her fingers in her ears again.

They're *still* not here.

This is so unfair. They're probably bogged down in their paperwork and haven't noticed the time. Mum and Dad are fantastic parents but when they're working, they forget about everything else. I even remember one evening when the headmistress had to phone Mum because she'd forgotten to pick us up. She hadn't noticed the time. Mum is a bit like Lea, very laid back. When there's a problem, she often just laughs.

It's a quarter to six. Augustin is the last one to leave. Sebastian pats me on the back, telling me not to worry, they'll be here soon. He knows I'm dying to show them my medal.

That's when Lea jumps up.

"Hey Morgan, what are *you* doing here?" she cries.

Mum's sister? What is *she* doing here? It's not like her to come all this way from Paris just to pick us up from camp . . .

And today she looks even weirder than usual. My heart starts pounding.

Lea rushes to hug her. Morgan smiles at Sebastian. Morgan never smiles at anyone. That's how it is in our family. My mum Emily laughs all the time and her sister Morgan is permanently miserable. It looks like she's glued a fake smile onto her face with Pritt Stick and it's going to fall off any minute. Morgan gently pushes Lea away, runs her hand through my hair and asks to speak to Sebastian in private.

I start to feel a bit sick.

Lea and I stay in the playground but I peep through the window and see Morgan in Sebastian's office, taking out what looks like her passport. She says something and Sebastian goes white and grabs the phone. I fiddle with my medal. Morgan turns around. I can see she is crying. I knew her glued-on smile wouldn't stay on long. I don't know what's going on but somehow I know I should take Lea to the swings at the other end of the playground. My heart keeps pounding and my legs are shaking. I can still hear the sirens in my head.

No, please, not that . . .

Lea jumps onto a swing. "Hey, come on, Elliot, I want to reach the sky! Look, I'm swinging all by myself, up and down, up and down. I want to go higher and higher."

A police car pulls up outside the school gate. A man gets out, says hello, and disappears into the office. I feel like I'm on the edge of a diving board—the high one that scares me—and have just been pushed off. I tumble down and down, with no end in sight, like Alice falling down the rabbit hole.

Lea is touching the sky while I'm plunging deeper and deeper down . . .

Lea calls for me to push her.

I can't breathe. The medal is choking me; I rip it from my neck and toss it to the ground. I jump when I feel a hand on my shoulder. It's Morgan. Her glued-on smile has fallen off.

And I just know ... I watch Lea swinging higher and higher, left right, left right, like a clock pendulum.

Up and down. Up and down.

I'm frozen to the spot.

Up and down. Up and down.

I look at Lea.

Up and down. Up and down.

My heart beats like crazy. Why can't Morgan just go away? I can't get the sirens out of my head. I wish I was as far away from here as possible.

"Elliot. There's been an accident. I'm taking you both back to Paris with me."

I stare into Morgan's eyes. They are light blue and so pale that I can almost see Mum and Dad in them. Mum's choc-olatey-brown eyes. Dad saying, "Hey, champion!" Mum who laughs everything off with, "It doesn't matter." Dad who runs his hand threw my hair telling me, "It'll all work out son." I carry on looking at Morgan. Her lips are quivering, and her eyes tell me I will never see Mum and Dad again. The ambulances were for them ...

I hear Lea's happy cries in the distance.

"Look Elliot, it's the moon! I can touch the moon!"

2

Morgan

Today started out just like any other day at the nursery. Well, almost . . . One of my colleagues was off sick, so I had to help dress and undress the little ones. And since then I haven't had a minute to myself this morning. I'd give anything for a nice cup of tea with a splash of milk; I've got that delicious ginger tea that Emily gave me. I breathe in my orange scented candle, the one I light when I answer my messages. I wish I was in my big armchair right now, my haven of peace. Though I'm technically in charge, it doesn't mean a lot. I'm only the manager when time permits, meaning when I'm not busy lacing up twelve pairs of tiny shoes onto two dozen tiny feet.

"Please don't put lace-ups on them," I tell the parents at the start of each term. But my plea always seems to fall on deaf ears. You can be sure that out of twenty-four shoes, there will be one that's gone missing, either lost or put on Zoe instead of Lola. Of course, Zoe refuses to part with it, has a tantrum and rolls on the floor. I run to fetch her cuddly toy and dummy to entice her to give the shoe back, and Cinderella springs to mind: the part where the two sisters are fighting over the glass slipper, screaming.

"It's mine!" cries Zoe.

"No, it's mine!" screams Lola, grabbing the shoe, and then it somehow ends up in my face.

The calm after the storm. I'm crouched in front of Zoe and she's trying to be helpful, standing still and pulling up her pink trouser leg. I show her the left shoe and she gives me her right foot. It's the same scenario each time. I gently tap her left leg, waiting for her to catch on. But unfazed and serene, Zoe is still perching on the wrong leg, an unflappable flamingo in pink sequined leggings. I wait and my loud sighs attract the attention of Viviane, who is struggling with Jules's trainers.

"Ah, the famous flamingo theory!" laughs Viviane, coming to my rescue. "Stands on one leg but never the right one. A child will never give you the right leg, no matter how many times you ask. Like the buttered toast that always falls butter-side down."

It's almost four o'clock by the time the children are ready to go in the garden. Luckily, it's July. Imagine what it's like in January, when you have gloves, hats and scarves to put on them as well! Amara and Nadège join us in the cloakroom with six other toddlers and they file out into the garden. I'm relieved to get back to my office. It may be sweltering, but the silence is golden. I open the window to the sound of the farmyard-like clamour below.

"Zoe," cries Nadège, "let go of Clara's plaits please!"

I breathe a sigh of relief. Though small, my office is my refuge amidst this infant turmoil. It may be right next to the cloak-room, but at least it's all mine. To brighten it up, I brought some cushions from home and photos of my sister Emily, her husband Niko, and their children, Elliot and Lea. Not to mention countless pictures of my beloved beagle, Snoopy, who I've had for seven years now. My poor darling, he must be roasting at home. I open my desk drawer and pull out an old magazine article featuring an exclusive kennels for sale just outside Paris: my dream job. I hardly need to mention that my salary wouldn't cover it. Besides, I'm not an expert on dog care. I trained as a nurse but should have been a vet.

I missed my vocation. But I'm not brave enough to start all over again at thirty-five.

I put the article back with the other remnants of my broken dream: dog home brochures, photos of Snoopy, a magazine on beagles, old job offers in veterinary clinics and the collar of my last dog, Droopy. I only had poor Droopy for three years; he got run over by a reckless driver. The culprit was never found. I was devastated. I stroke the metal name disk then slip it back into the drawer. The chaos outside seems to have eased. The heat must have made them drowsy. I can hear Amara and Nadège talking and giggling hysterically.

"Did you see Morgan trying to get Zoe's shoes on?"

"She really has no idea how to handle them, it's crazy! I thought she was going to throw a fit."

"What about the other day, when she was desperately trying to hand Jules to you because his nappy needed changing. What, change a nappy in a nursery? She wouldn't sink so low!"

"I can't fathom her out," adds Amara. "She must be the only nursery manager in the whole world who can't stand children!"

"You're too hard on her, girls!" says Viviane, trying her utmost to defend me. "As manager her role is to take care of admin and medical matters. I may be good with children but I'm disastrous with paperwork. Morgan's job is to manage the finances and deal with the parents, not to change nappies."

Try as she might to defend my cause, she is quickly outnumbered. A Greek tragedy springs to mind, in which I'm the sad heroine: an Antigone imprisoned in her office for not having been blessed with maternal instincts. I close the window. Better to be in a furnace than listen to that lot. I always hoped to become a vet and ended up running a nursery instead. I worked my socks off to get here though. I trained as a nursery nurse, then had a few years of hands-on experience before becoming deputy manager in a large nursery. I finally became manager of this nursery five years ago. Any dreams of becoming a vet fell by the wayside.

Despite the overwhelming heat, I could still do with a cup of tea, and put the kettle on. The parents will be here soon. I start to tackle the admissions I have to finish for the end of August. No matter how often I insist on the importance of submitting a complete application, half of the documents are always missing. So, who do we have today? Due to a cancellation, a certain Jean-Michel Rollin has just obtained a place in September for his daughter Alice. Up to now, Alice had been looked after by a childminder in La Villette, but now they live in Clichy. I detect a separation behind this move. The mother's name doesn't feature anywhere, another tricky situation. Father's profession . . . he works in a funeral parlour of all places; an undertaker, that bodes well! I hope he'll pay attention to hygiene and keep his macabre stories out of the nursery. I'd better deal with this promptly. The nursery closes in two weeks' time and all applications must be processed before then. I leave him an urgent voice mail.

Thank goodness it'll soon be the holidays! The heat is stifling. I reluctantly open the window. The farmyard clamour has ceased, though I prefer that to vicious gossiping any day. I'm so looking forward to the summer break. I'll finally be able to take Snoopy on some really long walks. Emily is leaving for Bavaria tomorrow to stay with her in-laws. I'm a bit sad she's going. Having her nearby is reassuring. She did invite me along but being around kids all day is not my idea of a holiday. Elliot and Lea are sweet children but they are still *children* and make far too much noise and commotion for my liking—especially Elliot, who is a football fanatic! I can always see them for lunch when they get back to Maisons-Laffitte. We can go for a nice long walk in the woods and Elliot can play ball with Snoopy. Meanwhile, time will drag till Emily's back. When we were teenagers, my sister and I were so close. We didn't leave each other's side the whole summer. We would spend our days on the beach in Marseille or in La Ciotat, from sunrise till sunset, sharing secrets, having fun, giggling and messing around. The blond and the brunette, a bit like Snow White and Rose Red. We wreaked havoc. We looked so different no one could tell we were sisters! Emily was Mum's favourite, the spitting image of her except for the eyes. I was the one who inherited our mother's blue eyes. I didn't care that Emily was her favourite. I was just happy to be me. Besides, I had a friend for life in my sister. I took care of her and pampered her. I nursed her when she was sick; I worried when she didn't come home on time. Then when I grew up and left home, and me and Mum drifted apart, it was Emily who was always there for me. No questions asked. So yes, I'd do anything for her. Except go on holiday with her kids.

Suddenly my mobile rings, startling me.

"Hello, Ms Morgan Mercier? This is Maisons-Laffitte constabulary. Are you the sister of Emily Mercier?"

"Yes, I am."

The sky is so blue today. But down here my world has fallen apart.

I hang up.

The noise around me resumes: children's cries, birdsong. The sun beams down. The earth is still spinning, but my heart has stopped.

I get up and leave in a daze, only to return to grab my bag. I blow out the scented candle. I tell my colleagues there has been an emergency. They are still gossiping about me. I somehow make it to the train station, walking blindly, on automatic pilot. I dive into the first train heading to Maisons-Laffitte. My phone vibrates: it's my mother. She is still in

Marseille but is taking the next train to Paris with my father. She is in floods of tears. She begs me to fetch Elliot and Lea and have them for the night. "Please don't be frosty with them, for your sister's sake!"

My mother has always considered me heartless. In fact, right now I am. My heart is in smithereens and the pieces have fallen to the bottom of my cup to be rinsed out with the tealeaves when the cleaner comes.

I get off at Maisons-Laffitte station and run frantically down the street, eyes glued to Google Maps. I finally arrive at the leisure centre. I put on a brave face and go in. I catch sight of Elliot. Then Lea is running towards me, calling my name.

"Hey Morgan, what are you doing here?"

3

Elliot

I was too hot all night and had a horrible nightmare. Mum and Dad were leaving forever to live on Mars and had left Lea and me alone in the woods with just a suitcase, a packet of crisps and the inflatable canoe. We can't use it without the pump though so we have to get to Oma and Opa's house and they can blow it up for us. I toss and turn. I can hear Lea snoring, humming like an insect. She's been restless all night too: it must be the heat. I'm sweating so much that my eyes won't open, they feel like they're stuck together. I'm back at the swimming pool. I jump off the diving board and tumble down and down, never reaching the water.

What's that scratching at the door? The floorboards creak, then I hear a clicking noise. It sounds strange, we don't have wooden floors at home. I suddenly feel something warm and heavy on my feet and stretch out my arm. It's Snoopy!

If it's Snoopy then I can't be dreaming. It must be true.

The medal at camp. Mum and Dad not arriving. Lea swinging higher and higher, touching the moon. The police car parked in front of the school gates. Morgan, Sebastian, the diving board and Morgan's eyes telling me Mum and Dad had gone forever. I start falling again until I open my eyes. It hurts so much . . . I wish the pain would stop.

"Snoopy, come here."

I lift up the sheet and the dog slides in next to me. I cuddle him. He stares at me with his big black eyes and starts licking my hand. It's all sticky but who cares. I bury my head in his fur to drown out my sobs so Lea doesn't hear. It's comforting to feel the dog next to me, even if it makes us both even hotter.

Lea calls out to me and sits up on the sofa bed where she spent the night. She looks as rough as I feel. When Morgan came to fetch us and told us about the accident, Lea didn't understand what had happened. She even tried to comfort Morgan on the train, telling her it would be okay and that Dad would look after Mum because he's strong. I didn't feel brave enough to explain. So I just said no, it's not going to be okay.

Lea grabs the cushions from the sofa and throws them on the floor. "I hate these cushions, they're scary!"

I see what she means. One of them has a big snarly wolf on it and on the other one there's a bear and a stag—at least *that* won't eat us. She slips into bed beside me, on my mattress on the floor. We're squashed in tightly like sardines and Snoopy clambers over us to get in the middle. Lea points at his eyes, saying they have a ring of black at the bottom like Mum's when she puts her make-up on. Snoopy falls asleep on us. Lea tries to pull out his whiskers and peel off his nose to see if they're real. He doesn't mind. Then she points at the curtains. "Look, it's like a forest, with the wolf and the bear again. Morgan likes scary animals. Have you been here before?" she asks.

I say maybe once or twice but I can't really remember. Then she asks if we're still in Paris, and I tell her that Mum used to call it "Les Batignolles" but I don't know where that is.

Suddenly Lea notices all the books around us. There's a big bookcase against the wall, with a small desk next to it with a computer on top. Mum gave Morgan so many books. I look at the titles; there are lots of children's stories, though I suppose that makes sense because Morgan does work in a nursery. *Tales of Perrault, Peter Pan* and even *The Legend of King Arthur*, a story I can't wait to read. And I've just spotted Lea's favourite book: *Where the Wild Things Are.*

When I show her, she snatches it from me. "Come on Snoopy, I'm going to read you a story," she says.

She reads quite well even though she's only six. Snoopy looks content. I carry on sifting through the books. There are quite a few boring ones that I've never heard of. Then I look at Morgan's collection of DVDs and CDs. She even has some old black vinyls, like Grandpa Paul's. I show Lea that there are two doors, one on each wall. "That's Morgan's room. And that's the living room. So we must be right in the middle. Let's explore while Morgan's still asleep."

We quietly open the living room door and Snoopy follows us. Lea feels safer with him there in case a monster jumps out. In here the curtains are open and the sky is bright blue. I'd forgotten it was still summer outside. Lea covers her eyes. I blink hard until I can see at last. We're beside a window.

"Look how high up we are!" whispers Lea.

What a view. We're on the top floor and can see for miles. There are no houses, just a park opposite, a railway track on the left and in the distance, some blocks of flats. I whisper to Lea that it's like being in a treehouse at the very top of a tree and the city is the jungle. "Look, there's a playground in the park opposite with a roundabout, see? And there's a train going past. We're right next to the station. Let's pretend it's a huge river with piranhas in that we can't cross!"

"No, that's too scary," protests Lea. "I don't like piranhas."

"Hey, look, our forest!" I say, and show Lea the miniature trees standing on a table, each in its own pot, beside the large window overlooking the balcony.

"They are so sweet; I've never seen such small trees before!" she says. "They would make a great forest for my Playmobil. But you'd have to put little pebbles in so they don't get lost." Lea then takes my hand and holds it tightly. "Let's pretend that we're lost in the forest too. And that Mum and Dad come and find us."

I jump, and Lea lets go. There's a noise coming from Morgan's room. We quickly tiptoe back, watching out for witches hiding in the bonsai tree forest and the wolf cushion snarling on the floor. I press my ear to the door. Morgan must have dropped her phone while talking to someone.

"Mum? Mum? Are you still there?" I hear her say.

She's talking to Grandma Cat! I would love to be in Grandma Cat's arms right now with my head on her stomach like a big soft pillow. She is so much fun. She wears loads of jewellery, has a really loud voice and always waves her arms around madly when she speaks. When she doesn't like something, she just comes out with it, like the time she asked the baker if he had made his bread with cat wee! Grandma Cat and Morgan do nothing but argue. Mum says they are like cat and mouse—worse than me and Lea. Apart from their blue eyes, they don't look anything alike. Grandma Cat is round and Morgan is skinny. Grandma Cat is dark-haired and tanned, and always has sunglasses perched on the end of her nose, while Morgan's skin is whiter than a ghost—even her hair is white—and she hates the sun. Mum really loved her older sister, though I don't know why. I find her weird. Mum always stood up for her when she had fights with Grandma Cat. Grandpa Paul just used to keep out of it.

I can't bear to think about Mum right now, it hurts too much. I try to concentrate on what Morgan is saying. She sounds upset. I hear sniffles, she must be crying.

"Are you serious Mum? You *are* joking? How dare you say such a thing? How could I have known that? Do you really think I would have asked Emily to give me custody of the children? Me of all people?"

After that, there's silence. Then something smashes against the wall.

4

Morgan

"So, you're taking them away from me too? I knew you were good for nothing much, but taking my grandchildren from me . . .?"

My mother knows how to strike right where it hurts. She has it down to a fine art. I didn't call her back. Having to face her in the cemetery is bad enough. And I won't respond to any of the insinuations she'll reel off once Dad's back is turned.

Here we are, all of us, side by side in the pouring rain, grief-stricken, trying to hold back the tears. I hold Lea's hand. I wish she would take my mother's hand, rather than grip mine so tightly. Lea may be adorable, but I can't do this. Why did Emily leave her children to me? I shudder at the thought of her pleading for paper and pen in the ambulance to note her final wish. Niko wasn't spared that extra time but Emily knew she was dying. It must have taken her last breath to make this request, but she knew what she was doing. Unstoppable. No doubt my mother will do everything in her power to get custody of the children but it'll probably be a year or two before the courts decide. I'm still stunned by my sister's decision. Why didn't she save her last breath and focus? Hold on? I would give anything to have her with me still.

Elliot is hanging on for dear life to Snoopy's lead. It's hard to tell who is pulling who, but he insisted on bringing Snoopy along. The dog's presence comforts him, so I agreed. I get it;

Snoopy has been a big comfort to me in the past. Besides, Lea did bring her cuddly toy. Next to Elliot is Niko's father, Georg. He is mumbling something in German, which I don't understand. He has just aged ten years, a mountain of a man reduced to crumbling rubble. He clings to Elliot's arm and Elliot clings to the dog's lead.

We slowly march forward, like an army of emperor penguins in our black attire. We make our way through the sea of graves in silence. My life has fallen apart. Or fallen apart *again*, I should say. Each time I start to get my act together and really build something for myself, everything comes crashing down like a house of cards collapsing. I walk with robotic precision. Lea holds my hand tightly. She may be very sweet, but she's still a nuisance. I can't believe Emily's gone. I feel numb. The undertakers guide us through the stone jungle to our family tomb. My father's ancestors were residents of Paris. Now they're residents of Batignolles cemetery, a mere stone's throw from my apartment. It took twenty-five minutes for us to walk here in the rain. We all trooped here together: Elliot, Lea, Georg and Annett, my parents and me. We walked past the carousel in Batignolles square, where the plastic horses were parading morosely, and the ducks were turning in sad circles. The few passers-by didn't appear to notice us.

So, this is where I say goodbye to my little sister, my best friend and confidante, my constant driving force and source of unconditional love. The one person to whom I could have told everything. Yet didn't. The one person I loved, who knew when to stay silent and when to listen. The mother I never had.

The ceremony comes to an end. We need to leave and get the children out of this depressing forest of gravestones. My Great-Aunt Josephine hobbles up to me and grabs my arm.

"Your sister made the right choice, I'm pleased for you," she says. "I can see your mother doesn't agree, but *you* know how to handle children. Besides, you're young. Between you and me, we all know that Catherine isn't all there. In her family all the women end up losing their marbles in their seventies. Plus your father has his prostate problems. Who knows how much longer he'll be around! Sorry to be so frank, but I call a spade a spade. Entrusting them with two young children would have been irresponsible."

I scan my shoes, then count the pebbles on the ground, unsure how to reply. My silence only seems to encourage her.

"And what's more these children were born here. We can't just uproot them and pack them off to the countryside!"

My dear Great-Aunt Josephine . . . The hardened, eighty-five-year-old Parisian, who believes that civilisation ends once you cross the Paris ring road. My thoughts turn to Corniche Kennedy, my parents' apartment with its balcony overlooking the ocean. I remember swimming in the sea, the winter sky, storms raging over the Chateau d'If. Memories of growing up in the mistral wind. Such happy times, till the day it all shattered. If I had children and something happened to me, I would like them to live there. Beside the sea, I mean. Not with my parents.

"You're right," I say, deciding not to hold back. "My parents' place doesn't even have running water, but they wouldn't want you to know that. Believe me, I was raised there. Life in sunny climes isn't all that it's cracked up to be. Plus the nearest school is twelve miles away. Not the best conditions for raising kids. Not that the residents of Marseille have any."

"Oh, really? I never understood what made them leave Paris," Josephine mumbles, limping off.

The undertaker comes to lay the wreaths. Lea's grip tightens when she sees his big round face and thick black beard. He looks at me as if he understands what I'm feeling. He seems decent enough. I am tempted to stretch out my arm so he can pinch me really hard and tell me that this is some sort of sick joke and that I'm going to wake up. And my sister will appear from behind the gravestone, everyone will jeer at me, shrieking, "She fell for it, she fell for it," and start clapping. And the kids will be able to go home. Please . . .

The undertaker walks towards me and my heart beats faster.

"Ms Mercier," he says, offering me his hand, "my name is Jean Rollin. I know this is not the time or the place, but my daughter Alice just got a place in your nursery for September. I recognized your name from the paperwork in my office. Please accept my sincere condolences." He glances towards Elliot and Lea, who have crouched down to stroke Snoopy and pick up pebbles. "Take good care of the little ones, they are such a gift. I can see there is bad blood in your family, but keep the kids out of it. It doesn't concern them."

I can't think of an appropriate response. We leave the cemetery in the rain. Elliot drops the small pebbles onto the road. Lea hugs me. "Auntie, your umbrella must have holes in it, it's raining on your cheeks!" she says, as she dries my tears with her hands.

When we get back to the square near my apartment building, Annett finds the energy to make an unusual suggestion. "Come on children, let's go on the carousel!"

"Yippee!" cries Lea.

"No, you're crazy . . ." mutters Elliot, a serious look on his face.

"It's not up for debate, on you get!" Lea orders.

Lea jumps onto a swan. Annett straps Elliot onto a motorbike and scrambles onto a horse, to the astonishment of the fairground attendant. Georg hands me Snoopy's lead and selects a proud steed. The attendant loses his temper and shouts at Georg to get off right now as he is too heavy.

"I'm sorry," stutters Georg, "we little speak French."

The fairground attendant stares at us all, in turn, perplexed. Observing our sad faces and the rain dripping from our hair, he finally presses the on button with a shrug and sends us galloping round. I can hear him grumbling from here. Georg clowns around while Annett cries, "Faster, faster!" And even Elliot is smiling. My parents and I watch them, frozen to the spot.

"Hi Grandma Cat, hi Morgan!" the kids call out.

I wave. Lea tosses her head back, chuckling. Elliot shouts to his grandfather that he's going to overtake his ridiculous horse.

Round and round they go, laughing in the rain.

My mother blows them a kiss.

Round and round, laughing in the rain.

My father waves to them.

Round and round, laughing in the rain.

We get dizzy watching them.

The horses finally come to a standstill. Lea throws herself into Annett's arms showering her with kisses. I stand there in awe of such grace and simplicity. Children make loving look so simple.

Annett takes them off to go and jump in the puddles. However hard I try, I'll never be like her . . .

When we reach my apartment, Annett comes to my rescue. "If it's any help to you, Georg and I can take the children for three weeks. That will give you a bit of time to get organized. It was the plan anyway and to be honest, it would be a great comfort to have them with us for a little while."

What a relief. Three weeks! Three weeks in which to learn how to be like Oma Annett. Mission impossible . . .

5

Elliot

Dear Mum,

Oma Annett gave me a cool notebook with Tintin on the front. I couldn't wait to start writing in it. I love writing, remember? I want to be a journalist when I grow up, as you know. So when I got this notebook, I thought of you. Oma said it would do me good to tell you all my thoughts. Maybe she's right.

At first, it was weird being here without you and Dad. Then Lea reminded me that we came here on our own last summer and we should just tell ourselves it's no different. Lea is so brave, way braver than me. There are times when it hurts so much that I tell her to quickly put on her swimsuit and we go swimming right away. We then jump into the lake from really high up, holding hands, screaming, and then it feels better. Oma and Opa are so kind to us. They are doing their best to give us a lovely time, so we try to smile a lot to please them. We know how hard it is for them too as Dad was their only child.

It's so much fun here, you would love it. Oma and Opa have rented a house for the summer. We swim every day and even go canoeing. Opa bought an amazing canoe. Dad would have been green with envy. Don't worry, we do wear life jackets! Lea is terrible at it, she doesn't understand how to hold the oars, but I love it. Her swimming is getting better though. I tried to teach her the crawl, but she goes under every time. Yes, I will be careful, promise!

Yesterday we played football with Opa. He is almost as round as the ball! We made him run so much that he turned bright red like a tomato. I actually thought he was going to explode! He even promised me that one day he would take us to see Bayern Munich play. It would have been nicer to go with Dad, but that's how it is.

I'm sticking a postcard onto this page. I bought it yesterday when Oma took us to visit the castle of a mad king. They say this king slept by day and lived by night. He even built a hut in his garden for a wooden bed, with wolf skins hanging every-where (real wolves, can you imagine!) and a baobab tree right in the middle of the garden. I would love to have stayed there a few nights, hiding under the furs, just long enough to forget. When I came out, the weather was nice, you could see the sun, the forest, the mountains. We ran through the park and found lots of dandelion clocks. Oma picked one to blow and told us to do the same, while making a wish. You are meant to blow it all away in one go. As we really, really wanted our wish to come true, though we knew it wouldn't, we blew at least fifty each. Lea was so bad at it that she ended up with a mouthful of dandelion fluff. It was so funny, Mum! We started laughing all three of us! I had almost forgotten how to laugh. In the end, there were so many dandelion clocks flying around that we lay down in the grass with Oma, watching them floating up to you and Dad in heaven. When we stood up, I could see Oma drying her tears. I pretended not to notice and took her hand.

I want to stay here forever. I don't want to go back to Morgan in Paris. Nor does Lea. She doesn't like the scary animal cush-ions. Plus we'll have to go to a new school … Mum, I know how much you loved your sister, but she really is strange and miserable. Oma said you made the best choice for us. But Grandma Cat seems angry about it. She wants to take us back to Marseille with her. I'd like that too. She calls us every day you know, while Morgan has only called us once or twice. But at least she is young like a mum. I guess that is why you chose her. There's less chance of something going wrong. I mean even in fairy tales children never lose their parents AND their auntie.

I must go now, Lea's waiting for me. I promised I'd teach her how to dive. And then we'll go play in the cabin that Opa built. I look after Lea, you know, and at night I sing your lullaby to help her fall asleep.

Twinkle twinkle my little star,
I wonder where the sweet dreams are.
Up above the world so high,
Time to close your big brown eyes.
Twinkle twinkle my little star,
Dream sweet dreams my pretty Lea.

She loves it. You should see her face, she does her big panda eyes.

Well, maybe Oma was right. I feel better after telling you all this. Give Dad a big kiss for me up in heaven and tell him I love him. Love you too Mum. Lea and I miss you so much.

Elliot

6

Morgan

The first days of August are always unbearably hot. My office is an oven, and I'm roasting like a joint of meat. I've spent all my time here since the children went to Oma Annett's. I work from seven thirty in the morning until eight at night. It calms me. I feel safe in these four walls, cut off from the outside world and my thoughts.

My phone beeps: it's a text from my mother.

I can come up the last week of August if you like. The nursery reopens soon, what will you do with the children? Love, Mum

For once, I appreciate it. To be honest, I hadn't even thought that far ahead. Everything has happened so fast. I'm on holiday for three weeks from this Friday and I'm planning to stay in Paris. I'll be alone for the first couple of weeks and then the children will be back around the 18th and we'll spend a week together before I return to work. My mother will judge and criticize me as usual, but I need her help this time.

Good idea. Thanks. Morgan

It's a battleground in the cloakroom as the girls prepare to take the tots into the garden. Shoes on, squeals, screams, hair pulling, laughter, tears, in other words *real life*. I'm still hiding away in my lair. I would love to just withdraw from the outside world. There are very few children in the nursery this week, about fifteen at the most. The other children are on holiday, so the staff won't be overworked. Viviane leads the procession of infants out into the garden, followed by Nadège and Delphine. Amara and Josée stay with the children who are napping. I can hear the animation outside, the creaky see-saw and the squeaky slide. I close Jean-Michel Rollin's file. Done. I just need to mark it with today's date. I search for the stamp. That kind-eyed giant rattled me, unwittingly putting his finger right on the problem. I have no desire to see him again, nor listen to his candour, but his file has been accepted by the administration so we will be welcoming his daughter Alice in three weeks' time.

The stamp is nowhere to be found. I open my desk drawer and catch sight of the red plastic folder containing my dream job, the exclusive boarding kennels. No point in opening it. I grab the stamp, complete the file and go on to the next one: Valerie Le Gall and her six-month-old son, Lucas. I get up to make some tea.

Down below the party's in full swing. It's so hot that the girls have brought out the inflatable paddling pool. It's perfect when we only have a small number of children like today. The little ones squeal with joy as they're undressed down to their nappies. I hope the girls have thought about sunscreen.

I can hear the water filling the pool. Cup in hand, I go to the window. I must admit they do look extremely sweet, standing in line, waiting their turn. Those cuddly pink toddlers who have no idea that they will grow up one day. Viviane sprays them with the hose, and Delphine and Nadège supervise them as they go in and out of the pool. They are chatting and my ears prick up when I hear my name.

"Morgan? She won't cope with her nephew and niece, that's for sure. It's not that she's unkind or anything, but she has zero compassion."

"She's so gloomy all the time! I find her really depressing."
They burst out laughing.

"Can you lend me a hand please?" Viviane interrupts.
"Do you not think that such a situation would make anyone
depressed? Some people are depressing even without all of
the problems she has to deal with!"

She hands them towels to dry the children. They carry on
their malicious gossiping regardless.

"At least she'll finally realize what we do every day, taking
care of so many small children, day in day out. She has absolutely no idea what it's like!"

"Maybe it'll make her a little less obsessive."

"She'll give us all a bonus at the end of the year, you'll
see!"

The tea suddenly scalds my leg. Damn! I was so upset by
what they said that I spilt it over myself, though boiling tea
hurts less than their malicious words. Who the hell are they to
judge me? Do they really think my life is so idyllic compared
to theirs? My hermit-like existence thrown into turmoil by
two confused orphans? Do they think that only children cry?
I've just lost my sister for God's sake! Can they not see that
I'm grieving and have no one to console me! Why do they
think I spend over twelve hours a day here? Just to see their
ugly faces? This time they've gone too far. I storm out intend-
ing to confront them. When she sees me coming, Nadège
suddenly goes quiet.

"What were you talking about? It was obviously very
amusing," I say, casually.

Silence. I look at Viviane.

"Can I see you for a few minutes? I'm sure Nadège and
Delphine can cope without you, if they concentrate on what
they're doing."

I leave them to mull this over. Viviane and I go upstairs.
What do I want with her? No idea. I just want the jabbering

to cease. I open my office door, searching for an excuse. Viviane stands there, waiting, looking surprised.

"Err. I'm going to need you, Viviane, you know, to head up the team. I really trust you, and from September onwards I'm going to have a lot on my plate."

"I'm sorry, Morgan," she says, visibly relaxing. "No one has dared say it to you, as you haven't said anything yourself, but we were all devastated to hear what happened. I'm here should you need me to do any extra hours. My boyfriend doesn't get back till late in the evening, so I'm flexible. You can count on me."

I thank her. Outside, the children are still laughing. Nadège and Delphine start gathering them up before the parents arrive.

"When are they back?" Viviane asks me.

"Who?"

"The children?"

"In two weeks' time."

"Do you need any help?"

"With what?" I ask, distractedly.

"I don't know, with getting things ready . . ."

Getting things ready. Those words irritate me. I divert my gaze from her big soft eyes, her white freckled skin, her sweet smile and wavy hair. She's waiting for me to answer. My mind goes blank. "To be honest, I don't know where to begin," I say. "I live alone, you know . . . I'm rather a solitary person, I like my own space, I'm not . . . err, do you have children, Viviane?"

"No," she says.

I tell her that children love her and that she is a natural with them. I offer her some tea, which she accepts. It's the first time I've asked a member of the team to join me in my office for a cup of tea. She is too polite to remark on it though. The staff normally get together in the meeting room for their breaks. I switch on the kettle and allow myself to sink comfortably into her warm gaze. Exhausted, I can't even think straight.

"How are you going to prepare for their return?" she asks me, gently.

"No idea," I confess. "What do I need to do? Schools are closed now so I'll register them at the end of August. Given the exceptional circumstances, I doubt there'll be a problem. They'll have to sleep in my study. There's a sofa bed and a mattress on the floor."

"Ah, you need to get down to IKEA rather promptly then," she says.

"Can you see *me* assembling an IKEA bed?" I retort.

She laughs and says no but I shouldn't worry as there is an assembly option. I say good, as I wouldn't even know how to use a screwdriver.

"Get two beds from IKEA," she says.

"What about the rest?"

"You need to jazz up your apartment a bit, get them some eye-catching kids' stuff, like *Cars* or *Snow White* duvet covers for example. How old are your nephew and niece?"

"Lea will soon be seven I think . . . And Elliot is ten. I feel more at ease with my niece. I'm not so sure about Elliot. Boys are difficult," I reply.

"Hmm, ten, in that case *Cars* might be a little too babyish for him. How about *Batman* or *Star Wars*? Will you be able to pick up a few things from their house, clothes, toys, etc.? I know you probably won't want to go there, but you must. Just don't let them go with you. Do you have the key?"

I nod.

She offers to lock up the nursery and tells me to go now, the earlier the better.

Viviane doesn't wait for my reply and heads back down. The kettle is still steaming. I forgot to serve her tea. Out of habit I open my desk drawer. I despondently take out the magazine article about the boarding kennels. I grab a match from the box next to my candle and set fire to it in the sink. Another pipe dream gone up in smoke. I grab my bag and dash to the station.

Maisons-Laffitte, late afternoon. I cross the town and the park in the sweltering heat; it's scorching. The outline of the house looms in the distance. It's painful seeing it. My hand is trembling so much that I can hardly get the key in the lock. I tell myself to be brave, then take a deep breath and slip inside, like a thief. I mustn't look at anything, mustn't break down, and mustn't think. I grab two large suitcases from the cupboard and dart towards the children's bedrooms. I open their cupboards and grab boxes of Lego and board games from Elliot's room, and Barbie dolls and Playmobil from Lea's. I seize handfuls of tee-shirts, underwear and socks, and bundle them all up. I catch my breath, as if I had stopped breathing for the last twenty minutes. My legs are shaking. I look down and avert my eyes from the smiling cuddly toys of a happy little girl, from Elliot's football dreams taped to the wall, and from all traces of their shattered childhood. I drag the two suitcases down the hallway as if I had lead weights attached to both feet. I don't know how I'm going to get them home. But I don't have a choice. It's surprising how much inner strength you find in times of adversity.

My sister's bedroom. My heart and feet stop in sync. I push open the door, and everything becomes a blur. I imagine Emily making her bed that morning not knowing that it would be the last time. Placing her book on the bedside table, kissing Niko, Elliot and Lea reaching up to kiss her too. Happy at the thought of their imminent holiday and their picture book happy life together. I notice a piece of jewellery on the desk. It's the golden shamrock I bought Emily for her last birthday. I tiptoe towards it. Why am I tiptoeing? Who am I disturbing? I snatch the chain and put it around my neck. *Emily, give me courage please.* I notice some rotting flowers in a vase in front of the window. Common sense suddenly takes over. My father stopped by just after the accident to pick up some stuff, but I guess he didn't think to throw them away. I take down the suitcases and pick up a bin bag from the kitchen, and empty the fridge of rancid butter, mouldy vegetables, decaying meat. I take the dead flowers out of the vase and tip the water down the lavatory. I take out the rubbish, slam the door behind me, without looking back, laden like a mule and overwhelmed with grief. A young man, on his way to the station like me, offers to help. I accept, without looking at him, muttering a quick thank you. Tears are rolling down my cheeks.

As soon as I get home, I order two single IKEA beds with the assembly option, even if it does cost an arm and a leg. I put my sofa bed up for sale on eBay and start frantically searching for a *Snow White* duvet cover. For Elliot, was it *Cars* or *Star Wars*? They have both, but I can't remember which one Viviane suggested now. Come to think of it, the red of *Cars* would clash less with my colour scheme, but next to the purple and blue of *Snow White* it'll be eye-watering. I take a deep breath and tell myself to get on with it. I confirm the contents of my basket and press *Buy now*.

7

Elliot

Morgan is a neat freak. All we've done since we got here is tidy, tidy, tidy . . .

"Can you clear away your Lego, please?"

"Can you make your beds?"

"Roll your socks into a ball so they don't get separated."

"Your toothbrush is on the floor, you know it belongs on the sink!"

"Why are your underpants under the bed, don't you know where the laundry basket is? Follow your sister's example, come on, it's not that difficult is it?"

She's chased after me with her stupid vacuum cleaner all week. As well as the big one that rolls with the long wire, she also has a tiny one that she uses when she notices any dust. And she even polishes the TV. It must be contagious because even Lea has started playing with the broom. Everything has to be just perfect. Lea says that's how Morgan likes it.

I told Grandma Cat about it last night on the phone. It was nice to speak to her. I love her voice, it's so cheerful and warm. And I love how she pronounces words, in a long, drawn-out funny way. I can see her in my head, with her big cushion-like tummy and dark glasses. I can almost hear the sea down the phone.

"Morgan is *obsessed* with tidiness," says Grandma Cat. "She always has been but she's even worse now. She's never lived with anyone except her dog, so she doesn't know what mess is. Besides, she's never at home because of the long hours she works, so her apartment is like a museum. But don't worry my angel, you won't be there forever. Would you like to come and live with us in Marseille?"

"I would love that," I reply.

"You'll have to be patient a bit longer my angel, it's just a question of time. Your mum thought she was doing the right thing, but . . ." her voice trembles and she coughs. "Grandma Cat will take care of it, promise. Meanwhile, do as Morgan says, tidy up and don't annoy her. Don't make her angry with you, that's the last thing you need. Did she tell you I'm coming next week?"

My heart leaps with joy, like a huge ray of sunshine that has just brightened up a cloudy day.

"No!"

"Typical. I arrive on Sunday. I'm going to spoil you rotten my darlings! Morgan goes back to work then, so it'll be just the three of us. We'll do lots of naughty things and *not* tidy up! I can show you your new school too."

"Love you Grandma Cat," I say, before hanging up.

Neat freak. Neat freak. Neat freak.

I throw myself onto my brand-new *Cars* duvet cover. It was nice of Morgan to buy us something, but *Cars* is so babyish. I would rather have had *Star Wars* or Harry Potter. Sitting on her bed with Snoopy on her lap, Lea is excited about the old doll in her arms. "It was Morgan's when she was small. Isn't she pretty!"

I ask her why she doesn't play with it as she doesn't have her dolls here.

"I wish I could, but she won't let me. She doesn't want me to break it."

"What, and stop her from playing with it?" I ask.

"No," she says, "it reminds her of when she was small so she wants to keep it . . ."

"That's rubbish," I say.

I turn over, Lea looks sad. I try my best to give her a big smile. What can I do to cheer her up?

"I've just had an idea. What about bowling? There are loads of empty plastic bottles in the kitchen and we have the football that Opa gave me. And Morgan is in the bath reading, so she won't know!"

Lea's eyes sparkle. I tell her to shush so Morgan won't hear us. I line up the empty bottles in front of the window near the bonsai trees and explain the rules of the game to her. "We stand in front of the wall and then try and knock all the bottles down in one go, get it? But be careful not to hit the bonsai trees, okay?"

"Promise."

Snoopy joins us, wagging his tail. He loves my ball. It must be because he supports Bayern; this dog has good taste.

"One, two, three!"

I throw the ball and knock down seven bottles out of ten. Not bad for a first attempt. I run to put back the fallen bottles.

"Now it's my turn!" cries Lea impatiently.

She throws the ball too high and hits the bonsai trees. Crash bang wallop! One even falls on the floor. She's so stupid! We'll get into trouble now! I should have known she wouldn't be able to do it. And I hadn't even thought about Snoopy causing any damage. He throws himself on the ball, hits the table and knocks over a second bonsai tree. She'll kill us now!

"Elliot, what was that noise?" Morgan calls out from the bathroom.

"Err nothing, just Snoopy knocking over a book."

Lea looks terrified. I push her into the kitchen. "Quick, go and get the small dustpan and brush you play with all the time and sweep up the earth!"

The first bonsai is still in pretty good shape and just has a broken branch. I cut that bit off and chuck it out of the window. Let's not make a big deal out of a few leaves on a stick. With lightning speed, Lea sweeps up the earth and tips it into my trainers. I pick up the second pot and my heart starts thumping. "Oh no, it's broken, Lea, what are we going to do?"

She thinks for a second and then says, "Let's turn the pot around so she won't see the crack and we can put a bit of tape on to hold it together."

"Perfect," I whisper.

We place it back on the table and turn the pot towards the window. There's a large roll of clear tape on the desk. I cut some off and stick it over the crack. Morgan will be getting out of the bath soon. She will think it's odd if she can't hear us. Adults don't like it when kids go quiet. We need to hurry. I'll hide the ball inside the desk.

"Everything okay? Elliot, what was that noise?"

"Nothing," I reply.

"Nothing," adds Lea. "And we definitely haven't broken anything."

I stand on my sister's foot to make her shut up. Morgan looks at us with bewilderment and goes back to drying her hair.

8

Morgan

I've never been so happy to go back to work! I've really missed my office: no footballs, no toothpaste on the walls and no Lego in sight. My knee still hurts after kneeling on a piece yesterday as I helped Lea put on her sandal. Who would have thought that such a tiny object could cause so much pain! I was so angry that I threw it in the bin. Elliot shouted at me, saying that he couldn't finish building his space rocket, but that's his problem. It had no business being on the floor! I heard him rummaging in the bin last night. I shouldn't really have thrown it away. I'm so hopeless at this and keep losing my temper over stupid little things. But Elliot doesn't understand that you can't play football in a living room, you can't bowl in the hallway and you certainly can't race Snoopy up and down the stairs. The poor dog will end up breaking a leg. Why can't he just sit quietly colouring like his sister? I printed out some drawings for them to colour in. Lea was delighted but Elliot, well ... I'm actually glad my mother is coming. Who knows, this whole episode might end up bringing us closer together.

My office is a haven of calm. Even facing hordes of anxious new parents seems like child's play compared to what awaits me at home. I prepare myself for the onslaught of endless questions and just for fun imagine myself replying to the hypochondriacal mother, "Yes, she'll no doubt get cholera, I expect. And I heard the blond lady say her child has worms. Would you like me to keep his nappy for you so you can check?"

Or to the laid-back mother who is always "just" ten minutes late in the evening, "No problem, just be aware that from seven thirty onwards we serve soup to homeless drug addicts. You don't mind your daughter being with us, do you?"

Then there is the neurotic father who doesn't want his son to have his afternoon nap next to that child with the runny nose, "Okay, I'll put him next to the one with the tummy bug, then?"

And the arrogant academic who wants to know what sort of educational programme we have planned for the two-year-olds and how we intend to evaluate their progress, "This year we're working on Kant and the resilience concept. It's a bit ambitious but given how precocious they are, it shouldn't be a problem for them."

There's enough material there for a novel, I'm sure!

The first week back, the parents behave like model students. They arrive on time in the morning, shower their offspring with kisses, linger behind the door for ten minutes until the screaming subsides, then finally depart with tears in their eyes, arriving extra early in the evening. But there's always the odd exception. Valerie Le Gall, for example, who always manages to squeeze out ten extra minutes at the end of the day, once the adjustment period is over. This doesn't go down well with the team. Delphine has to pick up her eight-year-old daughter every evening at eight o'clock over on the other side of Paris. Nadège has to go home and make dinner for her mother. Amara helps her sister with her four children and the other assistants have their own lives outside of the nursery. Viviane seems to be the only one who is always available. The first week was hardly out before Valerie Le Gall became the latest hot topic at the coffee machine. Today at breaktime, the girls were so wound up that they didn't hide it from me when I came down to get a box of tea.

"Have you seen how stuck up she is? She doesn't even say hello or goodbye to us. Who does she think she is, the Queen of England?"

"Victoria Beckham more like. Six stone and teetering around on six-inch heels!"

"Yesterday she almost threw her son Lucas at me from her stilts. He was allowed one tiny kiss but no more as she didn't want her blow dry messed up. And she followed up with, 'I'm in a hurry, I'll be late for my meeting.'"

"The poor mite, it's not his fault. I gather there's no daddy. At any rate, he's not on the list of people authorized to pick him up—there's just the grandmother and one or two friends."

The chorus is interrupted by the arrival of a hearse blaring out loud music.

"That's discreet," I mutter.

"Look, it's the doting father!" laughs Delphine. "At least someone respects the adjustment period. He's come to pick up his daughter after her nap as agreed."

"I personally find him rather sexy," giggles Amara. "He oozes confidence and strength. And apparently he's single!"

"Are you serious?" exclaims Delphine. "Can you see yourself with an undertaker? Just the thought gives me the creeps. I heard his girlfriend dumped him."

Amara is no longer listening. She pretends to be the singer Dalida, belting out *Itsi bitsi petit bikini* at the top of her voice in time to the music coming from the hearse. With her hand on her chest, she then kneels in front of Delphine, and flamboyantly hands her a bouquet of imaginary flowers. The girls leave in a flurry of laughter, almost drowning out the music itself. Our team would certainly do well at karaoke. One thing's for sure: Jean-Michel certainly makes an impression. His outspokenness caused quite a stir at the parents' information evening. He responded to a stressed mother who asked about the activity schedule for the day by tapping her on the shoulder and saying, "Schedule! What schedule? Give your kid a break, he's not even two years old. Let him play, he's got his whole life ahead of him to deal with that crap!"

The poor woman looked at me, dumbstruck, her question forgotten.

The music stops. I hear a car door slam. I go and open the door for Jean-Michel. Outside of official hours, someone has to act as security. "Next time, would you mind keeping the music down while the children are napping?" I ask him, rather bluntly.

He takes a similar tone, "Are you saying I make more noise than the ambulances that race past here at all hours?"

I don't back down but tell him that I find it a little inappropriate to say the least, given where he works.

"Make no mistake, Ms Mercier," he replies, "undertakers live life to the full. You need to relax! After work I laugh, sing, play, chill out. Who cares what other people think."

"Well . . . I'll let you get your daughter," I blush.

This new term promises to be interesting. I return to my office. I can hear Jean-Michel tickling his daughter Alice in the cloakroom. The child has hiccups she's laughing so much. They drive off in the hearse with Dalida at full volume.

When I get home in the evening, I'm greeted by a triumphant Elliot. My mother has bought him a new box of Lego to replace the piece I threw away. Parenting is going great so far.

9

Elliot

"My poor babies! Luckily Grandma's here at last to spoil you. Morgan is far too engrossed in her work . . ."

It's true that Grandma Cat really does take good care of us. When she arrived, she took a look around. She saw our bedroom, our toys, clothes, everything. She pulled a face when she saw the beds and the duvet covers. "I can see she has made an effort, Emily would be pleased. You know, my darlings, Morgan doesn't have any children and she has no maternal instinct whatsoever, so we are going to have to teach her everything."

"But she works in a nursery," I say, surprised.

"Well, my darling, it's easy to read books on how to look after children, but until you have one of your own you don't know what you're talking about. Look at these shelves full of books! But there's no substitute for real life experience. It's all just theory with her. You don't become a parent until you can change a nappy."

"Why?" I ask.

"Never mind darling. Do you have enough toys here? I can't see many."

"Maybe we could go home and fetch some more?" I suggest.

Grandma Cat stops in her tracks. She starts coughing and gets her honey pastilles out. She can't fool me. I can see tears in her eyes. She quickly puts her dark glasses on, coughs again and says, "Well, actually it's a bit too far for me, sweetheart.

I'm not getting any younger. And to be honest, I don't know if I could face it. Grandpa Paul and Morgan will fetch your stuff from home later on. I promise we'll bring your things back here. I just don't think it's a good idea for you to go there. Oh, to hell with the cost, why don't we go shopping for some new toys and other bits and pieces. What else do you need?"

"I don't have a school bag!" yelps Lea. "The one I had in the babies' class is rubbish."

Grandma Cat says we can get new school bags after our appointment at the school. She sits down and takes out her crossword. I sneak up beside her. I like her wrinkled hands, long red fingernails, big black ring, round belly and dark glasses, which always end up either on her nose or on her head. She strokes my hair. I twist the laces on her chair cushion. She puts her pen down and looks me straight in the eye. "Did you want to tell me something, sweetheart?"

"Yes, Grandma Cat," I reply. "We did something naughty and we haven't dared say anything to Morgan yet."

I show her the bonsai and the Sellotape over the cracked pot.

She bursts out laughing and says, "You repaired it yourselves? Grandpa would be proud of you; you've done a great job. Does Morgan scare you that much? Don't worry, I'll take care of it."

I'm worried she might tell Morgan but she promises not to. She then looks at the clock and tells us to hurry or we'll be late for our appointment.

When I try to put my trainers on, I see that they are still full of earth. I completely forgot! Never mind. We charge down the stairs while Grandma Cat ambles down slowly, puffing and panting. In the square, children are shouting happily. We look at them silently. Grandma Cat finally appears. "I must say five flights of stairs without a lift is exhausting. I hope Morgan feeds you well at least?"

The school isn't far away. When we arrive, I grip Lea's hand tightly. Once we're inside, we see walls covered in paintings of scenes from fairy tales. We see *Little Red Riding Hood*. Grandma Cat explains to us that the school is named after Charles Perrault, the famous author of fairy tales.

"I hope we won't see the snarly wolf," Lea whispers in my ear.

A beanpole dressed in green comes towards us. It must be the headmistress. Even her eyes are green although not her skin, obviously. She's really tall and skinny, even skinnier than Morgan and that's saying something! Next to her, Grandma Cat looks like a hot air balloon.

"Do you think she's the magic beanstalk?" asks Lea, staring at her and looking bewildered.

I shake my head. The headmistress points to some children's chairs for us and offers Grandma Cat an armchair. "I'm Carole Dubois, the headmistress. I'm delighted to meet you all."

"Well, thank you for agreeing to see us only one week before term starts," replies Grandma.

"Given the situation, it's the least I can do," she says. "We will do our very best to accommodate your grandchildren. We are just a small neighbourhood primary, you know. But we are here to help you. I think it would be good if we met regularly to discuss how the children are settling in and assess their progress, what do you think?"

"I agree," says Grandma Cat, "but it won't be me, it'll be my daughter. *She* has custody of them, not me. I live in Marseille. I would have preferred to have them of course, but it was decided otherwise. Though the current situation may only be temporary."

"Ah . . . well in that case, I need to see your daughter as a priority," says the headmistress.

There are even paintings on the wall in her office. Lea points them out and we play guessing games. "Look at the little girl next to the spring giving water to an old woman," says Lea. "She's beautiful, she looks like Mum."

"I know," I reply, "it's *The Fairies*, the tale of the two sisters, the good sister and the bad sister! And there, look at that one. The girl with a basket and red cape."

"Too easy," says Lea, getting restless. She leans towards me, whispering, "I don't like it here, there are too many scary pictures on the walls."

I tell her to stop being silly as they are not real, they're just paintings. She's worried the headmistress could be a witch too and says she's sad because she won't be in the same class as her friends Louise and Manon. She starts sobbing. I do my best to comfort her and hold her hand. "Everything will work out Lea. And if the headmistress turns out to be a witch, well I'll throw her in the oven, I promise."

"You promise? But what about Manon and Louise?" she asks.

"We can go and visit them! I'll ask Morgan. And don't worry, you'll make lots of new friends here, you know."

We finish the tour of the school in silence, holding hands. Grandma Cat has so many questions that the beanpole headmistress doesn't pay any attention to us at all. She then gives us a list of school supplies to buy and grabs a small square tin from her desk. "It's snack time children, do you like gingerbread?"

Lea looks at me in horror. The headmistress smiles at her sweetly and says, "Don't worry, Lea, it's normal to be a little scared when you arrive at a new school, but your teacher is very nice, you'll see."

After leaving the school, Grandma Cat takes us shopping. She says that Morgan can get the stationery on the list and she'll buy us our school bags. My heart races when I see a

Harry Potter backpack, something my mum would never buy me. Lea grabs a horrible shocking pink satchel that looks like candy floss, with a huge fairy on the front. Grandma Cat looks at the price and pulls a face. "Maybe you could choose a different one my darling, this one is ridiculously expensive."

"No, no, no," whines Lea, "I want this one, the others are all rubbish."

Grandma Cat gives in. Lea *always* gets what she wants. We set off, proud of our brand-new school bags. When we get back, Grandma Cat starts packing. I don't want her to go. She hugs me tightly and whispers in my ear, "Don't worry, it's not for ever darling. Cheer up and trust me."

When evening comes, Grandma Cat rushes into the hallway when she hears Morgan's key in the door and knocks into the table with the bonsai trees on her way out. The cracked flowerpot falls and smashes into a thousand pieces. Morgan stoops down to pick up her treasured little tree.

"Oh, I'm so sorry," says Grandma Cat. "I'll get you another one tomorrow."

"Wow, did you see that?" Lea asks me, wide-eyed. "Now Grandma Cat will be punished, instead of us!"

10

Morgan

Saturday is finally here. My mother was a great help but let's be honest, I'm not sad to see her go. We did our best to avoid each other all week. We haven't seen eye to eye for so long now. During her visit, once the children were in bed, I would pretend I had urgent work to do and shut myself in my room. It's still too painful for us to talk about Emily's death. Any discussion about it would have inevitably ended badly.

Elliot is standing by the front door looking tearful. He insisted on accompanying Grandma Cat to the station. At least that way Snoopy will get a walk.

He hugs his grandma tightly on the platform. He can't see her tears behind her big dark glasses as he whispers, "I'm really going to miss you Grandma Cat."

"And I'm going to miss you both too, my darlings," she answers. "Why don't you come to Marseille for the half term holiday? I'm sure Morgan would pay for your train tickets."

"Yes, what a great idea!" I say, trying to feign enthusiasm.

That's my mother all over. I'm cornered. How can I say no now? Though quite frankly, I'm dying to have some time to myself. It will feel like an eternity until the next school holidays. But she should have asked me first. If I say no now, they'll see me as the wicked auntie, worse than the wicked stepmother in fairy tales. And of course she'll be seen as the doting, loving grandmother.

The train is about to depart, emotions are running high. Snoopy starts to bark and pull on the platform, Lea holds him back with all her might. I breathe a sigh of relief as the carriages pull slowly away. I can see a big tear rolling down Elliot's cheek and I pretend that I haven't noticed, to spare his pride. We enter the underground in silence, with Snoopy at our heels, and get off at La Fourche. We head towards the office supplies store to buy the items on our list. The place looks like Aladdin's cave, festooned with glittery school bags and pencil cases. When I was small, I used to love choosing my pens and books, unwrapping them and lining them up ready for the big day. I remember breathing in the chemical fragrance of the crisp new white pages of my exercise books and greedily sniffing the Pritt Stick. In contrast, my mother dreaded buying stuff for the new term after the summer. She would moan that the shop was overcrowded, the stationery overpriced and the weather too hot.

Lea tugs my sleeve, dragging me back to reality. I pick up two large baskets. We dive headfirst into a tide of parents and children looking for the best textbook protective covers. The treasure hunt is on.

I pull out two lists as long as my arm. I can't do this alone. "Come on Elliot, it would help if you could choose your own book covers and folders, and I'll take care of Lea's things."

I hand him his list, having taken a photo of it first with my phone, and put a basket on his arm. I then set off down the aisle with Lea. Elliot says he'll race us. The one who gets everything in the basket first is the winner. Ready, steady go!

Easier said than done. The day before school starts back, the office supplies store is about as much fun as a commuter station in rush hour. To top it all, the list is never ending: three HB pencils for Lea, four for Elliot. Of course, they only sell them in packs of five. In that case, we'll have to take ten. Done! Ticked off. Three "large" glue sticks for Lea. What does that mean? They clearly state that it mustn't be fancy-coloured glue. Four small tubes for Elliot.

Lea interrupts me, saying, "Morgan, look at this ballet shoe rubber."

Damn, I've lost count. How many small tubes of glue again? How many large ones? Oh yes, four and three.

Lea repeats herself, "Morgan have you seen this rubber?"

"Lea, please, I'm looking for something! How many did I say of each?"

Too late: a tall lanky woman snatches the last packet right under my nose. I grab a special offer pack containing five large and five small tubes, one of which is pink and one purple, but never mind. If the teacher isn't happy, then I'll tell her to give me a list that doesn't resemble an encyclopaedia next time!

"Morgan, can I have this ballet shoe rubber? Say yes, please, say yes!" Lea is insisting now.

I panic when I see how full my basket is. How much is all this going to cost? And how many of these pencils will go astray in the first week? Honestly, I don't know how parents afford it. Plus my mother has just added the cost of three round trips to Marseille onto my bill, bang in the middle of the peak school holiday season.

Elliot appears, dragging his heavily laden basket. A bottomless pit of stationery. "I won!" he says. He is dripping with sweat and smiling proudly.

"Are you sure you need all that?" I ask.

"I have everything except the pink book protective cover and the 4 cm thick plastic pocket! I would rather die than have a pink book! So I took a black one instead," he replies.

Lea continues whining at me to buy her that rubber. I can't take it any longer. "Lea, honestly, I think that's enough don't you?" I snap.

She stubbornly brandishes the rubber under my nose. "Don't you think it's pretty? It's only four euros!"

"Four euros for a rubber! It's out of the question."

"Morgan!"

"Lea, I said no!" I holler.

I just can't get out of this store quickly enough; it's a gigantic oven full of rabid parents battling over glue sticks and crayons. I just want to get home and curl up on my sofa with a good book and a cup of tea, in silence, and daydream about how my life was before the kids came along.

Lea won't back down and stands there in the middle of the aisle, scowling with her arms folded. "No!" she says.

"No what?" I ask.

"No! I want this rubber. Mum would have said yes, I know she would. And so would Grandma Cat!"

A shopper turns round and stares at us unabashedly. This is not the Lea I know, normally so sweet that butter wouldn't melt in her mouth. I don't give in to her pleading. Besides, I'm not a bottomless money pit. I try to remain calm without backing down. "Maybe they would Lea, but from now on, *I'm* the one who decides, and the answer is no. Come on, we're going home!"

Lea stamps her feet and starts crying. She's no longer listening to me and starts shouting and screaming in the middle of the aisle. She then rolls on the floor; I still don't give in. I'm so ashamed. I close my eyes and let the basket fall to the floor. If only I could just disappear into a hole in the ground and never emerge.

"Please, Morgan, *pleease!*" she screams.

I hadn't even noticed that Elliot had sneaked off. Suddenly the tears turn into cries of joy. "Thank you! Thank you, Elliot! You're the best brother in the world. How did you pay for it?"

"Remember Oma Annett gave us some money? You bought sweets and cards with yours. Well I had some left over."

I open my eyes to see Elliot hugging his little sister, with a small plastic bag in his hand. Talk about taking the wind out of my sails. Elliot is the king of the castle, Lea the queen, and I'm the prize fool. I desperately rack my brains wondering how I can get my authority back. "Elliot, Lea, we're going to the grocery store. I want to get Snoopy some chocolate. The poor dog has been waiting outside for an hour!"

Lea asks if they can have some too. I tell her no, it's not good to snack between meals.

That's the best I could come up with: chocolate for the dog and not for them. It was clearly worthwhile all that time spent studying Françoise Dolto and child psychology. Plus you can't even give dogs chocolate. Elliot glares at me but doesn't dare get his money out. I finally hoist my two baskets onto the checkout and prepare for the damage. I can just about make out three figures on the receipt. Hopefully it's upside down and the zeros are before and not after the one. We finally leave the shop and Lea rushes up to Snoopy to show him her new rubber.

Elliot is delighted at having outwitted me. On the way home, he jabbers away, "Morgan did you know that sharks grow teeth throughout their whole lifetime?"

"No, great. Come along, it's going to rain," I answer.

"Did you know that octopuses have three hearts and nine brains? Crazy isn't it?"

"Yes, especially when you see how stupid an octopus is . . ."

"And did you know that owls can turn their heads 360 degrees? I read it in a magazine that Grandma Cat bought me."

"Incredible," I mumble.

I feel like I'm being interviewed for some wildlife documentary. We climb up the five flights of stairs while Elliot lists the many talents of the fire salamander. Exhausted, I dump my bags down and lock myself in the toilet. Elliot continues his banter from behind the toilet door. "Hey Morgan, the weirdest of all is the chameleon. It can see from all sides at the same time. Imagine that?"

"Amazing," I say, feeling sorry for myself. "My kingdom for a horse . . ." Or rather a book, tea, peace and quiet, or maybe some music. I go to the kitchen to switch on the kettle and listen to the rain outside. I go into the children's room to get my pile of records from the bookcase. Elliot is sitting on his bed reading his favourite magazine about strange wildlife facts.

"What are you doing Auntie?" asks Lea.

"I'm going to listen to some music."

"On that black thing?" she asks.

She wants to know how it works. "Ah, it's so funny. Is *that* a record? Can I choose one?" she asks.

I reluctantly show her the pile of records. She picks one out, humming to herself. "This one!"

"You know it?" I ask.

"No, but I like the cover."

"It's Barbara, one of my favourite singers," I say proudly.

"You mean like Babar the elephant?"

Lea watches me put the record on, amazed at this antique contraption. I can see in her face that she thinks I'm a hundred years old. I drift off to Barbara's dulcet tones, a cup of tea in my hand. I curl up in my armchair, grab a cushion and pick up the book beside me. I haven't even read one page in the last ten days. Normally I read one or two books a week. But with all the things I need to buy for the kids, I can already see my book budget disappearing, melting away like ice cream left out in the sun. Barbara's voice vibrates through me, as I savour her wonderful lyrics.

One day,
Or maybe one night,
Near a lake I had fallen asleep,
When suddenly seemingly tearing the sky apart,
And coming from nowhere,
Appeared a black eagle.

Peace, at last. I close my eyes. Lea is sat on a cushion chewing the ends of her plaits. Barbara's warm voice lulls me. My mind wanders and my thoughts turn to Emily. Emily, who could never understand why I loved this song so much. I submerge myself in each and every word, let my heart fill with the music.

"This song's rubbish."

I am jolted out of my reverie by Lea.

"This song's rubbish," she says again. "I don't understand any of it. And her voice is all sad and wobbly."

"No Lea, it's just that . . . well, it's a song for grown-ups," I reply.

"She's right, this song is well depressing!" shouts Elliot, from behind the wall.

Lea asks me to read her a story instead. Here I am, in my own apartment, not allowed to listen to my music. Okay. Hint taken. I abandon my book and put the record away. Welcome to my new life! Lea is already jumping around with a book in her hand. It's *Tom Thumb*. I'm not enamoured by her choice.

"Really? It's a grim story," I say.

She nods with a huge grin across her face. I begin to read:

"Once upon a time there lived a woodcutter and his wife; they had seven children, all boys. The eldest was but ten years old, and the youngest only seven. People were astonished that the woodcutter had had so many children in such a short time, but his wife was very fond of children, and never had less than two at a time."

"Ten and seven! Just like us! Hey Morgan, I'm going to be seven in September!" says Lea.

I nod and carry on reading. What a sordid tale. I had actually forgotten just what a chauvinist Charles Perrault was. In his fairy tales, all women are portrayed as silly wenches, witches, or just plain fools, and they all faint at the drop of a hat. Though I guess you *would* faint on discovering that your ogre of a husband has just slain your seven daughters. I slam the book shut.

"Lea, this is a gruesome story. Are you sure you want me to read it to you?"

"Yes!" she whines.

"It'll give you nightmares! Plus the author hates women; he does nothing but criticize the ogre's wife and treats all the women in the story as if they're idiots. I don't like it."

I close the book. Elliot says he'll read to her. He snatches it from me and says that I never like *anything*. His remarks are hurtful and humiliating. I don't retaliate. He's just a kid after all. Lea comes to my rescue, saying, "She *does*, she likes Snoopy!"

Some consolation! I get up from the sofa. *Tom Thumb* has stuck in my throat. It's seven o'clock. I'd better start making dinner.

I hear the end of the story from the kitchen. Elliot patiently explains the difficult words to his sister. "The 'moral' of the story is the end, Lea. There's always a lesson at the end of a fairy tale, which helps you to understand the story."

Lea is mesmerized.

"It is no affliction to have many children,
if they all are good looking, courteous and strong,
but if one is sickly or slow-witted,
he will be scorned, ridiculed, and despised.
However, it is often this little urchin
who brings good fortune to the entire family."

And they think Barbara is depressing! Time to serve our gourmet dinner: fishfingers and peas. Thank heavens for frozen food.

Only one day to go till school starts.

II

Elliot

Dear Mum,

It felt strange going back to school without you. You were always here for us on the first day of term to hear how it went. I liked that. So I'm going to tell you all about it now. Luckily, I like writing, as it's going to take a while.

On the first day back, Morgan took us. She picked us up at six o'clock too. She said she would pick us up every day but sometimes she may have to take us back to the nursery with her, if she has a lot of work. The nursery is not far on the underground. Lea likes going because of the babies. She would love to play with them. There is a nice lady there called Viviane. Lea helps her put away the cuddly toys and straighten the duvets on the little beds. She loves helping.

Right. Now it's my turn. A lot has happened this week. You will be a bit angry with me because I got into a fight with a boy at the new school and was told off afterwards. I won't do it again, promise!

On Sunday night before school started, I could see that Lea didn't want to go. When I asked her if she was okay, she said she was sad her friends would not be there and that she didn't like that school with its horrible scary paintings on the walls. So I had an idea. I let her choose her clothes for the next day, like you used to Mum. She is SUCH a girl. We took everything out of the wardrobe, and she chose her blue dress, the one with the big bows on the shoulders. She said you liked it and it's the one she wanted to wear. Then she asked Morgan if she could plait her hair for her in the morning. Morgan agreed, as long as we got up really early. Actually, Morgan is rubbish at doing plaits, but Lea doesn't tell her, as she doesn't want to hurt her feelings.

We got our school bags ready the night before, and I put our snack bars in. You always used to ask me to do it, remember? This time I did it on my own. Oma Annett called us just before we went to bed to wish us luck for the next day. So did Grandma Cat. But she calls us every day anyway.

When Monday morning came, we got up before the alarm went off. We stood in front of the school gates watching the other kids play and Lea whispered how happy the other kids looked. We just looked miserable standing there with our auntie.

You know, Morgan's skin is so white you can almost see through it in the sun. When she took Lea's hand, I could see that she had bitten her nails right down. Grandma Cat must have told her when she was small that nail biting is bad.

The other children started looking at us and so did the teachers. I don't like being stared at like that. But don't worry, we'll be okay. I like being the big kid at school, especially when I see the small ones in Year One who look like tiny beetles with their huge backpacks. It's a funny sight. Hey, you should see the amazing Harry Potter schoolbag Grandma Cat bought me; you would never have got me one like that!

At breaktime on the first day back, I found a surprise in my schoolbag. Lea had put a kiss bar in it, like you used to when I was small. A strip of paper with little hearts on, which you pull off one by one and hold when you feel sad. I pulled off a heart and squeezed it tightly in my pocket. Lea is so sweet, and never stops laughing, I don't know how she does it. When I asked her whether she felt sad sometimes, she told me that Snow White and Cinderella had no parents but were happy, so we could be happy too.

And now you are going to be mad at me because I got into a fight with a boy called Alex in Year Five. Thank God he's not in my class. He keeps bugging Lea because we're new. He pulls her plaits and steals her snack at breaktime, and on Thursday, just before lunch, he said something to Lea that really annoyed me. I don't know why really because what he said was more stupid than mean. He thought Morgan was our mum and said to Lea that she was so white, she looked like a panda in her black dress! I told him she wasn't our mum and that his mum was so fat she looked like a pig. Alex then called me a son of a bitch, so I punched him right in the face. It's the first time I have ever hit anyone, and it made his nose bleed. I called him an idiot and said that you were dead and that if he ever said it again I would smash his whole head in.

The beanpole (a.k.a. the headmistress) quickly came and took me into her office. I thought she was going to suspend me, but she was actually quite nice. She gave me a gingerbread biscuit and looked me straight in the eye saying that this must never happen again and that she didn't want any violence in her school. She said she knew I was going through a very difficult time, and that she would smooth everything out with Alex's parents and we would say no more about it.

That evening in bed, Lea gave me a big hug and she even sang your lullaby to me. I'm so lucky to have a baby sister like her. I would hate to be here on my own.

I'm sorry Mum. Hugs and kisses to you and Dad. Love you . . .

Elliot

12

Morgan

"Good evening everyone, I'm Morgan Mercier, I look after my niece Lea and my nephew Elliot, who is in Year Five."

Phew, it's over. I flop back down into my chair trying not to make eye contact with anyone, which isn't difficult as I deliberately took a front row seat. I can feel twenty-two pairs of eyes piercing my back. Running a marathon in mid-winter in a bikini would have been preferable to this parents' evening. I just don't fit in here. The chair is ridiculously small. I don't know how the other parents are managing to sit still for more than ten minutes. There's a father behind me who would have been better off taking two chairs for his oversized backside.

I can feel Emily and Niko's presence. The other parents know full well why I am here tonight instead of them. The teacher thanks me with a nod of her head and adds a touch of Disney-style charm to my speech. "Lea has just joined our school. I ask you all to give her your full support and kindness. Don't hesitate to invite her to your children's birthday parties; that girl is a pure ray of sunshine. I can see from her records that she will be seven years old in a few days' time. Would any of you like to bake a cake for the occasion? We shall be celebrating birthdays on the last Friday of the month and may I remind you that everything must be from the authorized list. So, no chocolate, no fruit tarts, no nuts, and of course, no sweets or fizzy drinks."

And this is meant to be a birthday? That's a joke. What does that actually leave, celery? Baking a cake for school appears to be incredibly complicated. I let the kids eat home-made chocolate cake at the nursery all the time. I mentally note to check on what date the last Friday of the month falls. Woe betide me if I forget the date, though I imagine Lea will remind me. I quickly glance behind me, managing not to catch anyone's eye. Lea and Elliot are busy playing in the book corner with another child whose parents couldn't get a babysitter. Good as gold.

I emerge from the meeting feeling overwhelmed by my new responsibilities and by the pile of textbooks waiting to be covered in plastic. I have to cover two for Lea and four for Elliot, for goodness sake! To top it all, Elliot hands me a list of additional items to buy: there's that 4 cm thick plastic pouch again, a 30 cm transparent ruler and of course the pink exercise book cover he didn't want. This last item is underlined twice. I'll deal with it tomorrow.

Once the children are in bed, I'm torn between Netflix and covering the textbooks. I'm rather tempted by Netflix but the scissors and roll of plastic are beckoning me. I have always been terrible at covering school books. I'm no good at cutting out either. My sister used to do both of ours. She already had a caring, maternal side to her, unlike me.

I grab the scissors, telling myself to get on with it, not to stab myself and to cut straight. Elliot will probably have the wonkiest book in his class. My crooked botch job will make him a total laughing stock. I cut the plastic and stick it down with tape. I think of Emily and how carefully she used to cut and tape. I remember us both at school, sat on the carpet surrounded by a pile of books. She would cover them, and I would pass her the tape. She used to make fun of me.

"So how will you cope when you have kids? You'll have to learn."

"Easy," I said. "I won't have any."

That was the intention anyway ... I close the book, and there's a nasty cracking sound. Blast, the plastic has just cracked all the way down the back of the book. I start again, cutting out and taping down, and close it shut. No cracking sound this time. But the corners have come unstuck, damn! *Emily, tell me how you did it, send me a sign!* The rebellious plastic begins lifting itself up from the book again. In a rage now, I tape the corner down hard, holding back my tears. *Emily ... Why did you do this to me?* I'd better start again. I pick up the tape and cut some off. Ouch! My finger is bleeding. I roll up the paper in a ball and hurl it across the room in anger. *Emily, why did you go? I don't care about these stupid books, but me, why did you leave me? You were all I had. And why choose me? You put me on a pedestal, which I didn't deserve. You always believed in me. But the truth is I am a hopeless sad old spinster who hasn't got a clue how to handle kids. I've never been good at it. There's so much I couldn't tell you, I was afraid you would walk away from me. I couldn't risk losing you, do you see? Please forgive me. I'm sorry for not telling you everything. I never imagined it would end like this, not even in my worst nightmares. And to think it was just a tree, a tree that took you from me. A mere tree.*

I break down in tears, my head resting on my forearms. Snoopy pushes my elbow off his nose. I didn't even see him there. *Maybe that's a sign from you Emily. I need a hug so badly. Thanks Emily.* I take my beloved dog's head in my hands and rub my cheeks against his. He licks my palms. I spring into action, bandage my finger, take a deep breath and get back to work. I glue the plastic directly onto the book. I know it's not allowed, but that's just tough. I'm not going to waste any more time on a geometry book. I hate maths anyway. It's never been of much use to me. I cover all the books then slip them into the kids' backpacks. Maybe Harry Potter and the pink fairy can use their magic to fix my disastrous handiwork.

I'm off to bed now Emily. I'll try harder next time, I promise. Don't forget I'm not you though, and never will be.

13

Elliot

I've got thirty-five marbles now. My old ones are still at home in Maisons-Laffitte, so my new friend Paul gave me two of his during the first week of school. I had to start all over again from scratch but have already won quite a few. I also found some in the playground. And the last five . . . well I didn't actually win them. That idiot Alex kept boasting about how many marbles he had and showing off to everyone, so I took some of his and now he's five down—serves him right. He keeps out of my way since I hit him. He didn't even realize I stole them from his bag while he was in the toilets.

"We're going food shopping for the weekend, Elliot," Lea calls out to me. "Morgan says we're going to make pancakes! Are you coming?"

I stuff the pouch of marbles under my mattress. Lea will never look there. I don't want her asking any questions or telling Morgan afterwards. I just have enough time to hide them before Lea bounds in all excited.

"No, I want to stay here," I say.

Morgan nods at me from the bedroom door and Lea runs down the stairs with Snoopy.

We've been here a month now and this is the first time I've been alone in the apartment. I don't feel at home here. I could try exploring, it might make me feel better. It's my sister's seventh birthday next Saturday and I still haven't got her a present. I only have five euros left from Oma Annett though, so I might ask Grandma Cat to give me some money. She never says no. I know Lea wants some elf Lego.

Morgan's bedroom door is wide open, so I go in. This room is different to the others. It's very colourful with lots of yellow everywhere. Strange for someone who only wears black. Her curtains have big grey elephants on them. And there is an enormous wooden elephant on the floor, which I guess comes from somewhere far away. I try to lift it. It weighs a ton.

I can't hear anyone on the stairs, so I continue exploring. Morgan's room is super tidy, of course; everything is lined up and spotless, with nothing lying around or on the floor. It smells of furniture polish. Suddenly there's a noise and I jump, but it's just me making the floorboards creak. I suddenly notice Mum's shamrock pendant on Morgan's bedside table and feel like I've been punched in the stomach. Morgan has been wearing it every day since we got back from holiday. She gave it to Mum. I have a sudden urge to pick it up, touch it and sniff it. It doesn't smell of Mum anymore. I put it back. I wish I hadn't eaten chocolate crunchies this morning for breakfast: I feel a bit sick.

The phone rings. It's probably Grandma Cat, as usual. I don't want to answer.

I try to open the drawer of the bedside table; it's stuck. I manage to pull out what's blocking it: a letter in an envelope with at least twenty other envelopes inside it. I've never seen stamps like these before; they are all really pretty with colourful pictures of flowers and birds. There's even one with a big green dragon on. That's so cool! It says "Vietnam", wow, that's the other side of the world! It's weird to hide so many letters in a drawer, like they're top secret or something. I know I shouldn't pry, but I'm dying to read them. The envelopes are all open anyway, so I'm not doing any harm just looking. I read the postmarks on the top ones; they're dated 2017, 2016, 2015.

I poke around a bit more in the drawer. The oldest one is from 2010. I open it and a photo falls out onto the bed. It's a picture of a little girl in a blue uniform, smiling. She has slanting eyes and black plaits. On the back of the photo it says *LINH, October 2010, Hanoi.* She looks about nine or ten years old. I open the letter, which is in French:

Dear Morgan,

    I began learning French in September. The teacher helped me write to you. Thank you for your letter and photo. I'm very happy to have found you. Thank you for everything you have done for me. Thanks to you, I have been able to start school in Hanoi. It's a long way from where I live, but it is my dream, even if I have to leave my little brother and my father behind. I will see them in the school holidays.

    Speak soon,

    Linh

I'm so startled by Snoopy barking on the stairs that I drop the envelopes. I scramble to pick them up and stuff them back in the drawer, keeping five of them, which I then run and hide under my mattress next to the marbles. I deliberately take the ones right underneath, so that Morgan won't notice they've gone.

"Elliot we're back!"

"Elliot! Look, we've bought some sweets! And they're not just for Snoopy! Come quick!"

I lie on my bed for a minute to make it look like I was there the whole time, then I join them in the living room.

"Were you bored without me?" asks Lea.

"No, why would I be?" I snap. "I was doing my homework."

Morgan is slicing bread in the kitchen. I'm curious to find out a bit more so I dive in. "Hey Morgan, have you ever been to Asia?"

"Yes. Why?" she asks.

"I was just wondering. Our teacher was talking about Vietnam in class. Do you know it?"

"I know it pretty well actually. I spent several months there doing charity work when I was eighteen. After that I travelled a bit around Laos, Cambodia and Thailand. That's where I bought the elephant that's in my room. Have you seen it?"

I pretend that I'd love to see it. I then ask her if she went alone and did Grandma Cat let her go. She said Grandma Cat tried to stop her, but she went anyway. I then ask her if she got into trouble. She says she was in Paris at the time and that Grandma Cat lived in Marseille. Then when she got back from Asia, she began training to be a nurse, and eventually Grandma Cat got over it. Morgan then tells me to go and have a look at the elephant.

I pretend to be really excited when I get to her room. I feel guilty at stealing five of her letters. This is the first time that Morgan has ever talked about herself to me. I really will put them back after, but I'm just dying to find out about the little girl and what's in the other letters.

The phone rings. Lea runs to answer it. "Grandma Cat!"

She shuts herself away in the bedroom with the phone, but I can hear her whispering about her birthday list, Lego and a Playmobil house.

14

Morgan

Six forty-five. The alarm goes off. Argh, already? Why do nights seem so much shorter than days!

I stagger to the bathroom. I like to get ready in peace before the children are up and the commotion starts. I start waking them, or rather *shaking* them, at seven fifteen. It's always a challenge to get them out of bed on school days. But on weekends, for some strange reason, they are wide awake at six thirty. Not being an early riser myself, it's a nightmare. Once they're up, things move quite quickly though; I don't have to dress them like the little ones at the nursery. We pick out their clothes the night before and then we're done. What I actually mean is that I choose Elliot's clothes as he couldn't care less what he wears, and Lea spends an hour deciding between her three dresses and two pairs of jeans. I'm going to have to get her some new clothes soon as she's had a growth spurt since the summer. Then there's the whole hairstyling routine of plaits, hair slides and bunches. I'm about as good at that as I am at covering school books, but luckily Lea is easy-going. I just make sure she doesn't look in the mirror afterwards.

This week has been hell. I spend my whole life racing against the clock and barely have time to breathe let alone think. Sometimes I even squirm for an hour in my chair before finally dashing to the loo; not wanting to waste even a single minute. I spend all day running around, from the nursery to the school to the underground, coping with this

grumbling father, that anxious mother and those over-
devoted parents. Not to mention Jean-Michel and his music,
Valerie Le Gall and her perpetual lateness, and the gossip
and jabber of the girls.

Thank goodness the week is almost over. I glance at my
calendar. It's already the 29th of September. The month has
flown past.

Lea can hardly sit still at breakfast. She seems to have ants
in her pants. Plaiting her hair is impossible when she's
wiggling all over the place like that. But Lea is far too busy
messing around to worry about her hair. I sense she is hiding
something. I would like to ask Elliot, but he has disappeared
into his room looking for something.

"Auntie, look, I'm wearing my best dress for today!"

"Yes, good. Look it's eight fifteen already! We'll be late!" I
say, distractedly.

"But Morgannn!" she pleads.

We grab our bags. Lea, sniggering, tells Snoopy one last
secret, and we run down the stairs. Then we file out, like the
tots at the nursery.

"Morgan. Stop!" cries Lea.

"Come on, we'll be late!" I try not to shout.

We make it to the school gates just in the nick of time, out
of breath and looking a bit ragged.

Lea stops, panting. "But Auntie, you've forgotten my
cake!" she wails suddenly.

How I wish that the ground would just swallow me up
right then and there. Of course, the cake! It's Friday the
29th of September. The last Friday of the month! I feel sick
to my stomach. How could I forget Lea's birthday cake?
Lea, the new girl, the one all the children stare and point at.
She doesn't have a mummy you know . . . I start trembling. I
thought we would be celebrating it tomorrow with Elliot
and Snoopy. Her actual birthday is the 30th after all. I'd

completely forgotten about the school celebration. I want to kick myself.

Lea picks up on my silence and starts crying on the pavement, without saying a word. This is the worst thing of all. I'm used to seeing kids throwing tantrums, rolling around on the floor, kicking and screaming. I do run a nursery after all. As long as they're yelling, they're probably alive, is my motto. But I worry a lot more about them when they go quiet. Overwhelmed with guilt, I try in vain to get myself off the hook. "Why didn't you say anything last night?" I ask.

"Because I thought you were going to give me a sss . . . surp . . ."

She can't finish her sentence. Tears roll down her cheeks, she chokes and sobs in despair.

Elliot looks daggers at me.

"Why didn't *you* say anything Elliot?" I say.

He shrugs his shoulders defiantly. I can see he is furious.

"How could you forget! Mum would never have done something like that."

Lea's sobbing resumes. I can almost feel the condemnation in the glances of the other parents as they watch us out of the corner of their eyes. *There's that terrible aunt who can't even bake a cake for her orphan niece's birthday.* Yes, the wicked stepmother has done it again. I wring my hands in despair. I'll be stuck all morning in a health and safety meeting, which I can't get out of. In desperation I ask Lea what time the party starts.

"I don't know," she mumbles. "In the afternoon I think."

"I'm so sorry, Lea. I really am. We'll have a party tomorrow, you'll see, you'll have a lovely present and I'll make you a chocolate cake, okay?"

Lea won't even look up. She frantically chews the end of her plait, her eyes glued to her wrinkled socks. I'm utterly hopeless. Elliot goes inside without speaking to me. The door closes behind them.

I haven't even had time to buy her birthday gift for tomorrow, but at least I hadn't forgotten. It's on my list, I had planned to buy it in my lunch break. But I have absolutely no idea what to get her. I frantically text my mother to ask for some ideas.

The hearse lurks in front of the nursery like a vulture stalking its prey. Jean-Michel is singing cheerfully in the cloakroom while he puts on Alice's slippers. Another parent arrives, carrying a large box that smells deliciously of lemon. Viviane greets me cheerfully, while I mumble hello and shut myself in my office. There's a knock at the door. It can only be Viviane.

"Can I come in?"

I shrug, which she takes to mean yes.

"You don't look too good, Morgan. Is there anything I can do?"

I can't even find the words.

She looks me right in the eye, like she does when she's scolding one of the infants. I hang my head and confess. "I forgot to make a cake for Lea's birthday party at school today. It's a nightmare. I left her crying her eyes out."

"Come on, it's not the end of the world! Go and buy one!" she says.

"I can't, I have an important meeting now. People from the council will be there, I can't possibly miss it."

She looks thoughtful and tells me not to worry about it any longer as she has an idea.

The meeting takes forever and the morning really drags. But it's over at last. I can't wait for them to go. It's one o'clock. Class resumes in half an hour. The odds of me finding a cake and getting to Lea's class in time are slim to none, unless a fairy godmother somewhere waves her magic wand.

But when I get back to my office, a wondrous sight meets my eyes. There's a lemon cake in a white box on the table. No chocolate, no gluten, and not a nut in sight, just as the school instructed. It's the most perfect cake in the world. There's even a number seven made out of Smarties on the top. It's slightly crooked, as if the number has been changed. There's a Post-it on the box:

There are two birthdays in the Dragonfly group today, which is one too many if you ask me. Half of the children here don't have teeth anyway, so why waste a cake on them. And it was a doddle changing the one into a seven. Enjoy!

I now remember seeing the mother arrive with the box this morning. I can't thank her enough. Actually, I'll never thank her at all come to that. What would I say? "By the way, I stole your daughter's birthday cake, thank you very much, it was delicious." I run towards the underground with the precious box under my arm. I beg the train to speed up and I eventually arrive at Lea's school, sweating. I ring the bell and give my name. The door opens. A tall thin lady welcomes me in; it must be the headmistress. She shakes my hand and leads me towards the classroom. Lea has just gone back into class. Her eyes sparkle with joy when I proudly hand the cake over to the teacher. I apologize for the delay and slip away, my heart thumping. I made it!

Not so fast. The headmistress is waiting for me in the corridor with a huge smile on her face. "Ms Mercier, I'm Carole Dubois, I run this school. I'm delighted to have met you at last. Have you got five minutes?"

I follow her reluctantly. I'm not used to this. As the manager, I'm normally the one who summons people into *my* office. I feel like a worried little girl about to be punished. And my punishment is swift in coming.

"Ms Mercier, I'm worried about your nephew and niece. Lea is not settling in well, and Elliot . . ."

"Yes?"

"Elliot's a little aggressive. There was an incident at the start of term, which I let go, but since then things have deteriorated. He often gets into fights. I do understand how difficult the situation is for you, of course. Most of all, I strongly believe that these children need lots of love and attention. Maybe we should try to see each other once in a while?"

"Absolutely," I reply.

I glance at my watch, aware of the time. I must get back to the nursery and I still haven't bought Lea's birthday present. I thank the headmistress for her concern. She lets me go.

My phone vibrates. It's a message from my mother with a gift suggestion:

A dinosaur of course! What else would a seven-year-old girl want!

Good idea, I wouldn't have thought of that myself. And with this new trend for gender-neutral toys, why not? I put my phone away. It vibrates again. I'll read the message later. I run to the toy store and buy the biggest and most impressive dinosaur I can find, which costs me a small fortune. Twenty euros for a plastic monster. Ridiculous. But if that's what my mother thinks Lea would like, then dinosaur it is. I grab some butterfly transfers and a kit for making bead necklaces, which reminds me of my childhood.

When I arrive back at the nursery, I read the message I missed. It's my mother again:

The dinosaur was obviously a joke. Get her some Playmobil.

Argh! How stupid can you get? It's not even my mother's fault; she sent the second message just two minutes after the first, probably feeling guilty about having set a trap for me which I literally walked right into. It's too late to change it now though. I'm back at the office. I'll have to get the children soon and due to the time I've lost today, I'll have to bring them back here for at least an hour.

I have no choice. I'll give Lea the dinosaur and face the music later.

15

Elliot

Lea is over the moon. "Thank you, thank you Morgan. Your cake was so yummy. Everyone loved it!"

I look at Morgan. How did she manage it? She was at work all morning, wasn't she? Sounds fishy to me. I'm still mad at her for forgetting Lea's cake but at the same time I'm happy that Lea got one in the end.

Morgan says we'll have to spend an hour at the nursery as she has too much work. As soon as we arrive, Lea hugs the freckled lady, who takes her to help tidy up a dormitory. I put my schoolbag in the cloakroom and pull out the book I took from Morgan's flat: *The Legend of King Arthur*. It's a huge book full of amazing pictures. I sit down on one of the tiny chairs in the entrance. I like watching people coming and going; I know who's who now. One of the dads is so tall, he has to bend over double to get in the door. One of the mums wears gigantic glasses. And I can hear the dad arriving in his funeral car. His music is so loud, you can hear him from the other side of the street. He's really funny. The same thing happens each time. He walks into the nursery singing or talking very loudly, and Morgan slams her office door angrily.

Here he is. I pretend to be reading. He looks pretty scary with that big black beard. And he works in a cemetery too, how creepy. If I wasn't at the nursery, I'd run away, but now it looks like he wants to speak to me.

"You okay, kid?"

"Yeah."

"Book any good?"

"Yeah."

"Do you know any other words apart from 'yeah'?" he asks.

That's how he is, straight to the point. I look up. "Don't know really, it's okay."

He carries on staring at me. What does he want? That I tell him how I *really* feel? Okay then. "It's not much fun actually, hanging around here, I'm waiting for my aunt. My sister's off having fun somewhere and I'm here reading a book . . . Oh, and my parents are dead. You get the picture?"

I don't know why I threw all that at him. He didn't ask for it. Maybe it's because he was at the funeral. He knows everything anyway. He crouches down in front of me and says, "Yeah."

"And tomorrow is my little sister's birthday," I go on, "and I haven't even got her a present. And Morgan, I mean my auntie, forgot to make a cake for school and it made Lea cry."

He puts his hand on my shoulder like the Big Friendly Giant. "Yeah."

"Don't you know any other words either?" I ask.

"It's annoying, isn't it?" he says. "Kid, for the birthday present, it's not that bad, you can always draw her a picture. As for your parents . . . You know it *is* possible to grow up without them. Believe me, it's not easy but it's possible."

I ask him if his parents are dead too.

"No. Yes. Let's say, as good as. They didn't want me. But there were other people who took me in and loved me as their own son and that's what matters. You see, there's always someone waiting for you. You just have to be patient. The most important thing is that deep down inside, you know that there are people who love you. You had your parents of course, there's your sister, and there's your aunt too."

"Yeah, right," I snap.

"She does love you. In her own way," he says, before disappearing.

Ten minutes later, he reappears with his daughter. He waves bye to me. Then his big black funeral car roars off, playing an Edith Piaf song that Dad loved. I know the words by heart. *The blue sky may fall in upon us . . .* The music fades into the distance. I stand there, the melody going round in my head. *No matter the problems.* What a joke!

I slam the book down and go and look for Lea. I find her in one of the bathrooms, sorting dirty towels with that nice lady. Everything here is minuscule, even the toilets. Lea is excited to see me. "Viviane, it's Elliot!" she shrieks.

"Hi, Elliot. What are you reading?" she asks.

I show her.

"Aha . . . Did you see there's a fairy named after me?"

"Yes. And there's also one called Morgan, who's a witch. Funny, isn't it."

Viviane has a coughing fit. "It depends which version you read. In some, Morgan is nice. Believe me, thanks to my name, I've read them all."

She glances at Lea then whispers to me, "Your aunt is doing her best you know. It's not easy for her, becoming a mum overnight."

I don't answer. Morgan will never be like a mum. Lea can't lift the basket of dirty laundry, so I take it from her and give her my book in exchange.

"Keep up kids, it's already a quarter past seven and the nursery closed fifteen minutes ago. I'll take you back to the cloakroom; your aunt must have finished," says Viviane.

In the entrance hall, another lady from the nursery is holding a child in her arms and talking to Morgan. They look angry.

"Is everything okay, Delphine?" Viviane asks.

"Lucas's mum is late again. It's just not good enough," she complains.

"This can't go on," says Morgan.

"She shouldn't have had kids, if it's too much of an effort for her," adds Delphine. "Every evening it's the same, we stay an extra quarter of an hour because of her! We've got a life too!"

The door opens. It's Lucas's mum. She is dressed in a long skirt, lots of necklaces and wears a large scarf on her head. The ends of the scarf blend in with her hair and tumble down her jacket. She doesn't know what's in store for her. *She* doesn't know the real Morgan yet!

My aunt asks her to come to her office. I'm sure Morgan's going to kick off, I wouldn't want to be her . . .

Delphine carries on complaining, still holding the child. "You saw her, Viviane, all dolled up in her scarf with her nose in the air. Does she think she's on the catwalk or something?!"

The office door opens. The lady in the scarf comes out, apologizes and takes her son. They leave.

"I think she got the message. I made myself very clear," says Morgan.

"Was there a reason for her lateness this time?" asks Viviane.

Morgan shrugs and tells us to get our stuff. It's the weekend, yay!

Lea wakes me the next morning jumping up and down on my bed. "It's my birthday, it's my birthday!"

She dances, jumps and then gives the dog a kiss. I search under my pillow and pull out a round package I made from a sheet of paper I coloured in. "Here, they're my marbles, but you can have them. I'm sure you'll like the colours. Look, I picked out the pink and red ones for you."

Lea rushes to hug me.

The doorbell rings. It's the postman with two enormous parcels. Lea squeals with joy when she sees the dress made by Oma Annett, "It's Elsa's dress from *The Snow Queen!*"

And from Grandma Cat there's a huge box of elf and dragon Lego. Lea jumps and hops up and down in excitement and ends up dropping everything. Morgan finally brings in her presents, looking a bit scared. Before handing them over she says, "Look, I didn't know what to get you, but we can always exchange it if you don't like it."

Lea takes an enormous dinosaur out of the box. I'm so jealous.

"It's a Velociraptor! Wow, it's awesome. Can I borrow it?" I ask.

"No, it's mine! All mine!"

I'm sure she prefers the transfers and the bead set but she likes having a gift that she knows I want. And she deliberately won't let go of it, just to annoy me.

"Morgan, I really like your present," she says. "I'll take it to school and it'll protect me against those horrible scary paintings on the walls and Alex who keeps annoying me."

Morgan is swift to react. "What, someone's annoying you at school?"

Oops. I don't want Lea to tell her everything. "Just at the beginning, but he's stopped doing it now," I say quickly.

Morgan calms down but warns Lea, "If someone is bothering you, you must tell me. I won't tolerate harassment or injustice in any form and I won't let anyone make fun of you or hurt you, do you understand? I don't want you suffering in silence. You must tell me if this happens again. The same goes for you, Elliot."

I've never heard Morgan speak in this way before. She sounds so serious.

We phone Grandma Cat and Grandpa Paul in the evening. I tell them all about the day. "Morgan's actually super cool, she gave Lea a dinosaur, can you believe it!"

Grandma Cat bursts out laughing. "She actually bought it? What is she like?! That's priceless!"

16

Morgan

It's four o'clock in the morning. Another broken night with Lea screaming and crying. Even when she drifts off, I can hear her sobbing in her sleep. She looks the part in the daytime though, cheerful as a lark, singing, dancing, playing and running around with Snoopy, pretending to be a princess or a pirate just like other little girls of her age. Yet at night, she wakes up terrified from her nightmares and in the morning I have to shake her awake so we're not late for school. Sometimes I find her in Elliot's bed, snuggled up to him. Last night she even slept with Snoopy, both of them curled up under the duvet.

Feeling groggy, I watch the leaves swirling outside. Autumn is my favourite season. The trees dance in the wind and the whole of Batignolles square is ablaze with splashes of purple, yellow and orange, shining like car headlights. Though the leaves appear grey at night, I know these October colours off by heart. Lea's sadness reminds me of the falling leaves: faster and faster, redder and redder, devouring everything in its path.

Lea likes to spend hours drawing, sitting at my desk. She then tapes her pictures to the wall in front of her. After the *Cars* and *Snow White* duvets, I gave up trying to maintain my colour scheme and had to admit defeat. They have covered the white wall in their room with rows of triumphant faces, which grin slyly at me. First, the wall was a sea of princesses and knights. Then Lea's dinosaur appeared too. And now there are family pictures of Mum, Dad, Elliot, Lea and Snoopy. I feature in some, right at the back in the corner behind the dog.

Once, I did appear in my own picture, but as Lea explained kindly to me, "Morgan, here's you as a princess. And I've drawn a prince charming for you because you don't have a husband. So you can stop being sad."

What can I say? My nursery nurse training didn't cover this sort of thing. At least it'll soon be the holidays. Maybe Grandma Cat will find a way to soothe Lea's pain. Failing that, I know Oma Annett will. I wish I were like Annett. My technique for consoling Lea is just to buy more felt tips and paper. I even found some tape that was the same green as the curtains. Try as I might, this whole thing just doesn't come naturally to me.

"Morgan!"

Lea is restless again. This time she is calling for me and not her mother. I leave my herbal tea on the table and slowly go into the bedroom. She's asleep with Elliot snoring quietly by her side. I go up to her. Her face is wet and the pillow-case is drenched. I gently lift her head to remove the pillow then fetch a clean one. When I slide the pillow under her cheek again, she grabs my hand and mumbles groggily, "Hug me."

I've never hugged a child before. At the nursery, we try not to hug the kids, try not to replace their parents. I look at her profile in the twilight: her big apple-like cheeks and her long eyelashes. I squeeze her little hand in mine and gently stroke her hair so as not to wake her. She smiles and turns her face towards me. "It's okay, I'm here now," I say softly.

I run my hand all the way down her plaits, which she wears in bed to stop her hair tangling, then I work my way up to her face, which I pat dry. I grab a tissue from a box at the bottom of the bed and wipe her nose. She looks just like Emily with her huge dark eyes and chestnut hair. My dearest Emily, who was the opposite of me with my white skin and blue eyes.

That's impossible, you can't be sisters!

No one believed us. We were like chalk and cheese. Yet opposites are drawn to each other and need each other, as proved in her dying hour when she entrusted her children to me, believing it was for the best. I take Lea in my arms and lie down beside her. She snuggles up to me. I stroke her hair, intoxicated by the sweet smell of her strawberry shampoo. Tears roll down my cheeks, but I catch them before they land on her.

My sweet little niece. You have woken me up every night for the last three weeks. I'm at my wits' end, I can't concentrate properly at work anymore. I have too much on my plate all day. At the nursery I'm getting short-tempered, the girls have even pointed it out to me. Do they think I don't hear them whispering about me? I was mad at you, for waking me up every night. But here you are, snuggled up in my arms. Just a tiny little girl who has lost her mummy and daddy. As for *my* mummy, well it's complicated. Not only have I made nothing of my life, but I've managed to destroy everything I did have too. That's why I work with children, so I don't forget. The only prince I've ever had is the one you drew me and the only man I've ever known was anything but charming. I just want you to be happy, Lea, despite everything. I hope that one day you will have children of your own, that you can love them, cherish them and watch them grow up.

I continue stroking her hair. She finally drifts off, dreaming that a knight mounted on Snoopy saves her from the jaws of a dinosaur.

*   *   *

When morning comes, we are still in each other's arms. Elliot turns over under the duvet. I can't really remember what I'm doing here. I tiptoe out of the room and manage to step on a piece of Lego. It bloody hurts.

17

Elliot

HOLIDAYS!

I was so afraid of missing the train that I woke everyone up at seven o'clock in the morning. Yippee, we're off to Marseille at last! Morgan will take us there, then go straight back to Paris because the nursery is still open. But she'll be back to get us the last weekend of the holidays. I think she is secretly pleased to have some time on her own. I did my own suitcase and packed my swimming trunks because sometimes it's so hot there in October that you can still swim in the sea. I even pack my sunglasses so I can be like Grandma Cat.

I race down the stairs with my suitcase. Morgan shouts at me to be careful but I'm already at the bottom.

Saint-Charles station, terminus.

I'm the first off the train. Grandma Cat is waiting with her arms out to greet us. It's boiling. Snoopy is just behind me, barking. We jump in the car heading for La Corniche. It's so windy here! Waves of white foam beat fiercely against the fortress and the islands. It looks amazing! I take a deep breath. The air smells salty and the seagulls are screeching overhead. Lea clutches her plaits so that they don't fly away. From Grandma Cat and Grandpa Paul's balcony all you can see is the beach. Even though there are lots of other people in the building, it's like being on a big boat, alone in the middle of the ocean, it's so cool. Lea laughs and I join in. We hold each other's hands and jump up and down on the balcony singing, "Holidays forever!"

We sit down to have a drink and a snack in the sun. Grandma Cat is wearing her dark glasses and Grandpa Paul is watering his flowers.

"I've put the house up for sale," says Grandma Cat to Morgan. "The agency will take care of it. All we have to do is clear it out when it's sold."

My heart misses a beat. Grandma Cat may be hiding behind those huge glasses, but I can see her hand trembling and she sounds sad. I suddenly feel sorry for her. She hasn't stopped comforting us right from the start but she has no one to comfort *her*. Maybe she's as sad as us? I've never thought about this before. Same with Morgan. Both of them really loved Mum. Though Mum was Grandma Cat's favourite, which must have been tough for Morgan, I guess. I would have hated it if my parents had preferred Lea to me.

I look up at Grandma Cat. She looks older. I take her hand. A tiny tear rolls down her cheek and she dries it quickly. Poor Grandma, who will take care of her? Not Morgan, and not Grandpa Paul, he's too busy with his roses. He's hardly said a word to us since we got here. He is even less talkative than before. Maybe he tells his flowers how sad he is? I don't want to think about our old house, my old bedroom and my toys. Lea didn't hear what Grandma Cat just said. It all goes quiet and then Grandma Cat changes the subject. "Morgan, did you know that our neighbour is coming back?"

She startles Morgan, who was lost in thought. "Which neighbour?"

"What do you mean which neighbour? The one next door, who left seventeen or eighteen years ago, I can't remember exactly. About the same time as you. He helped you find a room in Paris, remember? My God, he was a lovely man! And handsome too! He must be old now, like the rest of us, especially as he spent all those years travelling round the world."

"Morgan, you look ill," says Lea, her mouth full of dried sausage. "You've gone white."

Morgan places her glass on the stone table. Grandma Cat continues, "Well whatever, it'll be fun to see him again. His tenants moved out last week. They're going up north to Lyon. I can't imagine leaving Marseille! I don't know how long he's going to stay, maybe just long enough to get the apartment spruced up? Unless he's back for good. They said the end of the month. Maybe he'll still be here when you come back for the children, Morgan! We could ask him round for drinks. That would be nice, wouldn't it?"

I take some crisps and hand the dish to Morgan. She refuses, saying she feels a bit sick from facing the wrong way on the train. She really does look odd and she's trembling now. She gets up and says she is going to unpack her case. I hear the door of her room close.

Grandma Cat pours me a large glass of Coke and grabs my shoulders. "I'm going to spoil you rotten, my darlings. It can't be easy for you living in rainy Paris with Morgan. She's only been here five minutes and she's sulking already. Is she still obsessed with keeping things tidy?"

I nod.

"Well, while you're on holiday here, you don't have to tidy up a single thing, is that okay for you?"

I nod again. Sounds good to me.

It's Sunday. Morgan leaves tonight. She argued with Grandma Cat yet again yesterday. This time it was because she wanted us to come back using the special rail service for children travelling without grown-ups. Grandma Cat said it was reckless of her to let us travel on our own.

"Mum, that's how it is I'm afraid. Something has cropped up and I won't be able to come back and collect them."

"What, something has come up on a Saturday?" I hear Grandma Cat snap.

"I do have a life you know. I'm going to cancel my ticket and get the kids' tickets exchanged. Unless you'd rather bring them back yourself? But no, I can't come back."

"All I can say is those poor children! You don't exactly put yourself out for them. They have to travel alone just because you say so," replies Grandma Cat angrily.

Deep down I'm really excited about it. We've already flown back from Germany on our own. So it'll be fun taking the train.

When it's time to say goodbye, Lea doesn't want Snoopy to leave and gives him at least a thousand kisses. She hugs Morgan and says, "I really like you, look after Snoopy and my dinosaur."

Suddenly I'm worried: I hope that Morgan won't find the marbles. I shoved them under the bed; I won so many that the pouch wouldn't fit under the mattress. Damn, the letters! I completely forgot about them too. She'll be furious if she finds I've hidden them.

We are having such an amazing time at Grandma Cat's, it's so cool here. She even took us to the funfair. Every day she says, "Don't you just love being here, children? Wouldn't it be great if you never had to go back?"

When she says that, Grandpa Paul just stares at her. He's always out on the balcony, watering, cutting and pruning. I help him sometimes. He doesn't talk as much as Grandma Cat, which is nice. I'm used to peace and quiet at Morgan's house.

Grandma Cat kept her word. She won't let us tidy up a thing. I don't make my bed or pick up my dirty socks. It's great! And I can watch TV whenever I want. At night in bed, I often hear Grandpa Paul and Grandma Cat talking, and it's usually about us. "You should have seen how much fun we had at the fair today. The little ones were laughing their heads off. Poor kids, it does them good to relax a little. Emily was so much fun to be around! And Morgan is just the opposite, it can't be easy for them!"

"Give your poor daughter a break," says Grandpa Paul, who is always nice about Morgan.

"Paul!" she snaps. "I'm worried about her and about them! It breaks my heart to see a beautiful girl like that all pasty-faced and skinny, her skirts hanging off her, always looking so sad. I really don't know what Emily was thinking of. I mean, you no longer have prostate trouble and I'm as fit as a fiddle with not the slightest sign of dementia."

"What about your cholesterol?" he asks.

"What about it? Do I look like I'm ill? No, I'm giving these poor children time to get to grips with things then I'll get the courts to settle this ridiculous situation."

I creep nearer. Lea is already asleep. Grandma Cat is crying now. I can hear her blowing her nose. I would love to just go and hug her but I would get told off for listening at the door.

"I'll never get over it, Paul, never . . ." sobs Grandma Cat.

"Having the children won't make things any better. I admire your energy, Catherine, and I love Elliot and Lea very much. I know that you'll try everything to get custody of them, but why can't you respect Emily's decision? We're too old, I've been very ill and Morgan is a good girl. She's just a bit complicated that's all, like lots of young women her age. She's always had a rebellious streak, that's how she is, that's all. Having the children could do her good. You know how Morgan absolutely worshipped Emily. She's as broken as us. Elliot and Lea will put some sparkle back into her life, you'll see."

He has a gentle voice. I didn't even know he could talk this much. Grandma Cat is still crying. "Paul, you don't know her like I do. I'm her mother. She is not at all maternal."

I close the door quietly. I'm tired and don't want to hear any more. I look at my suitcase, sadly bursting at the seams. Lea sleeps deeply. She's happy to be going back. She can't wait to see Snoopy again.

18

Morgan

The silence hits me, I'm not used to it anymore. I put some music on to drown it out. I was so looking forward to two weeks of peace and quiet. I even drew up a list of everything I wanted to do: see a good film, cook some gourmet meals, repot one of my bonsai trees, take Snoopy to the grooming parlour, listen to my favourite records. And I ended up doing none of it.

It was a nightmare week at the nursery. Two of my colleagues were off sick, plus there was the daily routine and a ton of admin to take care of, so I worked late every night. Then on Friday evening, just before the nursery closed, someone gently tapped on my office door. I found myself face to face with Jean-Michel, who was fiddling with his cap. "Hey, Ms Mercier, I know it's none of my business, but are the kids away at the moment?"

I stare at him in a stupor. How must I appear to others, dragging the kids here every day after school to the point that their presence is taken for granted?

I find myself babbling, as if to apologize. "Err no, actually, no, they're on holiday."

He laughs loudly. "But of course, how silly of me! Good, well, I'm sorry to have bothered you. I was worried, I mean not seeing them all week, I just wanted to check that everything was alright. It's not easy for them, or you of course. I was afraid something else might have happened."

Seeing my astonished gaze, he adds, "I know it's not my place to say anything, but it pains me to think of what's happened to your kids. Forget what I said. I'm off, my Alice is waiting for me."

One big guy with one big heart, someone who simply cares about others. Come to think of it, our work is not dissimilar. Our jobs are both entwined with the circle of life itself. The difference being that I come in at the beginning, looking after sweet, pink-skinned babies, while he comes in at the end, dealing with sorrowful, grief-stricken families. You would think that I have the most human contact but I don't really *see* any of the kids that I look after all day long, while Jean-Michel clearly connects with the grieving families he looks after. He seems concerned about Elliot and Lea; I haven't even rung them since they've been away. I bite my lips. I'll call them tonight.

I open my office door and come face to face with Valerie Le Gall, who has clearly made a tremendous effort to arrive on time. I say a quick hello. Viviane is right, she doesn't look good. Raising a kid on your own while working all hours is just impossible. She's a prime candidate for a burn out. According to Amara, her child's father abandoned her shortly before the birth. How classy is that. Though I feel sorry for her—now that I know what it's like to work full-time and raise kids—I cannot tolerate her lateness every evening. The girls are entitled to leave on time.

The week is so intense that when I get home all I want to do is snuggle up on the sofa with Snoopy on my feet and fall asleep. Forget about films, gourmet dinners and grooming parlours. The dog can splash around in the bath next Sunday with Elliot and Lea, they will be delighted—Snoopy too. I dread to think what state the bathroom will be in afterwards.

I use the weekend to tidy up the apartment, which looks like a bomb has hit it. The bedroom is a mess with pens and socks everywhere. I clean the school bags, throw the pencil sharpenings into the rubbish and sign off their work. Elliot got 12/20 in history and 15/20 in French. He'd already told me about the French. I'm not surprised, he's really good at writing. He wants to be a journalist when he grows up. I'm more surprised by the 5/20 he got for maths, which he failed to mention! We'll deal with that when terms starts. I change the duvet covers, wash the sheets, dust and polish the furniture, and remove the dirty washing. The laundry basket is a bottomless pit and the more I empty it, the more it seems to magically fill up.

When I put Lea's duvet cover back on, I discover one of her favourite cuddly animals lodged between the bed and the wall: a small pink fox she is extremely fond of. I can smell the lingering scent of her strawberry shampoo on its fur. I put the fox back in the bed, its head on the pillow. And now for Elliot's sheets.

As I grab both ends of the duvet to put it in the duvet cover, I suddenly feel a pain in my right breast. It's not the first time either. I can feel a small lump—probably just a cyst—but I'd better get it checked out. Now that I have two children to raise, I can't take any risks. I already worry about contracting Alzheimer's as it runs in our family. Who knows if I will still be around to see Elliot and Lea's children grow up? I've never asked myself this up to now but becoming a senile, grumpy old spinster never bothered me before. I touch my breast again and shudder at the thought of having to be examined by the gynaecologist. Lying there with your legs in the stirrups pretending to have a relaxed and polite conversation is hardly the best way to spend an hour, but I really should get myself checked out.

Elliot's duvet cover is finally back on. I spot a sock under the bed and bend down to pick it up. It's covered in dust! I grab the vacuum cleaner but it gets stuck almost immediately. Flat on my stomach, I pull out a notebook and a fat misshapen fabric pouch from under the bed. Tintin waves at me from the cover of the notebook. Could it be his personal diary? I find it touching that Elliot confides in someone or something. I carefully put it back. I wouldn't dream of opening it and reading his innermost thoughts; I prefer to let him deal with his grief in his own way. If he hasn't told me, it's because he doesn't want me to know. The large fabric pouch interests me more. There are about fifty marbles inside. I didn't bring any back from their house in Maisons-Laffitte, but maybe his grandparents gave him some this summer? He's very secretive and my mother would do anything to ingratiate herself to him as she already proved with the Lego. There are an awful lot of marbles though. He must have won some of them at school.

At the bottom of the pouch, I find a dozen felt-tip pens, a green fluorescent marker and a football team pen. This is not the stationery I bought him. Maybe it's some trade-off between friends. I close the pouch and put it back under the bed, next to the Tintin notebook. I spend the rest of the afternoon listening to Barbara and Edith Piaf, and sipping tea.

The next week goes by in a blur. I finally pluck up the courage to phone the gynaecologist, and get her secretary. She's a real dragon and keeps offering me appointments at ten thirty on a weekday, before snapping that I need to make myself "a bit more available" if I want to see the doctor. We end up finding a slot at the beginning of December during my lunch hour. It's Friday at last. I get home satisfied; everything is clean, neat, polished and tidy. The children are back tomorrow. I take a look at their perfect room and stroke Lea's cuddly toy. I'll be happy to have her back.

19

Elliot

Dear Mum,

I wanted to write to you sooner, but Lea and I were staying with Grandma Cat and Grandpa Paul in Marseille. We slept in your old bedroom and Grandma Cat showed us some photos of you when you were small. Morgan was even smiling in some of them.

It was hard going back to Paris. I hate November, it's so cold and rainy and it was tough after the sun and our games on the beach. Plus I got some bad marks at school again and I haven't shown them to Morgan yet. You know what, Mum, I feel like my brain has stopped working. I had it all sussed before, but now it's like everything has broken. It's because of the new school too. I got 5/20 in maths just before the holidays, which is really bad. And Lea keeps getting the little red stamps on her exercise book saying "best in the class". I'm sorry, Mum, I know you will be angry, but it's not my fault. I never get marks as bad as this, even when I forget to revise. In Marseille I needed a break and didn't do any of my homework. It was so cool with Grandma Cat and Grandpa Paul. And they didn't ask me to do any.

Morgan is worried. She wanted to know why I didn't mention that I got a bad mark in maths. It's because she scares me. Also I'm pissed off that she went through my bag. I'll have to tell her that my brain has stopped working.

I wish you were here to explain to her and tell her I'm not okay and that when I get my head fixed, everything will get

*better. But I don't like my teacher, which makes it harder. And
the other kids are always provoking me and making fun of me.
I keep getting in fights in the playground.*

*When I'm feeling down, I call Grandma Cat. I don't tell her
everything though, in case she tells Morgan. She talks about
the seagulls and the sea, which makes me feel better.*

*Luckily, Morgan hasn't found the letters underneath my
mattress. She would have been mad at me. So I decided to put
them back. I really was going to, I swear. The Saturday after
school started, when she went out to buy bread with Lea and
Snoopy, I took out the letters. But before putting them back, I
decided to take one last look at the little girl's face. I still wonder
who she is. I took out her picture and then I figured it wouldn't
be so bad if I read the other letters. I read one from April 2011
and there was another photo of her. Her name is Linh. I'm not
going to tell you everything she said, Mum, it would take me
hours. Basically, Linh said that school was great, that she
missed her daddy and her little brother very much and that she
would like to become a doctor to treat sick children because no
one could save her sister. In the other envelopes there were more
letters and photos. The last one I read was from 2014. She
wrote it herself in French. And you know what? She loves
Morgan, how about that!*

*I jumped when I heard the key turn in the lock and quickly
put the letters back under my mattress. But I can't stop thinking about her. Who is this little girl? Morgan said she went to
Vietnam when she was eighteen. Could Linh be her daughter?
She'd be sixteen or seventeen by now. It's true that they don't
look anything alike but I have a friend whose dad is Chinese,
and even though his mum is from here he has slanting eyes and
black hair. But why would Morgan leave a child over there?
And if she did, why would she give her money when she says
she can't afford to buy us anything because everything's so*

expensive? And Linh never talks about her mum there, just her dad, so maybe she doesn't have one?

Oma Annett was right; it makes me feel better telling you everything. I'll try really hard to get some good marks and make some friends, I swear. Give Dad a kiss from me in heaven and tell him I love him. Love you lots Mum, so does Lea.

Elliot

20

Morgan

I can't sleep a wink. I pace up and down like a caged lion between the living room and the bathroom. I can't get it out of my head. When I picked up Elliot tonight his lip was split and bleeding. He told me he had walked into a door. What sort of idiot does he take me for? He is lying through his teeth to me with a lip that swollen. At home, while he was in the shower, a terrified Lea confessed to me that "two big boys from Year 5" had beaten up Elliot just outside the school gates. Elliot made her promise not to tell me. I'm beside myself with rage just thinking about it. I mean really, two older kids beating up a new kid, how low can you get? And he is clearly petrified and won't tell on them. I can't believe that there is no one watching the kids as they leave school. If there's one thing I can't stomach it's violence of any sort. It makes me feel sick to my stomach. I can't leave it, can't calm down. *Emily, I'm ashamed. I'm so sorry ... I know I'm not perfect and that I make a lot of mistakes but I will never ever let anyone hurt Elliot again, or Lea. Only those who have suffered understand how dreadful injustice is. But don't worry, I will be in the headmistress's office at eight thirty sharp tomorrow morning. Emily, I'll make that beanpole of a woman react. And I swear she'll never let your son get beaten to a pulp again.*

I wake up on the sofa with a splitting headache. I'm going to need a painkiller to calm down and face the headmistress without losing my rag. I take a deep breath and try to look normal in front of the kids. They mustn't pick up on my anxiety and Elliot must *not* find out his sister let the cat out of the bag. There's enough tension between us already, without adding to it. I drop the kids off at school, pretend to leave and once they go in, I approach the security guard. "Good morning, I need to see the headmistress. It's urgent. A serious incident occurred yesterday."

"You're out of luck," he replies. "On Thursdays, she has back to back meetings and won't be free until later. Come back between four and five. What's your name?"

"Morgan Mercier, I'm Elliot Bauer's aunt. I'll be there, thanks."

I spend the morning preparing my ammunition and fine-tuning my argument so that both offenders get maximum punishment. I'm hoping that there'll be an official warning and their parents will be summoned to the school.

Right, I read off my notes: "Violence is totally unacceptable, whatever the reason. I would also like to remind you of my nephew's unique circumstances. I don't doubt he is difficult to deal with, but he is going through a hard time and can't cope. I think it would be a good idea to ask all of the children to show some kindness and tolerance towards him. I will have to report this to the authorities if it happens again."

No, I'll have to do better. Time's running out. My phone rings loudly. It's the school! I drop my pen in surprise.

"Ms Mercier? It's Carole Dubois, the headmistress, here. I was told you wanted to speak to me urgently. I took the liberty of calling you."

"Yes, that's right," I answer.

Caught off guard, I can't find my words. I'm a bundle of nerves and drop my notes. I tell her I was shocked to hear my nephew was beaten up yesterday just outside the school gates. According to his sister, it was two boys from Year 5

called Alex and Tristan. I say that I will be there at four thirty
to discuss things face to face.

She says that what I suggest is a very serious accusation
indeed and that she was taken aback herself to see Elliot's
swollen lip this morning. He turned his head away as soon as
he saw her. She says she will be waiting for me at four thirty
and in the meantime she will make some enquiries to try to
get to the bottom of this.

Phew, that's the first step over with and I'm satisfied. I gave
her no leeway, telling her firmly that I will be there at four
thirty. I pick up my notes. My stomach is in knots still. And
what if those two creeps start picking on Lea? I make notes,
then cross out and rewrite them. I'm shaking with nerves.
Viviane reminds me of the rush orders for nappies and wipes
I was supposed to place this morning. It completely slipped
my mind. I send her to the nearest supermarket to get a few
packs to see us through till Monday. I forget to eat lunch.

Here I am at last, in front of the school, my stomach churning and my anger raging. I'll prove to Emily and my mother
that I'm up to the task. If my mother finds out that Elliot's
been beaten up, it's all over. She would do anything she can
to take the children off me, even if it means defying my
sister's wishes.

The headmistress greets me with a forced smile. I go
straight for the jugular, forgetting about the notes I spent the
whole day writing. "Look, there was an incident yesterday
just outside the school gate. Elliot was beaten up by two other
kids. His lip was split and bleeding. I know they weren't technically on the school premises, but they go to your school.
His little sister Lea recognized them."

The headmistress nods, elbows on her desk, hands folded
in front of her mouth. She doesn't say a word. Her silence
starts to annoy me so I continue, "I'm waiting for an

explanation. I will not tolerate bullying and violence, especially given Elliot's circumstances. I will not allow such a thing to happen again. I demand that the two boys in question be punished accordingly."

The headmistress takes a deep breath and says, "I understand. Unfortunately, all this has happened quicker than I feared."

"I beg your pardon?" I answer, confused.

"I want to reassure you of one thing: no acts of violence are allowed within the school grounds, or even in front of the gates. I spoke with Alexander and Tristan today and they admitted what they did. I will be taking the matter up with their parents."

"Thank you," I say. "I hope their punishment will reflect the seriousness of what they did to my nephew."

She interrupts me a bit too quickly for my liking. "I will deal with it personally. Nevertheless, as I told you, I was half expecting this to happen."

"Well, why didn't you do something about it then?" I ask.

She sighs. "Elliot is a very aggressive child. He constantly gets into fights and has been ostracized by all the other children at school. So far I've been extremely tolerant, but . . . I've always kept a close eye on him, to protect him, of course, and to protect the other children."

I tell her she obviously hasn't been vigilant enough.

She says she has more to say and I should listen carefully. She states that if there is no change in Elliot's behaviour, we are heading for something quite serious that could threaten the stability of the whole school.

I can't believe this. So it's up to Elliot to change his behaviour? Isn't it to be expected that he is a little disturbed? I lose control. "The child has just lost his parents! Do you not think it's understandable that he is having trouble adjusting to a new school?"

The headmistress looks me right in the eye. Her calm exasperates me. I'll listen to her but I'm ready to pounce if necessary.

"Ms Mercier, let's focus on the cause rather than the consequences. I've spoken to Alexander, Tristan and Elliot, individually. I've also spoken to a few other children from the class, as a matter of routine. I asked a lot of questions and received a lot of answers, that unfortunately all tally. Not only are the other pupils fed up with your nephew's aggressive behaviour, but there is also another more pressing issue. They say that Elliot is stealing from them."

I almost choke at the thought of such an accusation. "They're lying, you didn't believe them I hope!" I shout in dismay.

"Let me finish, please," she continues. "They claim that things like marbles, pens and small items such as erasers and fluorescent markers have been disappearing from their school bags. Nothing of value, but it's still property theft, or rather petty theft."

I sit there dazed. In my mind's eye I see the pouch underneath Elliot's bed, bursting with marbles. There were pens, too. So they didn't come from my mother or Annett. What a mess! I came here seeking justice and now I'm the one in the firing line.

"Alexander and Tristan supposedly caught Elliot red-handed stealing a baseball cap. Their reaction was unacceptable. They will be held to account for their violence and their parents will be involved. But we must find a way to help Elliot. This is our absolute priority."

I need to get out of here, I can't breathe. My mind goes blank. A pigeon sits in front of the window and coos at us, mockingly. She offers me a cup of tea—which I refuse—then a gingerbread, as if to soften the blow she just dealt me.

My throat tightens. The pigeon flies away, bringing me to my senses. "What did Elliot say?" I ask.

"Naturally, he denies it all," she replies.

I have no choice but to tell her. I try hard to string a sentence together. "I found some marbles at my apartment. I don't know where they came from. He even gave some to his sister for her birthday. I thought his grandparents had given them to him. He doesn't tell me much you know."

I wait for her to put me out of my misery. She's going to suspend him, I can feel it. But instead she says calmly, "Elliot is not a thief. He is in a lot of pain. Kleptomania is common and is not necessarily a conscious act. Above all, it is a cry for help. He urgently needs our help. We cannot let him sink any deeper into this unhappiness, or just sit back and watch him withdraw from the other children. So far we have had five or six children claiming he has stolen from them. Tomorrow it'll be twice that many. It must stop now. No one will judge him."

My silence encourages her to go on. "I know an excellent therapist. Here is her card. I suggest you make an appointment with her as soon as possible. Elliot needs help, and so do you. I need you to get things back on track as quickly as possible."

I don't dare look her in the face and stammer, "So, so, is he suspended then?"

She scalds herself with her tea. "No, of course not! It's not Elliot's fault. The child is in pain. Our duty—yours and mine—is to help him through this. If we can put an end to it rapidly, it'll blow over. That's how children are. Talk to Elliot tonight, one-to-one, in private. Tell him that you know what happened but show him that you are not judging him and that you understand him. Say that you'll make an appointment with a specialist to help him move on."

She looks at her watch. "It's already five thirty. Do you want to collect Elliot and Lea now?"

I nod and stand up, stumbling against the leg of my chair. I cling to the desk, rapidly losing the little dignity I had left. My bag spills over and a cheque book and picture of Snoopy fall out. The headmistress picks them up and hands them to me. I mutter a shameful thank you. Humbled, I remember the scolding I gave Valerie the other night, which was just a cold shower compared to the ice bath I've just taken. Mrs Dubois accompanies me to the classroom. Lea is surprised, but Elliot acts like nothing's wrong. The other kids watch him get up. I imagine I can hear them cursing us, "Hey it's them, the thieves! Give us back our marbles and pens and get lost and don't ever come back." My head is buzzing with their insults. I tell the children to hurry as we are leaving.

The door is so heavy that it literally throws us out into the street. I feel both humiliated and ashamed. I can't hold myself back any longer. "So you like marbles do you, Elliot? If you'd just told me it would have saved us all a lot of bother. I'd have bought you a packet and you wouldn't have had to . . ."

He turns to me and shouts, "What, *you*? Buy me a pack of marbles? You'd buy them for Snoopy but not for me! You've never even bought me a chocolate bar. And you weren't capable of getting Lea a proper birthday present! What do you care anyway, you don't give a toss about us!"

He is consumed with anger. I reel under the force of his attack. Lea comes up to me and takes my hand. The other parents start to arrive, glancing at us with polite curiosity. I don't want to make a scene. I tell the kids we are going home. Lea follows me and starts to cry.

21

Elliot

"What, *you*? Buy me a pack of marbles? You'd buy them for Snoopy but not for me! You've never even bought me a chocolate bar. And you weren't capable of getting Lea a proper birthday present! What do you care anyway, you don't give a toss about us!"

I don't know why I threw all that stuff at her. I'd have been better off saying nothing. It's because I wanted to make it go away so that Mum would come back. I hate her! It's all her fault. If it wasn't for her, we'd be living with Grandma Cat and everything would be so much easier.

People are staring at us and Lea starts bawling. That's the worst bit, seeing what I've done to my little sister. Morgan turns her back on me and rushes off. I cover my ears—at least inside my head I do—so I don't have to hear her horrible voice anymore.

We walk home in the rain. I kick the stones; I feel like smashing something. I hate November; it's so cold and wet. It's hard getting up the stairs, my feet feel heavy. Morgan goes in without looking at me and Snoopy rushes to greet me. At least *someone* is pleased to see me. Lea runs down the corridor and I hear her rummaging around in the bedroom. She comes out holding her birthday marbles. "As they weren't really yours, I'm giving them back to you, but I'll keep the paper you wrapped them in."

I leave the marbles on the living room table, throw myself on my bed and bury my head in the pillow. I wish I could stay there all night but Morgan then comes in to nag me about having "a serious talk", as she calls it. Does she think she's my mum or what? Except that Mum never got angry, she understood everything, I never had to explain anything to her. Mum was beautiful and Morgan is ugly. Mum laughed all the time and Morgan is miserable all the time. Plus my head wasn't broken then. I had good grades and didn't steal other people's marbles. I was happy so Mum had no reason to punish me.

Morgan has a real go at me, "Do you have any idea? Do you want all the other kids to hate you? You think we don't have enough to deal with as it is? You, me, Lea, maybe it's not enough for you, so you have to add to it, steal, get beaten up?"

I sit on the bed staring at my trainers, waiting for it to pass. Hopefully, I'll wake up at home tomorrow morning and discover it was all just a bad dream. I pinch my arm. It hurts. Tough luck, it must be true. I look out the window. The rain beats hard against the glass. I hate the rain. Morgan has gone quiet. She must be tired. I won't look at her.

She finally spits it out, "I know you're not a thief, Elliot. But this has got to stop now. I think what you need most of all is someone to confide in and tell them what's on your mind. Listen, I'm going to make an appointment for you to see a specialist. It should help you get your thoughts straight."

She leaves but almost immediately she's back again. She kneels down in front of me, puts her hand on my knee and says, "I'm sorry I lost my temper like that. I was incredibly angry."

I still refuse to look at her. She gets up without speaking and this time disappears for good. Peace at last. Suddenly Lea taps me on the elbow. "Elliot ... Elliot. Have you seen Snoopy?"

"He's in the living room, isn't he?"

"I can't find him," she says in a panicky voice.

"Well, look again, it's not exactly massive in here."

Terrified, she leans over to me and whispers, "Elliot. The front door is open. I think Snoopy ran out while you were arguing, he doesn't like shouting."

This is the last straw. I explode. "Lea, you were the last one in, weren't you? You did close the door behind you, didn't you? You're such an idiot!"

Lea's lips start quivering, I can see that she's about to cry. I'm not going to argue with my sister on top of everything else, so I pluck up the courage to knock on Morgan's door. She already hates me, this won't change anything. "Morgan, is Snoopy with you?"

I clench my fists really hard. Please let him be there! Lea is chewing the ends of her plaits, looking really upset.

"No, why?"

Right now, I feel a bit like Louis XVI about to have my head cut off. We learnt about him in history. Morgan will kill me. She comes out, looking even whiter than usual. Lea stands there shaking like a leaf. "Morgan, I think I forgot to close the door."

Morgan looks like she is being chased by a giant bee. She runs around screaming, "Snoopy! Snoopy! Tell me this is a joke!" She even looks under the sofa, shouting, "I can't believe it! That dog isn't a toy you know!"

Lea tries to console her saying we'll find him. She feels guilty, as it's all her fault. Even I feel sorry for Morgan, seeing her like this: her hair stuck to her cheeks wet with tears. She grabs her coat and hands us ours without a word. We get soaked outside in the rain searching for the dog in the dark. It's freezing too. We go round and round the square and then along the railway tracks shouting, "Snoopy!" But nothing.

Once we get back, I help Lea into bed. Her hair is drenched but I don't dare ask Morgan for the hairdryer, much less get it myself. I pull my *Cars* duvet cover over my head. I'm cold. I guess Lea has done the same. Morgan is sitting on the living room floor next to the dog basket, crying her eyes out. She is mumbling. I don't understand it all and she's worrying me.

"Snoopy, Snoopy. My darling dog. I'm sorry, Emily, I'm sorry. I just can't cope. Please come back Snoopy. Please come back Emily, I beg you."

Lea wakes me up sneezing. She is sniffing and her eyes are still shiny with tears. She asks me if I think Morgan has found Snoopy. I say I hope so and that we should go and see if he's in the living room. But there's no dog in sight, just Morgan, who's fallen asleep sitting up with her back against the window. We startle her as we go in. Her eyes are bright red. We get dressed without saying a word. I make us each a strawberry jam sandwich and we grab our schoolbags. When Lea opens the door, she jumps for joy, shouting, "He's here, he's here!"

Morgan bursts out of the living room and covers him with kisses. "Snoopy, my love! You came back! Thank you, thank you, I'm so happy! But you're limping? We'll get you to the vet as soon as possible, I promise, we'll take good care of you."

She squeezes him tightly. At the bottom of my coat pocket, I can feel some paper. It's the old kiss bar from Lea. I quickly tear off a small square and clutch it tightly.

22

Morgan

The sun is finally shining again after a dreadful night. Snoopy found his way back and I can finally breathe. After losing Emily, the thought of never seeing him again either was unbearable. That dog is my life. I make a vet's appointment for the next morning as well as one for Elliot with the therapist. She sounds ancient on the phone. I hope she really is as good as the headmistress made out.

And now back to the daily grind: whingy parents and a mountain of paperwork. One of the dads is complaining that his son picked up a tummy bug from the child he sat next to at lunch. A mother bluntly informs me that her son's cuddly toy has disappeared "yet again" and that she can't keep replacing them. I finally get round to ordering the nappies. The arrival of the hearse marks the end of my working day. When I hear *Itsi bitsi petit bikini* at full blast, I know it's time to pick the kids up.

I grab my coat and leave. In the entrance hall I pass Amara, who is shimmying along to the music as she prepares the plastic shoe covers for the parents. I bump into Valerie on my way out. What, she's here already? It's only five forty! Is she feeling okay?! "Oh, sorry," I say.

She looks deathly pale and miserable, as if she hasn't been happy in a long time. Did I hurt her? I hardly touched her really. Then Jean-Michel bounds in, singing; he has a lovely deep voice. He grabs Amara and starts waltzing with her. She giggles with joy. It's a madhouse.

Valerie steals past them like a ghost, oblivious to Jean-Michel's buoyant mood and polite greeting. I run outside, impatient at the thought of cuddling up to my dog. The children are as good as gold the whole evening. Lea draws a picture of Snoopy in hospital, which she sticks to the wall with my green tape. She says she's not hungry and takes herself off to bed. Elliot hides behind an edition of his wildlife magazine that he's already read at least a hundred times before.

On Saturday morning, Lea complains of a headache and struggles to get out of bed. I even have to help her get dressed to hurry her along. Poor Snoopy has to be carried to the vet as he can't walk; he's heavy but it's wonderful to feel him in my arms. When we arrive, I go up to the receptionist. "Good morning, we've got an appointment with Dr Deprez."

"Lancelot Deprez? Very well. I'll notify him," she replies.

"Lancelot? Like the knights of the round table?" asks Elliot.

I nod.

"Really, imagine being called that!" he says. "Some parents are weird. Plus it's a bit pretentious, isn't it?"

"Is it?"

I almost drop Snoopy. I turn round to see a man in his forties staring at us coldly. He eventually holds out his hand for me to shake. "Lancelot Deprez, veterinary surgeon. Your name?"

"Morgan Mercier. And this is Snoopy. I think he sprained his paw."

"I can see that . . . Morgan. The knights of the round table, eh?"

He beckons us into his office. I follow him proudly, head held high, Elliot and Lea at my heels. This man is about as friendly as a grizzly bear and looks ready to attack. He examines Snoopy, then announces that he needs to X-ray him and takes him away without waiting for my reply. Lea collapses onto a chair by the desk, complaining she still has a headache. When the vet returns, he confirms my diagnosis. "Your dog has indeed sprained his paw. He's going to need to rest for a few days. Limit outings to the strict minimum and keep him on a leash. I'm also prescribing him an anti-inflammatory that you can get at the pharmacy. Come back and see me if he doesn't improve."

"Thank you, I was so worried!" I reply, the relief making me grateful despite myself. I turn to Lea, who is slumped on the desk, her head between her arms.

Dr Deprez goes up to her. "Do you have a headache?" he asks.

"Yes, it hurts here and here," she mumbles.

He places his hand on her forehead and says to me, "Your daughter is burning up, have you not noticed?"

"Err no. In fact, she's not my daughter, she's my niece. But I look after her, I mean. No, I hadn't noticed." I'm getting tangled up in knots.

He frowns, looking annoyed. "I'm trying to tell you this child is ill." He glares at me as if I were the witch in *Snow White* or rather the wicked stepmother who cares more about her pooch than her child. He pulls a thermometer out of his drawer and brandishes it like a sword. Lea leans back in fright.

"Don't worry, Miss," he says softly, "it's for people, not animals!"

She has a temperature of 39.8 degrees. "It appears your niece is in a worse state than your dog," the vet says accusingly.

"I, err ... I'll take care of her ... I'm a trained nurse," I stammer. "I'll monitor her closely and if she gets worse, I'll take her to the doctor."

"Is that right?" he says sceptically. "In that case, I'll leave you to it then. The dog will recover, you'll see. Goodbye."

I feel hurt and humiliated. I turn to leave without uttering a word. What does he know about me? Nothing at all. Men, argh! Always keen to criticize how women look after children! I liked this surgery as it's not far from the apartment. Hopefully this arrogant idiot will move on soon. I pick up Snoopy while Elliot helps Lea out of the chair. On the way home, we stop off at the pharmacy to stock up on paracetamol and the dog's medication. To console his sister, Elliot recites "The Raven and the Fox" to her over and over again. He is learning it for his school Christmas play; La Fontaine is the theme this year.

"A bit too late, Sir Raven swore,
The rogue should never cheat him more."

When we arrive in the lobby of our building, we run into the postman, who hands me some envelopes. I see a brightly coloured stamp with a red flag and a yellow star on it. Elliot hovers next to me excitedly. "Can I see where it comes from?" he asks. Before I have time to answer, Snoopy, finally released from my arms, tries to climb the stairs and collapses, bumping his nose against the step and whimpering.

23

Elliot

Dear Mum,

Today I went to see a lady to get my broken head mended. She's about a hundred years old but she's nice. She resembles a big, fat owl with huge, round glasses and really short hair that looks like grey feathers. I stayed on my own with the owl while Morgan and Lea went shopping. I thought she was going to give me some pills or medicine to take to mend my head and then it would be over, but she didn't. She asked me loads of questions, and every time she asked me something, she stared at me from behind those gigantic glasses.

"Your aunt told me she looks after you?"

Why is she asking something she already knows the answer to, I wonder. I reply, just to be polite, "Yes."

"And she also told me you had some bother at school?"

Okay, so that's what this is all about. I don't want to talk to her about it, I don't even know the woman. So I just sink deeper and deeper into the big green chair that reminds me of a huge green frog.

"I know you're not a thief," she says. Her eyes are smiling behind her goggles. "Well, can you tell me about the marbles?" she asks then.

Why should I? I've nothing to tell her, it's because my head is broken, that's all. It started off as a game to get my own back on that idiot Alex. Then when the other kids started teasing and annoying me, I decided to punish them too. Instead of answering, I ask, "Are you going to give me any pills?"

"No, I'm going to let you think things over," she replies.

Great, that's really going to work. I stay silent, so she goes on, "I think you just need us to pay you a bit more attention. And you're quite right! You're going through a particularly difficult time right now. Tell me how it's going with your aunt. How are you feeling Elliot?"

This is the first time anyone has asked me that question, Mum. Even the beanpole headmistress never asks me how I am. She's nice, and always says "I understand", but that's it. The lady just keeps looking at me without speaking. I stare at my feet. It's easier to talk to her like that. "You know, Morgan likes my sister Lea, but I think she hates me. Actually, I don't think she likes boys at all, except her dog. I'd prefer to live with my grandma."

"And is that not possible?" she asks.

"No. My mum wanted it this way."

"Do you know why?"

"I guess she was afraid our grandparents would die too."

"I think we're on the right track but I'd like you to think about it. I'm interested to hear more. And then next time, maybe you could bring your marbles with you?"

I have no idea how this lady is going to fix my head; she hasn't actually done anything yet. All we do is talk. She didn't even give me a prescription. Morgan let me walk home on my own because it wasn't very far. Notice I said "home"; this is the first time I've ever said it, though it doesn't feel like home one bit. It was great walking back alone in the street with no one spying on me. When I got back, Snoopy was the only one there. He was snoring with his head on the cushion. His paw is still injured and he can't walk very well. Morgan's still worried, like you were when I broke my wrist. She's been looking after him constantly and gives him loads of hugs. And Lea loves pretending to be his nurse. If only you could see her! Morgan said her dream was to run her own boarding kennels and Lea said she would help her take care of all the dogs. She even suggested that Morgan ask the vet to help us do it. But Morgan said that was out of the question.

While I was waiting for them to get back, I lay on my bed reading my Asterix comic and then suddenly I just had to look at the marbles again. So I took them out of their hiding place and opened the pouch. But when I saw them, they seemed so ugly and horrible that I put them straight back again. I then slipped my hand under the mattress and pulled out the letters. This whole kid-on-the-other-side-of-the-world thing kind of bothers me. I remembered the letter that came yesterday. I slipped into Morgan's room and opened the drawer quietly. The letter was there and it had been opened! Linh has just had her seventeenth birthday and wrote to Morgan herself in French. Now that she has a bike, she will be able to go to university next year. "Thank you for everything you do for me Morgan. You're like a mum. Without you I wouldn't have any of this. I hope we'll meet each other one day."

She sure is lucky. Morgan doesn't give a toss about me. It feels like my heart hurts. I put the letter back in the drawer.

In the evening, Grandma Cat called to give us some good news. She and Grandpa Paul are coming for Christmas and they've got a special surprise for us. Morgan won't have to do a thing. They're actually coming to clear out the house because it's been sold; I overheard them talking. And it's made me so sad. I know it's going to be hard on them, so I've decided not to say anything. I hope they sell everything, even the furniture. I don't want to see any of it again.

I can't get to sleep. There's too much stuff going on in my head, Mum. First there's you and Dad, I miss you both loads. I can't stop thinking about you. It starts in the morning when I wake

up, then all morning and all afternoon at school, then all evening at home. I didn't realize just how much I loved you both.
And then of course, there's this marble thing. I'm so ashamed, I
don't know why I stole them. And now the house. That's why
I'm writing to you using my little torch, I need to clear my
head, like Oma Annett told me to do. By the way, did you know
we're going skiing with them in Germany at half term in
February?

Morgan saw that we were feeling unhappy tonight and agreed
to let Snoopy sleep in our room. His basket is right next to us
so I can stroke his ear from my bed.

I love you both so much Mum, big hugs and kisses.

Elliot

24

Morgan

Gosh, it's midday already. I have my appointment with the gynaecologist today although I almost cancelled it. I have absolutely no desire to strip off and lie naked in front of a stranger. I haven't set foot in the doctor's surgery for at least four years. If it hadn't been for Elliot and Lea, I would have cancelled, but I'm responsible for them now: I can't be the old sick auntie. Fortunately, my gynaecologist is over seventy, blind as a bat, and a real chatterbox who never asks me any questions. That's what I like about her.

I dash to the underground. Not long now till Christmas. Streets and shop windows are beginning to look festive, and people have started putting up Christmas decorations. I've never really been a big fan of Christmas but this year I think I'll do a tree and some tinsel. I saw lots in the supermarket—advent calendars too. I'm sure the kids would like that. Ever since the marbles episode Elliot has been withdrawn. He won't even tell me how it went with the therapist. It's like there's an impenetrable wall between us. A Christmas tree might just help things.

I battle against the icy draught blowing down the underground tunnel as I exit. Frozen stiff, I charge headlong into someone who appears as if from nowhere. "I'm really sorry," I gasp.

"Are you always in such a hurry? How's your niece?"

Oh no, it's Sir Lancelot himself. The knight in shining armour who rescues poor orphans. Just my luck ... My gynaecologist happens to be right next to his clinic. I should have thought of that.

I try to stay calm. "Oh, she's been fine for three weeks now, thank you. I nursed her back to health."

"Fantastic. What about your dog?"

"Snoopy is slowly but surely getting the use of his paw back. I don't wish to appear rude, but I have an appointment. Thank you for asking after them. Bye." I dive into the building next door.

"See you soon, then!" he calls.

I sincerely hope not . . . The waiting room is empty. I take off my coat and pick up a magazine only to put it straight down again. I stand up to read the leaflets displayed on a shelf: *Overcoming Breast Cancer, All you need to know about the HPV Vaccination, First Steps in Birth Control.* Not exactly feel-good reading . . . I wonder whether I'll have to discuss all this with Lea one day. I don't think I'm the best person for the job. I suppose I could ask my mother, or even Annett? As for Elliot, let's not even go there. I just hope I manage to instil in him the need to treat girls with respect.

My gynaecologist is fifteen minutes late and I'm all jittery. She's going to come down on me like a ton of bricks when she realizes I haven't been having my yearly check-ups. The door opens at last and an old lady hobbles out. My God, I wouldn't inflict myself on any gynaecologist at that age. Then a prepubescent boy in a white gown offers me his hand. This can't be happening. Where's my gynaecologist? "There must be a mistake, my appointment was with Dr Moreau," I stammer.

"Yes, that's me! I took over my grandmother's practice three years ago," he replies. "We have the same name, which can be a bit confusing for patients. Come along in. I don't think we've met before, correct me if I'm wrong?" He smiles at me.

"What, she's gone? I didn't know," I say, still reeling.

"Yes, she's taken a well-deserved retirement. I was delighted to carry on the family tradition." His cheerfulness is really annoying me now. "So, what brings you here Ms Mercier?"

"A pain in my left breast: right there. But since I made the appointment, it's actually got a bit better. Probably not worth checking out."

"Are you joking?" He walks around his desk and leans towards his computer screen. "I can see that your last appointment was four years ago. I'm going to need to examine you; prevention is always better than cure. In fact, I think a thorough examination would be best. We'll start with a smear."

I find his enthusiasm infuriating. He must be fresh out of medical school. The perfect doctor, following the rules to the letter. There is nothing more embarrassing than having to see a male gynaecologist. What could this rosy-cheeked youth possibly know about real life and real women? Thrush, contraception, childbirth—how could he know what any of this feels like? He may have a string of diplomas, but he's still a man. How can men possibly understand what women go through? It's just an abstract notion to them.

He then says he needs to ask me a few questions to update my file. "You are thirty-five. The date of your last period?"

"Err. Two weeks ago."

"Are you using any contraception?"

"No."

"Are you in a relationship? Do you have a regular or occasional partner?

"No."

"Do you have children?"

This Sherlock Holmes in a white gown is starting to piss me off. "No. I imagine this is all in my file if you take a look," I say, exasperated.

"Nine months is all it takes . . ." he replies, laughing. "Right, let's examine you. Can you remove your top?"

He can feel a cyst but doesn't seem worried. He recommends following it up with an ultrasound scan and then shows me towards the examination table. Getting undressed in front of this stranger is mortifying. It's no big deal to him; he sees naked women all day long. I lie back, find a point on the ceiling and try to fix my gaze on it. If I can just pretend this isn't happening . . . But I feel increasingly uncomfortable and can't concentrate.

"You said you don't have children, is that right?"

"Yes, I already told you!" I snap.

"Hmm, strange. Your cervix doesn't resemble that of a nullipara. There are always exceptions of course."

I smile nervously. Doctors and their medical jargon . . . At last it's over. I get up rather clumsily, eyes still fixed on the ceiling, and grab my underwear. I can feel his inquisitive look. This man is really very annoying. I tell myself to calm down, it's only a check-up. I pull my clothes back on as fast as I can, grab the prescription for an ultrasound, settle up with his secretary and get the hell out of there. In my haste, I bump into Lancelot returning from his lunch break. "Sorry!" I blurt out, not waiting for a reply. I just want to be back at my desk sipping a nice cup of tea, or maybe a nice whisky. Something to blot it all out. It wouldn't go down well at the nursery though. Besides I hate alcohol. My grandfather was an alcoholic and Dad was completely traumatized by it.

Back at the nursery I'm greeted by the voice of Johnny Hallyday bellowing from the hearse. Of course, who else? Since the singer died last night the whole of France has been in mourning, and our famous undertaker is no exception. At least it makes a change from Dalida. But what is Jean-Michel doing here at this time of day? I'll have to tell him that he can't just waltz in whenever he feels like it. You can come and go as you please in a graveyard. But corpses don't need an afternoon nap . . .

I open the door and see Viviane decorating our little Christmas tree in the hallway. "Tell me Viviane, do you think I should get a Christmas tree for the kids? Is it important?"

"Yes, it's the most important bit! It's the run up to Christmas Day that makes the whole thing so exciting, don't you think?"

"What about advent calendars? Should I get them with chocolate or without?"

"Definitely *with* chocolate, Morgan, every time."

I go and put the kettle on.

25

Elliot

It'll soon be Christmas and I can't wait! Lea is sad because at home—at Morgan's, I mean—we still haven't done anything Christmassy at all. Mum really loved Advent. On the 1st of December we always bought the biggest tree they had, which used to annoy Dad, who would say, "But Emily, it'll never fit in *dieses Auto!*" Dad never said "car", he only ever said "Auto" in his German accent. Yet we always got the tree into the car. Next, we used to make a crib and manger and then Mum would buy us each an advent calendar from the newsagents. It always took me ages to choose. Last year, there were two I couldn't decide between: one in the shape of a train, and one in the shape of a big green crown, which I finally chose. I figured I could get the other one next year, which is now this year. But it doesn't look like I'll be getting it at all now.

On Saturday morning, when Morgan suggested we go and buy a tree and some decorations, I was so excited I got goose bumps. Lea rushed to hug her, shouting, "Thank you, thank you, you're the best auntie in the world!"

Morgan was really nice to us in the store. She let us choose anything we wanted from the red and gold decorations. Lea wanted purple, but Morgan said it would look awful with her colour scheme. I put back a black *Star Wars* bauble with Darth Vader on it.

It's not easy carrying back a Christmas tree plus baubles, tinsel, a star and the dog. Morgan bought a fake tree that came folded up in a box, so that we can use it again next year as well. She says it's better for the planet. It's not the same as a real one and it won't smell like a Christmas tree but it's better than nothing.

We finally make it home. Morgan then gleefully pulls out a big plastic bag. "Hey kids, I've got a surprise for you!"

She hands Lea a Kinder advent calendar in the shape of a Christmas tree. My sister is thrilled. She jumps up and down like a kangaroo and puts the precious calendar on the shelf above her bed. I wonder if Morgan got me the train shaped one? My heart beats fast with excitement. I didn't see it in the store this time, and she doesn't even know I like it. "I've got one for you too, look!" she says.

We're not really speaking at the moment, but for once, she's actually smiling. Ever since the whole marble episode, I live in fear of being punished. Oh, it's a Kinder calendar in the shape of a house. It's sweet, but nothing like the train one. But there's no way she could have known I liked it. It's not her fault, it's just that I really wanted the train. Mum would have figured it out for sure. Without thinking I say, "Thank you, Morgan, but I'm a bit too old for it. Why don't we give it to Snoopy?"

Morgan snatches it from me. "Okay," she snaps.

Her smile has fallen off. Idiot, I hurt her feelings and she was only trying to be nice. I can't say sorry though. I try to make up for it by helping with the tree and singing along. I put on the tinsel and Lea dances as she hangs the baubles. A couple of them fall on the floor and break. Morgan has shut herself in her room. I think she's sulking.

There, the tree is finished now. It looks beautiful. There are far too many decorations at the bottom and hardly any at the top, but apart from that it looks cool. Lea runs to get

Morgan to show her. Morgan's eyes are red and puffy; she says she fell asleep. She asks us to make a list for Father Christmas. I don't believe in Father Christmas, but if it makes her happy to think we do, then okay. Morgan gives us pens and paper. Lea quickly scribbles hers down. I'm stumped. I can't really put marbles—marbles of my own, I mean. A dinosaur like Lea's? No. Ah, I know: live with Grandma Cat. I hesitate. That would really upset Morgan. At the same time, if Father Christmas *does* exist, then this is what I want. I write it down.

In the evening, Lea is still excited about the tree and her list. "I put Lego, a Playmobil clothes shop, a lady dinosaur so mine can get married, a treasure chest, beads, plastic bracelets and an Indian costume. What did you put Elliot?"

"Nothing. The only thing I really want is Christmas with Mum and Dad. If I can't have that, then I'd like to live in Marseille."

"Morgan will be really sad if you put that," she says.

"I know."

Lea's right. And I gave Morgan my calendar back, which was the first and only present she has ever bought me. I snatch the list from under my pillow, rip it up and throw it in the bin, then jump into bed.

Lea gets in and snuggles up to me. "You know what Elliot? We could make a secret list, just for us, which we won't show to Morgan or Grandma Cat."

"A list of what?"

"A list of everything we'd like to do with Mum and Dad. And maybe Father Christmas will find it."

"There *is* no Father Christmas," I say.

"Who cares, I like him anyway," she retorts.

"If that's what you want."

I take out my Tintin diary from its hiding place and start writing:

A list of everything we **REALLY** *want for Christmas*

I try not to make any spelling mistakes and I underline 'really' twice.

Live in Marseille with Grandma Cat and Grandpa Paul (Elliot)

Lea nudges me and says, "I want Mum to do me some pretty plaits from the top of my head all the way down. Morgan can't do them."

Pretty plaits starting from the top of her head (Lea)

I chew my pen. "I want to play football with Dad," I say.
"And dance with Mum like we used to sometimes!" adds Lea.

Play football with Dad (Elliot)
All of us dancing together in the living room (Lea)

"And I'd like Mum to sing her special song," she says.

Hear Mum sing Twinkle twinkle my little star *(Lea and Elliot)*

"Do you remember that time we did the Smurf dance in the street, all of us holding hands together? It was so cool wasn't it!" I whoop.

Smurf dance in the street, all of us holding hands together (Elliot)

We keep going.

All of us watch a film together on the sofa (Elliot)

Play in the Wendy house while Mum and Dad read on their sun loungers (Lea)

I notice a tiny drop on my hand. Lea is crying as she tries to read over my shoulder. I put the notebook under the bed and give her a hug. We fall asleep in each other's arms, dreaming about the Christmas tree.

26

Morgan

I'm utterly hopeless. I hate myself for reading Elliot's diary. It was a slap in the face and serves me right. I'll just have to turn the other cheek: good practice for when my mother arrives.

I promised myself I wouldn't do it; secrets are sacred and everyone is entitled to their own secrets. But it just happened. I put my head in their room to see if they were sleeping. They looked so sweet together, asleep in each other's arms. I gently pulled Lea away from her brother and carefully slid her under her duvet. Barefoot, I stepped on a pen, so I bent down to pick it up. That's my obsessive side, everything has to be in its rightful place. Without so much as a second thought, I gathered up everything that was lying around, the toys, the dinosaur, their drawings. There were even some odds and ends right under Elliot's bed including the pouch of marbles that I'm leaving for the therapist to deal with. And there was his Tintin diary. I'm paranoid about people going through my things, so what made me open it? Maybe because, as a teenager, I would have given anything to have someone understand me. I thought that knowing Elliot's innermost thoughts might help me win him over. I was incredibly hurt when he threw the advent calendar back in my face. His words cut me like a knife. I was only trying to please him, patch things up, reconnect. Why does he reject me each time I reach out?

As for the diary . . . I actually only read the last page, but that was enough. What Elliot really wants for Christmas is:

"to go and live in Marseille." *Grandma Cat* this, *Grandma Cat* that. I could understand him fawning over the wonderful Annett, but my mother? Elliot, if only you knew how she has been weaving her web all this time, luring you in. And now she's succeeded! It's easy for her, spoiling you for two weeks at a time in the holidays. She doesn't have to deal with the everyday stuff, your moods, your stress, your bad school marks. Oh yes, she has the easy role. Elliot, do you really think that Grandma Cat is the only person capable of raising and loving you? As if! Emily chose me for a reason. She knew Grandma Cat couldn't do it. Grandma Cat was never there for me when I needed her, Elliot, do you hear me? She never wanted to listen to me, understand me, reach out. She saw me as a liability, not good enough, not pretty enough, not anything enough for her. I was just an embarrassment, so she shunned me. Because I didn't want to be like her.

As for Grandpa Paul? Well, he spent his days in his rose bushes away from us, on the balcony, keeping out of it. He reminds me of the three wooden monkeys that I brought back from Vietnam. He hears nothing, sees nothing and says nothing. You know, Elliot, when I was a teenager, Grandma Cat was so hard on me that I never dared confide in her or tell her about any of my problems. I was petrified of her. She only cared about Emily, the beautiful and perfect Emily. Keeping up appearances and what the neighbours would say were all that counted. I wasn't beautiful or cheerful enough for her liking. In fact, I was the ugly duckling, the swot, who came top of the class in everything (except maths). I was serious and uptight. She would say, "Come on Morgan, you could be so pretty if only you would make an effort, style your hair, smile." Then my confidence would take a battering when she added, "What? You can't possibly go out in that! Take a leaf out of your little sister's book. By the way, your school report was good darling, but quite frankly you need to do something about your maths. This can't happen each time. The neighbour has offered to help you with it, you know he is a teacher. I'm not asking you, I'm telling you, so accept his kind offer politely and don't forget to thank him."

My mother would then hide behind the solace of her dark glasses. As for my father, he was too busy treating his patients in his ivory tower.

I so wish I could tell you all this, Elliot, but I can't . . . I'm riddled with fear, remorse, shame, anxiety and on top of all that, I now have the huge responsibility of raising and protecting you both. It's tough you know. So no, I'm *not* Grandma Cat, and I certainly don't want to be like her. I'm sorry if I'm not the person you want me to be, but I'm really trying my hardest, believe me. You just see me as the wicked Morgan who won't let you eat chocolate and who drags you off to the therapist for more punishment. Grandma Cat wants everyone to think she is the doting grandma, baking cookies and pampering you all day long. Here I am, in tears, sitting against the wall, while you dream of living in Marseille. There is so much I want to tell you yet can't.

The other items on your Christmas list are delightful and typical of Lea. She's such a happy little girl—I would collect her sweet smiles and bottle them if I could. When I saw the tear ink smudge, something tugged at my heart. I never got to have any of those moments you're dreaming about. I may not be Emily or Father Christmas but I would like you to teach me. Lea, teach me how to do the Smurf dance. It sounds fun but I have no idea what it is . . . Teach me how to hold hands and dance around the living room. I haven't danced in so long . . . And teach me how to be like you, happy at any given moment, whatever life may choose to throw at you. I can't remember the last time I was happy.

It's late now. I get up and catch sight of the Christmas tree. I laugh when I see how all the baubles have been put on the bottom of the tree, at exactly Lea's height. I rearrange a few of them. Isn't this what Christmas is all about? I would have preferred to spend Christmas alone with the children but I know how much my parents mean to them. I'll just have to make the best of it.

27

Elliot

"Hey Lea, we can go to Disneyland, I've found Morgan's necklace!" Actually I knew where it was the whole time—I'm the one who hid it. Okay, I lied, but Morgan deserved it this time, so I don't feel bad.

I spent the whole of December waiting for Grandma Cat and Grandpa Paul. Every morning, I checked Lea's advent calendar to count the number of days left until the 20th of December. I just couldn't wait for them to arrive. I knew they were also coming to sell the house but I was just so excited to see them. But as soon as they got here, Morgan and Grandma Cat started arguing. They are ten times worse than Lea and me. To be honest, Morgan had been acting strange the last few days anyway. She kept going round the apartment, tidying up even more than usual, getting angry and then putting on Christmas music and trying to dance with us. Sometimes I would hear her walking around her bedroom late at night and once I even heard her crying. I know that she and Grandma Cat don't get on. But all I wanted was to snuggle up against Grandma Cat's big soft pillow belly.

On Wednesday evening, as soon as I heard the intercom buzz and then Grandma Cat grumbling in the stairwell about how many floors she had to climb up, I ran down to meet her at breakneck speed with Lea and Snoopy at my heels. We flung ourselves into our grandparents' arms, almost knocking them

over. Morgan was waiting for us upstairs with her fake smile
glued on. You could see from her eyes that she wasn't happy.
Grandma Cat and Grandpa Paul kissed her and then sat
down on the sofa for drinks and nibbles. Over dessert, they
came out with some amazing news. "Morgan, Elliot, Lea, we
have a Christmas surprise for you all!"

"What?" I asked, all excited.

"We've booked two days at Disneyland Paris! The 24th
and 25th of December! For all five of us!"

Lea jumped up, I shouted with joy and we began dancing,
holding hands.

"Lea, we're going to Disneyland!"

"We're going to see Snow White!"

Even Mum and Dad had never wanted to take us.

Grandma Cat couldn't resist saying that it would obviously cost her an arm and a leg. Morgan nearly dropped the
little snacks she had bought fresh that day from the bakery.
She didn't look too pleased. "Couldn't you have asked me
first?" she said.

"No, it was meant to be a surprise!" replied Grandma Cat
gleefully. "In any case, spending Christmas here was out of
the question, darling. Especially given that this year will be
difficult for us all anyway."

I could sense an argument brewing. Grandpa Paul had
already switched off. He had returned to the sofa and
immersed himself in his crossword. Grandma Cat got up
to take the plates into the kitchen and Morgan followed her
with that same angry look on her face that she had at the
nursery when she told off the mum who is always late.
What a killjoy she is. Disneyland is so cool! I went to stand
near the kitchen door.

"Mum, you could have consulted me first. We were
supposed to spend Christmas here . . . *I'm* in charge of the
children, don't forget."

"And *I'm* their grandmother and I have the right to give them a surprise, don't I? Besides, this is my Christmas present to all of you, you won't be getting anything else. Any of you. And I'm equally responsible for them as you are."

"No, you're not. Emily entrusted them to me; I'm their legal guardian. I'm in charge of their education, I look after them every day and it's not easy for them or me at the moment. I need to establish my own set of rules, at the same time as consoling them and keeping them happy. And I don't think that showering them with expensive gifts is the answer."

Grandma Cat went on to tell us that the situation was only temporary and that we were going to live with her in Marseille. She also said that Morgan didn't want us anyway.

"No, Mum, you're wrong there, *I do!*" snapped Morgan.

Grandma Cat turned sharply to face Morgan, looking furious. "Since when?"

"Since Emily entrusted them to me and since you started reminding me of how incapable I am. I decided to have faith in my sister's choice. I'm their carer and I will not let you turn them into nasty spoiled brats. Disney is a nice idea, but not this year, thank you. We have far too many issues to settle before then. You can postpone it to next year. Let's show them that life carries on as normal and that losing their parents doesn't mean they can do as they please and live without rules."

I couldn't believe what I was hearing. Clearly, she'd gone crazy! I had always dreamt of going to Disneyland. Grandma Cat was very upset, so she told Grandpa Paul they were going back to the hotel. Lea started crying. I was so angry that I ran to my room and slammed the door as hard as I could. Why would going to Disneyland turn us into nasty spoiled brats? That's exactly why I want to live with Grandma Cat: she lets us do what we like!

Grumbling, we got ready for bed. Then Lea started sobbing again and asked Morgan why she didn't want us to see Sleeping Beauty's castle. Morgan was cross and said that Grandma Cat should have asked her first and that the most important thing was to spend this Christmas at home as a family, rather than get distracted by an amusement park.

Yeah, right. Without Mum and Dad there, it wouldn't be a family thing anyway. Morgan was just jealous because Grandma Cat's present was better than hers. That's why she was being mean. I'd already gone through her wardrobe, so I knew exactly what she'd bought us. It was all cool stuff actually, she's learning. She got Lea the Playmobil clothes shop and a bead kit like at school, and she got me an amazing dinosaur fossil dig kit. But compared to Disneyland, no contest. She just couldn't bear that Grandma Cat got us something bigger and better.

I brushed my teeth without saying a word. Okay, so if she won't let us go, then we'll have to make her. And I've already got a great plan.

We switched off our light. I waited till I could hear Morgan running water in the bathroom. She spends hours in the bathroom at night. I crept into her bedroom. I found exactly what I was looking for, right there on her bedside table: Mum's small pendant. Morgan wears it every day and would really hate to lose it. I snatched it and hid it in one of her socks in her chest of drawers.

The next day, I saw that my plan had worked! Morgan went crazy trying to find her necklace. She was even crying. I felt bad about it but I stayed strong, reminding myself I was doing it for me and Lea. She searched everywhere: under the bed, in the hallway, in her coat pockets. When we got back after school, she started looking everywhere again, going crazy. I waited a bit then said, "Would you like us to help you find it? I'm sure if all three of us look, one of us will find it."

"Thank you, Elliot, yes, you know how much it means to me. I would like Lea to have it when she's older."

"Okay, we'll hunt for it. And if we find it, can we go to Disneyland?"

"I don't want to get into all that again . . . And I don't like bargaining. But this necklace means the world to me. So, okay, it's a deal. If you find it, then we can go."

I chuckled to myself thinking how easy this was going to be. Lea really was looking. She even went through all the earth in the bonsai pots. Morgan was getting more and more worked up. Grandma Cat and Grandpa Paul were due to arrive any minute. When she went to cook dinner, I sneaked into her room, took the necklace and put it on the floor just under her window and shouted, "Hey Lea, we can go to Disneyland, I've found Morgan's necklace!"

My aunt hugged me and kept thanking me. I did feel kind of guilty but I don't regret it. When Grandma Cat and Grandpa Paul arrived, we celebrated. Morgan didn't say a word, but we could all see the necklace shining brightly around her neck.

We had the most fantastic Christmas. I wish Mum could have seen Grandma Cat's face on the Big Thunder Mountain. I thought she was going to have a breakdown! Morgan spent most of her time at the hotel pool. She's not really into rides. Grandpa Paul came along though. He even came to the haunted mansion with us, so Grandma Cat wouldn't get scared. We had so much fun that I'll never feel bad about lying.

A few days later, Grandpa Paul went to our old house in Maisons-Laffitte to take care of a few things and then went home. Grandma Cat stayed on a bit longer. She took us to lots of cool places and we even went up the Eiffel Tower. And then it was time for her to pack her case. My heart started feeling heavy again.

28

Morgan

The kids are sound asleep, silence at last, sheer bliss! My mother goes home tomorrow and she is already back at her hotel, phew. In the end we managed to get through the festive period without too many arguments.

At nine thirty I put on a record and lie on the sofa with my book. I read a lot at Disneyland beside the pool. The hotel was amazing, I could never have given the kids such an expensive present, not that it would have occurred to me anyway. Strapped upside down in a roller coaster next to my mother isn't exactly my idea of having fun. And in any case, she encouraged me to take a break. I could really feel the distance between us, all those unsaid words, all that time. We managed to keep out of each other's way: her on the adrenalin-fuelled rides and me in the spa. Tomorrow I'm planning a film night with the kids for New Year's Eve. We'll go and buy a DVD together and watch it in front of a nice TV dinner. We won't stay up all night—they've already had a pretty action-packed Christmas holiday.

My phone vibrates:

Morgan, I'm going to drop by in about ten minutes. I think I left my yellow shawl by the window. Thanks.

Oh no ... I turn to look. The shawl is indeed there ... I thought I had seen the back of her! Anxiety hits me again like a boomerang. Dad has gone, the children are sleeping, it'll just be the two of us. This hasn't happened in years; eighteen to be precise.

The intercom buzzes. I let her in. I hear footsteps in the stairwell. She catches her breath, stops, starts again. My heart races. I should take the shawl, run down the stairs, hand it to her, tell her not to go up for fear of waking the kids and then flee. Instead, I stand there frozen to the spot and she walks in, breathless, looking theatrical in her big black coat, perfect blow dry and shiny manicured nails. Her bulk and imperious demeanour are so intimidating I feel like a small kid again and back away slightly.

"How do you manage to live so high up?" she gasps.

"I'm used to it, plus I'm thirty years younger than you don't forget," I reply.

"Yes, but with the children, I mean. It's a lot more complicated than being on the ground floor. Ah, there's my shawl. I've been looking all over for it. It was a present from Emily, I couldn't bear to lose it."

"I know. I would have posted it on to you. It wasn't lost," I say.

She just stands there looking at me. Her hands crumple up the precious shawl.

"Did the children like Disney?" she asks.

"I think so. I wanted to thank you. It was a good idea. I wouldn't have thought of it myself. Sorry I wanted to cancel it."

The shawl is in a ball now. I sense the impending attack. It's too good an opportunity for her to miss. "Tell me, were you serious when you said you wanted to keep the children?"

Here we go. My heart begins to pound. "Why wouldn't I be? After all, Emily did entrust them to me."

"But . . . it was obvious to me you wouldn't want them . . . It's a huge burden for a single woman like you with no children. What if you meet somebody? No man in his right mind would want to settle down with a woman with two children in tow, you know that! At your age, you're only likely to meet a divorcee who's had their fill of changing nappies. Divorced men just want their freedom."

"That's perfect then," I retort, "as I'm not planning on settling down. I'm quite happy as I am."

Mum places her bag on the table, pretending to look for something. She's actually regaining her composure before launching another assault. I slip into the kitchen to switch on the kettle and calm myself down.

"Morgan. Be realistic. We both know that you are not the right person," she calls out to me.

"But Emily chose *me*, Mum."

She violently zips her bag closed. It tips over and lands on the floor.

"But Emily didn't know about it!" she hisses.

Okay, so there go my hopes of a calm discussion over a herbal tea. I go back into the dining room. I'll have to tackle her with guns blazing. The time has come: we are about to have the discussion we have been avoiding for eighteen years. My legs feel wobbly. I'll fight her tooth and nail on this. She'll refuse to listen or understand anyway, so I've got nothing to lose. I go in for the kill. "Mum, Emily was aware that you are sixty-six years old and that all the women in your family eventually go senile. Plus Dad is in remission from prostate cancer. Who knows what will happen over the next few years? You are clearly not ideal candidates. That's a fact. Whether you like it or not."

Silence. Her mouth tenses up. She is about to cross the point of no return. I feel sick to my stomach; I know what she is about to say. Her eyes are screaming it at me already. Her hand trembles as she opens her mouth. I wish she would just leave. Right now. Before she starts spewing her venom at me.

"Morgan, you know as well as I do that had Emily known . . ."

I put my fingers in my ears before snapping, "Shut up, stop it, you know that this conversation is going too far. That has nothing to do with it!"

"But it does," she says gently, *too* gently. "Let's talk about it. Emily would never have left her children to you if . . . If she had known . . ."

"NO!"

". . . that you had abandoned yours."

"NO! Stop!" I scream in a whisper. I can't do this. Everything goes blurry. I grip the dining room table, bent over and broken inside. Her words pierce me like an arrow, penetrating deeper and deeper. "Don't say that. You have no right!" I gasp.

"I think a judge would be most interested to hear it," she smiles triumphantly.

"You can't prove it. There's no paperwork, no files, nothing!" I sob.

After avoiding each other for eighteen years, the terrible truth had to come out one day; I couldn't silence the fear, the anger and the shame forever. She's been waiting for this moment too all these years: waiting to watch me perish and finally surrender. She wasn't going to sugar-coat it either. I feel like I've shed every single tear in my body. "You don't know anything, Mum, you know nothing of what happened."

My mother turns her back to me, gazing out the window. The silence buzzes in my eardrums; I see her shoulders trembling. She suddenly pivots to face me. Her eyeliner has smudged in furrows on her cheeks. Though she is furious her voice is calm and composed. We mustn't wake the children, that would make this nightmare even worse. They don't need to know that I . . . that I abandoned the child I gave birth to at seventeen. My mother hovers over me, lifts my chin up and forces me to look her in the eye, gripping my cheeks. I wish I were dead . . .

"I know what you did, Morgan, I was there, remember, trying to talk you out of it? It was good of me to keep it all to myself, don't you think? Do you know what it's like to live with so much pain all that time?"

"Yes," I sigh. Yes, I know *only too well* what it's like.

I slide down, my back against the wall, my face buried in my hands. I can't look at her. I find myself on the floor. She crouches down in front of me heavily. There's no escape. She shakes me by the wrist, forcing me to meet her eyes. "You know why I never said anything? Not to protect you, no, I would have thrown you to the lions if I could. But because I was ashamed. In fact, I was so ashamed of you that I preferred to suffer in silence all these years, keeping your dirty little secret, rather than telling your father. Legally you were no longer a minor, I couldn't stop you. But one thing is for sure. I will never leave my other grandchildren with you! You understand? Never! You've already ruined my life once. And Emily's death just about finished me off. I won't let you take away what's dearest to me. I'll take it to the courts if I have to, believe me."

I pull away. Saint Catherine, utterly fearless and beyond reproach! Little Miss Innocent, it has *nothing* to do with her, does it? One would think the Holy Spirit got me pregnant. I'm so enraged I want to retch. She's so quick to judge, yet never once did she take the time to listen or hear me out, she was always too blinded by her own anger. How could she let me sink so low? Her own daughter! Why would she never talk to me or listen to me?

"Emily would never have judged me on something that happened almost twenty years ago. She would have listened, tried to understand. *She* would have forgiven me," I hiccup.

"Oh, you think so, do you?" A strange grin distorts her

face. I wish she'd leave her sunglasses on; her eyes scare me. "She would have been appalled!" she whispers. "Like everybody else. Her beloved sister who sleeps with every Tom, Dick and Harry and then gets knocked up and runs off to Paris to hide her own disgrace? Ah yes, studying in Paris! Great smoke screen, I almost fell for it too! Till I realized you were avoiding us and that something was wrong. You stopped phoning, you wouldn't visit at Christmas, the official version being that you were 'doing your charitable bit for the homeless'. Maybe I shouldn't have even cared and just left you to your own devices. That way, I would never have known about your sordid little secret. And my life wouldn't have been in tatters for the last eighteen years, every day of it spent mourning my lost grandchild. And now, Emily . . . I've got nothing left. I've lost everything. Everything!"

She flops down onto a chair. I'd never seen her cry before, except at Emily's funeral. I'm seething with rage. I hate her for passing sentence on me without ever bothering to hear my version of events. She is miles away, lost in her own fury. She can't hear me, she never could . . .

"Mum, you never . . ."

"Shut up! And listen to me for once, now that you can't hide behind your nephew, niece, or sister! If I hadn't come to Paris and found you slumped in your bed, puking your guts out and terrified—understandable at more than six months pregnant, even when nothing shows . . . If I hadn't called a doctor and asked him to give you a blood test, I would never have known. That's how I knew when the baby was due. And yes, I came back, deliberately. I stayed two weeks, right up until the due date. I could see how upset you were. But you didn't say anything and still kept your belly concealed from me. You knew I knew, but you refused to speak to me, gave me no explanation, until I finally wormed it out of you and made you admit you were pregnant."

My back is against the wall, eyes half closed, I feel feverish, I can't move. I was so young, just seventeen. What else could I have done? Who was really looking out for me?

Seeing me on the floor, Mum stands up to deliver the final blow. I whisper frantically to myself, "Emily, Emily," as if she could fly to my rescue and whisk me away on her big white wings. My mother continues to rant. "And when you left. When you went to the hospital, without even telling me, despite me begging you to let me keep the child." Her voice stops sharply, drowned by her sobs. "The child . . . that you didn't want . . . I didn't even know where you were."

I give it one last shot. "So you never caught on? Never saw anything? Never knew anything?"

That's what I find intolerable. That she never opened her eyes to see what was right in front of her. It's too much for me. I laugh nervously. I can't stop. I don't know who I am anymore. I'm laughing but I'm dying inside. "You should have taken off your dark glasses for once in your life," I say bitterly.

The truth wants to come out, it hovers on my lips before I swallow it back down. I'd rather she think of me as a slut than a victim. I'm still afraid of him—especially now that I know he's coming back. The person I hate more than anyone in the whole world. I'm still as scared today as I was then. I was petrified whenever I saw him, be it night-time, daytime, passing him in the street, or in the lift. The way he ingratiated himself to my parents made me cringe with disgust. He would say, "Is your daughter having problems with her maths? Send her to me!" I was so afraid that I couldn't even speak. Mum threw me to the wolves herself. "You've got your lesson today, sweetheart, the neighbour is waiting for you. Be a good girl and remember to thank him." The bastard seized any opportunity he could, as and when he wanted. I lived in fear of her finding out and accusing me of nymphomania, of

lying and seducing him. And what would the other neighbours think? I was afraid she would abandon me. Which she
ended up doing anyway. But most of all, I was worried sick
about Emily. I couldn't stomach the thought of him doing the
same to her. I sacrificed myself to save my sister.

I cackle and babble like a madwoman. "But I didn't want
to be like you . . . I couldn't bear to be a mother like you. A
mother who never sees what's going on . . . Turns a blind
eye . . . I couldn't love like that."

"You're mad!" she barks. She grabs her bag and coat and
turns to leave, hurling one last threat my way. "You won't
take my grandchildren away from me again, I swear!"

The door slams. I remain frozen, glued to my piece of wall.
I swallow the truth back down. The truth I've never managed
to utter out loud. But what if he really is back for good? What
if he takes it out on Lea? I can keep quiet for another twenty
years if I have to, I've gone this long. Because of course he
knew everything. When I found out I was pregnant, it was
already too late. He was the one who found me a room in
Paris at the last minute. "We need to get you away from here!
Tell them you want to go and study in Paris!" He took what
there was to take and tossed me aside like an old sock. There
I was, hidden away and heavily pregnant, living in permanent
fear for Emily. I was so worried about her that I couldn't
sleep. He promised me he wouldn't touch her if I didn't say
anything. I believe he kept his word. That is the only thing
I'm proud of: my ultimate declaration of love for my sister. I
would have been too ashamed to keep the child. I could never
have hugged it, kissed it, or even looked it in the face. I
preferred to give it to a woman who wanted it. I truly believed
that once the baby was born, my new life would begin. But
the baby's first cry took away my last breath. The day it was
born was the day I ceased to exist. My shame later gave way
to remorse, burning, violent, white-hot remorse, scarring my

body and soul forever. My heart had forgotten how to love. Until Lea came along. Until that happy little girl with her dark eyes and infectious smile showed me how simple it is to be happy.

My mother has gone, too bad. I still had so much I wanted to say. Never mind. I'll tell her anyway. "You know what, Mum? The day I left that child, I knew you'd turn your back on me forever. And yet I still made that choice." I giggle nervously. I stagger to the kitchen in a daze and dig out an ancient bottle of vodka. Where did that come from? I hate spirits. It's party season though isn't it? Celebrate the new year and all that? I chuckle to myself.

"But it didn't really change anything, did it Mum? I'd already been dead to you for years anyway." I pour myself a small glass. Ugh, it's disgusting! I try hard not to spit it out. Come on, make an effort Morgan. I pour myself another. Then another. It would be better if I took some pills with it maybe. I drag myself to the bathroom and open the medicine cabinet. I pick out a coloured tube. I've always been drawn to pretty things, even if they're meant to help me die. I swallow two pills, then start crying. No, I don't want to suffer that long. I put the tube back. I'll find something quicker. I think about my sister and feel the regrets start to crowd in. "Please forgive me, Emily. I wasn't the right person, can't you see? Elliot hates me, Mum hates me, I've got no one. No one even cares whether I'm alive or dead."

I close the cupboard with a bang. Boxes of pills fall on the floor. I don't care. I pour myself some more vodka. It tastes vile, but they say it helps to drink when you're down so there must be some truth in it. I can't stop laughing. Why are there two glasses on the table now? I leave them with the bottle and go to find Snoopy who is asleep in my bedroom. He is so handsome, even with five legs. Or six, for that matter, I'm not sure. I never noticed before—strange. But I shall never go back to that awful vet, the dog will have to stay like that. I kiss him and thank him for his unconditional love. I reach out to grab the rejected Kinder advent calendar. I rip open the windows and devour the chocolates. It's a shame to waste them. As I turn around, I'm drawn to the big dark blob in the park I can see from the window. Looks like a lake I could drown myself in, taking my sordid secret with me. Elliot would be delighted. He could go and live in Marseille. My mother wouldn't miss me. And I would be with Emily ... Maybe I'd finally find some peace. My sister would forgive me, she would understand. Besides, someone like me doesn't deserve to live. How can you live with yourself after abandoning your own flesh and blood? Or expect others to? My head is spinning. I start laughing again and my own voice sounds bizarre to me. To think I run a nursery, what a joke! Wiping other kids' bottoms to help me forget my own kid. Unbelievable. Come on, have one more drink, or maybe two and it'll start to feel better. I bump into the table. One of my bonsai trees falls off and the pot shatters. I pick up another one, laughing now, and smash it on the floor too. Destroying things is so fun. We're having a great time tonight, aren't we? The glass sliding door in the living room beckons to me. I open it and am greeted by a cold draught. The night creates shadows that I'd recognize anywhere: the merry-go-round, the children's games, the mini bridge. In the distance I can just about distinguish the murky outline of the Batignolles cemetery. I'd better tell Jean-Michel to take good care of me when I'm there: put a flower on me from time to time and let me rest near my sister. And I don't want to hear that awful Dalida every day. Silence would be nice, please. Just plain silence. No Dalida singing, *I want to die on stage*. I just want to die full stop. Away from the limelight. I gulp some more vodka and I can see Emily waving at me. I wave back and approach the railing.

"Morgan. Morgan. Help me."

"I'm coming, Emily! I've looked out for you all my life, so I won't let you down now!" I just have to straddle the railing, I'm almost there.

"Morgan . . . I'm scared."

I jump. Why is Emily talking to me? No, it's coming from the bedroom. It's a child's voice. Strange, I don't have a child. Wobbling like a skittle, I let go of the railing. I leave the door open and slip into the bedroom. Elliot and Lea: are they still there? They didn't go with my mother? I thought she wanted to take them. Lea is crying in her sleep. She is agitated and calls out for me. Me, not Emily. Me!

"Morgan. Morgan."

I hold her in my arms as if it were the last time, my tears drench her hair. She takes my hand and hugs me tightly, then falls asleep murmuring, "I love you, Morgan."

Her words vibrate through me like an electric shock. I cover my mouth to muffle my cry of joy. I sober up instantly. Tears stream down my cheeks. I go and close the sliding door and come back to hold her hand. "Thank you Lea. Thank you. Thank you. I love you too. Thank you."

I kiss her cheek and drag myself off to my bed, my stomach in knots and my head in pieces. *Orphan. Stepmother. Unworthy. Guilty. Disgraced. Pariah.* I am all of these things. But I also love that little girl asleep in the next room more than anything. And that little girl is not even mine.

I didn't know it was possible to love like that.

29

Elliot

I woke up at nine. That's strange because normally Morgan is the first one up. I always hear her walking around the living room, with Snoopy at her heels. Today all I can hear is Lea snoring. I can't see her face, just her hair sticking out of the duvet. I creep over the wooden floorboards so they won't creak. I need to go to the bathroom. When I get there, I see boxes of pills strewn across the floor. That's dangerous, what if Snoopy were to eat them? I put them back. I need to get some juice. The living room looks chaotic—what happened here? Someone has thrown Morgan's bonsai trees on the floor! She'll go bonkers when she finds out, and worst of all, she'll think it was me! I run to fetch the dustpan and brush and sweep up the earth then place the little trees back on the table. Maybe if she buys some new pots they'll be okay. I see an empty bottle and dirty glass on the table. The label says: VODKA. It smells awful, like the disinfectant you get at the doctors. I don't know who was here last night, but they clearly aren't very polite. Morgan hates it when people don't tidy up their mess.

I get a comic from the bedroom and curl up on the sofa. Snoopy comes to greet me wagging his tail and tries to jump up next to me. He can't manage it, so I help him up. Looks like his leg isn't quite healed yet.

Lea slips in unnoticed and startles me. She rubs her eyes. It's already ten o'clock. "Elliot, where's Morgan?"

"Come on, let's find out," I say. "But don't make any noise."

We slowly open her door. It squeaks. I hold my breath.

"Well?" whispers Lea.

"Nothing, I can just see her feet." I push the door a bit more. "She's not even in her pyjamas! She's still in the clothes she wore yesterday!"

In any case she is fast asleep. By eleven we're getting bored and decide to make some noise. We play with Snoopy, sing to each other and start preparing some games for New Year's Eve.

Then at midday, Morgan finally gets up. By that I mean she *wakes* up, she doesn't get up properly. She mumbles hello without looking at us and walks like a zombie, bumping into the furniture. I can see black marks under her eyes. She doesn't even moan about the broken bonsai trees and just throws them in the rubbish. She is really white too, even whiter than usual. Lea asks her if she is okay and when we are going to eat as we've been up for hours. She just replies, "yeah, sure" and hands us a bag of crisps and a packet of ham, and lets us eat what we want for dessert. Then she goes back to bed. We can do whatever we like, yay! I pour us both a glass of Coke. I get the impression that she wouldn't even care if we jumped up and down on the sofa today. I wonder whether we should call the doctor. Suddenly she springs out of bed and rushes into the toilet. Ugh, she's throwing up now. I'm a bit worried.

"Lea, I think she has a stomach bug . . . And they're really contagious, so don't go near her!"

The day drags on and we get bored again. I end up asking Morgan if we can go and play in the square on our own just this once. "You can see us from the window, look, we won't move, promise."

"Okay," she mutters.

Lea tucks in Morgan, who is already half asleep, and feels her forehead. "Poor Morgan, she is so poorly," says Lea. "Do you think we'll still be able to get the DVD for tonight? And the TV dinner?"

"No, I don't think so," I reply. "But we can watch *Home Alone* again. It's really funny."

We behave ourselves down in the square as promised and go back to the apartment when it starts getting dark. It's a good thing I took the keys because Morgan is still in bed. She's not asleep but keeps listening to that awful song she loves about the black eagle. That woman's voice is so depressing, it won't make her feel any better.

The phone rings. When it's the landline, I always know who it is. "Hey Grandma Cat, what's up?"

"Did you get home safely?" I hear an odd sound coming from Morgan's bed, like a bear growling.

"Oh yes, Grandma Cat, it's all going well. We haven't done much today but me and Lea did go and play in the park."

"What alone?" she asks in surprise.

"Yeah, it was super cool."

Grandma Cat doesn't seem to be in a very good mood. She asks me again how Morgan is and if we are okay.

"Yeah, we're fine. But Morgan is ill, she has a stomach bug, she keeps being sick."

Grandma Cat just says, "Poor thing, so she's sick now. You must leave her to her rest. Apart from that is everything alright?"

I don't know why she keeps asking. There's still all that mess in the living room but I don't know if I should tell her about it. I hesitate then end up whispering, "Yes, everything's okay except that this morning when I got up there were two broken bonsai trees on the floor and Morgan didn't even get angry about it! I put the little trees back on the table next to the empty bottle of vodka and the glass."

"Next to what my darling?" I hear Grandma Cat roar down the phone.

"Err, next to the empty vodka bottle and glass," I whisper again.

She then bellows down the phone so loud that it hurts my ears. She ends up telling me that it can't go on any longer and that she's going to take care of everything. I hang up. Meanwhile, Morgan has run herself a bath. Luckily, she didn't hear our conversation. I get the feeling that I goofed up somehow, but so what, it can't be that bad. Lea and I begin getting the sofa and cushions ready for our film night.

30

Morgan

Going back to work has been a blessing in disguise. Thank God I didn't have to go to the nursery the day after that horrific night though. I can't actually remember what we did the second week of the holidays. The kids spent a lot of time watching TV and playing in the square. Sometimes we all went together, sometimes they went on their own. I feel like the survivor of a shipwreck, which is ironic really as I'm the one who sank the ship. Little Lea saved my life, bless her. Her chocolate brown eyes are like a beacon in the night, bringing me back to shore. Elliot has been nice to me too. I think he was pleased to have a bit of freedom, without me tagging along for once. I'm normally on their backs all day long, not letting them go anywhere on their own, always worrying that something will happen to them. That's my own paranoia of course. I see the street as a jungle where ogres and vampires lurk, ready to pounce on children if you take your eyes off them for a split second.

This morning Lea was happy to see her friends again. Elliot looked a bit anxious. He's seeing the therapist again this week, let's hope she can get something out of him. She wants to see me too, but I'm not ready for that. I always find an excuse to put it off.

Back at the nursery, Viviane has taken down the Christmas tree and the girls have brought in king cakes for the older children. There's a lot of laughter, shouting and general commotion. I feel much more at ease here at the nursery, protected in my office, high up in my fairy tale tower, like one of Lea's princesses.

Meanwhile, life goes on at the nursery: tantrums, nappies, illnesses, annual reports, cheerful parents, cranky parents, house moves, new arrivals, Jean-Michel and Dalida, the disco hearse and Valerie "late again" Le Gall. I get collared by two of the girls when I go down to the coffee machine after lunch to get some sugar. They look distressed and Delphine begs me to intervene, "Morgan, please could you talk to her again?"

"I've already told her several times, Delphine."

"I know, but enough is enough. We have to stay fifteen extra minutes every night because *Madam* isn't capable of getting here on time! All the other parents manage it . . ." she moans.

"It's not every night though is it?" I ask.

"I have to pick up my daughter at eight o'clock sharp at the Porte Dorée. It takes fifty minutes to get there by underground. So, you tell me, just how am I supposed to get there on time?" she retorts.

I sigh. I totally understand her, but I just can't face another altercation right now. I give in, reluctantly. "I know, it's unacceptable. Though I am the last one to leave as I lock up most of the time. But I *will* speak to her again. The rules apply to everyone."

I return to my tower. I really can't face clashing with Valerie in the first week back. I would give anything to have a bit of peace and quiet. The prospect of another heated discussion rekindles my anxiety. My mother has reopened the wound that I hoped had been healed by time and solitude.

The day goes on. I mentally pray that Valerie will be on time this week, just this week, so I get some respite. At five forty-five I pick up Elliot and Lea from school and explain to them that I need to talk to one of the mums. We get back to the nursery at six thirty. I settle them in my office so they can start their homework. The last parents to arrive put on their kids' shoes. Delphine is champing at the bit. She is putting on Lucas's coat in the cloakroom. It's seven o'clock and Valerie is still not here. I tell Delphine to go home. She is reluctant to leave, she probably wanted to be a fly on the wall while I battle with Valerie. At ten past seven I finally see Valerie Le Gall approaching, walking slowly. This is just out of order. She has lost a lot of weight and has "burn out" written all over her. She looks like a junkie. I jump on hearing a door slam behind me. Viviane is getting her coat on. Oh no! A witness. I take a deep breath. Valerie pushes the door open looking flustered. I realize I don't know much about her, except that she lives alone and has a high-flying job in a luxury cosmetics firm. This has caused tongues to wag and the girls delight in jabbering about her life as an endless whirl of champagne and jet set parties, which would explain why she is always late. If she didn't party so much, she would be less tired and more punctual. I rest my case. Lucas gets up and squeals with joy upon seeing his mother, and clumsily attempts to walk a few steps towards her. When she bends down to him, I pounce. "Mrs Le Gall, it's only the first week back and you are already late. I'm sorry to keep harping on this but it's just not acceptable. I'm getting complaints from the team. Your son won't be able to stay in our establishment if the situation doesn't resolve itself quickly."

She gazes at me distractedly. Little Lucas finally throws himself onto her and clings to the big scarf she is wearing. It slowly slithers down, revealing her head underneath. She is almost entirely bald. I go icy cold and just stare at her face, her deathly pallor. A wave of nausea comes over me. All we have done is criticize this poor woman, her looks, her clothes, her weight. I'm so ashamed, ashamed of us all. Only Viviane had the intuition to sense something may be wrong. All I could see was some sophisticated, career obsessed glamour puss, whose kid cramped her style. Just who am I to judge another woman's maternal love? Valerie seems to be fading away with each chemo session.

Viviane comes up to us. "You don't live that far away do you? I could bring Lucas home in the evening, if it helps? I'll leave my mobile number in his backpack tomorrow."

Once again, Viviane saves the day and the nursery's reputation. I am eternally grateful to her. Valerie's eyes are blurry, her lips are trembling. She mumbles a faint "thank you" and turns round. Viviane straps the child into his pushchair. Quick, say something nice, Morgan, I tell myself.

"Err, Mrs Le Gall, I just wanted to say we had absolutely no idea that . . . And we want to help you, of course. How long have you been ill?"

Valerie gives me a vague smile. "Since October," she replies. "I didn't realize it would be this difficult. I hate to think everyone is pointing their finger at me. But I'll get there, you'll see. Thanks to Lucas . . . *For* Lucas . . . Please don't tell anyone. Thanks for your kind offer, Viviane, but I will pick my son up every day. He is the only thing that keeps me going."

We watch her walk off down the street slowly, leaning on the pushchair to keep her balance, her long scarf blowing in the wind. I watch her frail silhouette fade into the distance. I'm utterly distraught. I totally misjudged this poor woman, who is fighting for her life so she can see her kid grow up. While I fought to never see mine again. Who am I to judge her?

The door opens, Lea takes my arm. "Morgan, I want to go home now."

I gaze at her, her smile, her hair. She is the spitting image of Emily. I take her hand. "Yes, sweetheart, let's go."

I think about Niko's mum, the wonderful and gracious Annett. I knew right from the start I could never be like her. But I *can* be a fighter like Valerie. When I left my child behind all those years ago, I didn't fight. Now that Emily has left her children behind forever, I can and I will.

31

Elliot

Dear Mum,

It's been way too long since I last wrote to you, but with Christmas, New Year, Grandma Cat, Grandpa Paul, Morgan's stomach bug and going back to school, I haven't had a second to myself. It feels good to take out paper and pen and speak to you again. I love writing to you.

We had so much fun at Disneyland. If only you could have seen Grandma Cat's face on the Big Thunder Mountain. I thought we were going to end up in A&E!

Today is Saturday. And it was such a cool day. I'll tell you all about it. Lea jumped on me as soon as she woke up, she was so excited! She told me to open the curtain, and then, big surprise . . . everything was white! It had snowed in the night. Well, not enough to ski of course and there's no ski lift in Batignolles. But we couldn't wait to go out and roll in it anyway.

"Elliot, Elliot, look, it's as pretty as a sugar pancake!" shouted Lea.

"No, like a white page! We could write a story on it!" I said.

Lea knocked on Morgan's door to wake her up. "Morgan, it's been snowing, can we go outside, please?"

"Kids, it's only seven thirty!"

She didn't look too pleased. Sometimes she looks so much like Grumpy from the Seven Dwarfs. Still, she finally got up and made us breakfast. We had already put on our wellies over our pyjamas and had to take everything off again. We gulped

down our hot chocolate. Lea splashed hers everywhere. We got
dressed in a flash, then had to wait. To speed things up, I asked
Lea to do her panda eyes, and it worked! Morgan finally let us
put on our coats and hats.

We ran behind Snoopy into the square. I made a snowball
and threw it at Lea. It was so tempting; I'm sure Dad would
have done the same. She wailed loudly like a fire engine siren
and Morgan glared at me. But I didn't care and ran to hide
under the slide. Except you'll never guess what! A giant snowball hit me right in the neck. And guess where it came from?
Morgan! She never plays anything with us but she's actually a
really good shot! Lea burst out laughing, which was mean, but
it was great to see Morgan playing like that.

We said hello to the ducks who looked like they had cold feet
and we ran after Snoopy who was chasing a pigeon. And then
I had this sudden urge to see you. It's true, we haven't been to
the cemetery once since you moved there, so I asked Morgan.
She seemed annoyed at first, and said it was too far, then
changed her mind. Lea nodded and took me by the hand.

It took forever to walk there. The snow was so beautiful that we
didn't want to take the underground. I didn't recognize a thing
under the white blanket. It was like my first time there. I felt
sad that we didn't bring any flowers, so Lea and I decided to
make a snowman especially for you. We went to look for small
stones for the eyes, mouth and coat buttons, and bits of wood for
the nose and arms. Snoopy followed us and Morgan stayed
behind to keep you company.

I turned round to look at her. She was crouched down. I
could see her lips quivering. I crept towards her quietly, while
Lea was counting her stones. Morgan didn't hear me and I hid
behind a large gravestone with lots of names on it. She kept
drying her eyes and whispering to you, "I'm so sorry Emily, for
not living up to your expectations. At first, you know, I was

angry with you. I wondered why you would do this to me? Why me and not Mum? There is so much I haven't told you. Things I couldn't tell you because I was so ashamed, things I did to protect you. I loved you so much Emily, I never loved anyone more than you. You were the only person who didn't judge me. Life is so tough without you. And you can't even imagine how hard it is for Elliot and Lea."

Hearing those last words made me want to cry. But it would have made too much noise, so I told my tears to go back inside my eyes and carried on listening.

". . . You know, there's this mum at the nursery who has cancer. She's not even thirty-five and she's fighting for her life for the sake of her little boy, who she's raising on her own. Meeting such a strong woman gave me the slap in the face I needed. And I want to thank you Emily. Thank you for making me see the light. And trusting me with Elliot and Lea. I swear to you I will do everything in my power to make them happy. It won't be easy, I have so much to learn still. And there's been some collateral damage, which I need to repair: Elliot's in a bad way and he doesn't like me. He wants to go and live with his grandmother. And . . . I have baggage of my own to fix, before my heart can truly start loving again. But I promise you I'll get there."

I was pissed off that she told you I was in a bad way. Okay, so my marks are still bad and I don't have any friends at school because of the marbles, but I'm a lot better now Mum. I haven't stolen anything from anyone since, I swear. I talk about it a lot with the owl lady. I got goose bumps when I heard Morgan say how much she loved you. I thought she only had room in her heart for Snoopy. Now I can see she also has a place for you and Lea. And maybe for me too one day?

Morgan also said, "You know Emily, I had a terrible argument with Mum. It had been brewing for years. I don't think she's ever going to speak to me again because . . ."

"*Morgan, Morgan, Snoopy's foot is stuck in a snow hole!*"

At the sound of Lea's voice, Morgan ran off. It was nothing serious, but it was his bad paw so she freaked out a bit. I was annoyed as I wanted to hear the rest. But Morgan didn't return to the grave. With everything Lea had found, we could start building our snowman. We drew a smile with little pebbles and made arms out of bits of wood. Morgan helped us, and Lea drew a big heart on the snowman's belly. He was handsome and we were proud of our work.

As we were leaving, I wanted to do something for you, so I said, "I'd like us to hold hands and say goodbye to them."

I took Lea by her mitten, Morgan took my hand too and we blew you a kiss. And I promised you that I would try my hardest too as I felt really sad seeing Morgan crying in front of you. I know I haven't always been nice to her and that I don't talk to her much. I shouldn't have given her back the chocolate calendar or hidden the necklace just to go to Disney. And most of all, I'm worried about telling Grandma Cat about the vodka bottle. I know that Morgan never drinks alcohol, but Grandma Cat will think she does now.

When the girls turned around, I quickly drew a heart in front of you and Dad, and wrote our three names inside it with my finger: Lea, Elliot and Morgan.

We didn't talk much on the way home. When we arrived at the square, the merry-go-round was already spinning. Morgan looked at us and said, "Go on, I dare you!" I jumped onto a motorbike, Lea chose a giraffe and Morgan rode a pig. We goofed around, laughing our heads off. Morgan really made an effort today, Lea was happy, and I promise I'll do my best, Mum.

I love you both very much and miss you to the end of the earth and back.

Elliot

32

Morgan

Now that I'm determined to forge ahead, I'm going to need some help, and who better to ask than Viviane? Naturally, it's humiliating for a nursery manager to have to ask for child-care advice, but Viviane is sweetness personified. She always has an artful trick or two up her sleeve too, for dealing with difficult situations. But how can I broach the subject? I can't just summon her to my office for a quick lesson in "How to be Mary Poppins rather than a slightly rubbish stepmum . . ."

While the kids are having their nap, I loiter in the corridor. Luckily, she isn't on dorm duty today. I see her enter one of the washrooms and rush in after her. A large dolphin hanging from the ceiling silently encourages me. "Hi Viviane, how are you?" I ask.

"Good thanks, Morgan. Just doing a bit of cleaning while it's quiet. What about you?"

"I'm doing inventory; nappies, wipes and milk today. It's taking forever."

She says she is not cut out for paperwork and chose a nursery career because she loves working hands on with the kids. She finds children *irresistible*. I wish I could tell her that I'm also there for the kids but for different reasons. But this is not the time for confessions. I must wait for the right moment. She appears upset about something and scrubs the changing mats with gusto. Surely, they can't be *that* dirty.

She says how sorry she feels for Valerie as a single mother, being ill and on her own, and worries how the poor woman will cope. She offers to stay later every evening till Valerie arrives, as she has nothing pressing to rush home for. I really appreciate her help.

To justify my presence, I open the cupboard and count the packs of nappies inside. Viviane is now disinfecting the sinks.

My ears prick up when she enquires after Elliot and Lea, saying she hasn't seen them for a while as she no longer locks up. I say they're fine, and that Elliot is a bit better than he was. Then I bite the bullet. "This may sound silly, but I'd love to lift his spirits somehow. Would you have any ideas?"

She bursts out laughing. "So I'm an expert on pre-teens now? I'm flattered by your faith in me Morgan but . . ."

I had heard she looked after her fifteen-year-old niece on a regular basis but I feel a bit ridiculous now to be honest. She looks at me, changes sponges and heads towards the mini toilets. "Now let's see. What about the cinema? You must have already thought about that yourself?"

True, why did I not think of it before? I'm such an amateur.

She goes on, "It's simple, a film with popcorn and Coke. There must be a Star Wars or a Disney on?"

"Yes," I say, "but I fear *Star Wars* might scare the hell out of Lea so I'm trying to avoid it."

Viviane smiles warmly at me, her freckles lighting up her face, before saying, "The most important thing is to spend quality time with them. Cinema, Disneyland, presents, all that stuff is fun but superficial. They need *you*. Free up some time for them, you work far too much! It probably doesn't come naturally to you, but you must make time for them."

I see her point. Though I don't know how I can. In the week I'm the one who locks up the nursery. My weekends are spent going shopping, doing laundry and cooking. Should I teach them how to iron so we can spend some quality time together? All those fun evenings to look forward to ... I still haven't figured out how all those picture-perfect families you see on TV manage to spend their days happily playing board games together.

Viviane then asks me what I have planned for the February half term, implying it could be a good occasion to do something with the kids. I didn't spend the last holidays with them in Marseille. We had Christmas at Disney, though I hardly saw them; I spent my days at the side of the pool while they were hanging upside down from various roller coasters. As for that dire second week, I prefer to blot it out entirely. I shudder at the thought of what could have happened.

I tell her that I'm thinking of sending them to camp for the first week and that they will spend the second week skiing with their grandparents who have a mountain chalet in Germany. She suggests I go with them. The idea would never have occurred to me. Besides, I haven't been invited. Viviane tells me to invite myself along, that this could be the quality time together we all need. I point out that I would have to take the week off. She says it doesn't matter as I never take any time off outside of the official closing dates, before politely adding that the nursery will survive without me. Her warm smile and bright eyes spur me on. She puts her spray down, having washed away my doubts. I feel like a lost child who needs their hand held.

There, in the privacy of the bathroom, amidst the swinging dolphin, the starfish on the walls and the plastic lobsters languishing in fishing nets, my confidence bounces back. The holidays will soon be here! It doesn't seem two minutes since term began. How are parents expected to get any work done with all these holidays? Yes, why don't I give Annett a call? If there's room in the chalet, I'm sure she won't refuse, even though we hardly know each other. I mean we do have a lot in common.

I take a deep breath before firing my final question at her. "Viviane, I have something to ask you but it's a little strange. Do you know how to do cornrow braids?"

"Yes, I do, as it happens."

"Do you think you could teach me?"

"Certainly!"

Viviane's cheerful laugh echoes off the plastic shellfish on the bathroom walls. She asks me if I'm free tomorrow for my first lesson. The afternoon nap is over now. I thank her and cast an eye over the gleaming sinks, my fictitious inventory forgotten.

Viviane oozes kindness, compassion and generosity. In addition, she is good natured and gentle as a lamb. Her benevolence never fails to amaze me, and I tell her that she will make a wonderful mother someday. She turns around to face me. Her smile disappears and she looks tearful. I can see a deep sorrow in her eyes that I was unaware of before, which tells me something is wrong.

You could cut the atmosphere with a knife. I wonder if I hurt or offended her in some way? I just wanted her to know that she is a natural with children, so I tell her that I thought she wanted children one day. She replies that she probably won't be able to; she has an acute form of endometriosis, which her and her boyfriend have known about for some time. I'm speechless and try to comfort her. If only her spray could magic it all away. Even when I try to be nice, I always put my foot in it. She bravely puts on her chipmunk look and sweetest smile and tells me that she chose to work in a nursery so that she has the patter of tiny feet around her, and, when she gets home, she has her boyfriend Matthew. "He absolutely loves his job as a sports teacher, and one day we hope to open a club for underprivileged kids in a tough neighbourhood integration through sport type of thing."

"Ah, so you're really sporty then? I didn't know that," I say. I clutch at straws in my attempt to put her at ease. It hits me that I know practically nothing about her. I then learn that she was regional gymnastics champion, which is no mean feat. She wanted to become a sports teacher too, till she found out about her illness, which prompted her to work with kids instead.

"You see, Morgan, the nursery makes up for it. I have a great life, don't worry about me."

I feel guilty now for asking her help, as she already has her share of problems. She offers to teach me cornrow braiding tomorrow and tells me to bring some rubber bands.

Life is so unfair. I had a child I didn't want, and she wants a child she'll never have. Despite it all, she remains happy and cheerful while I'm a basket case on the brink. It's uncanny, but my past and her future share a common denominator: remorse over a lost child.

That very evening, I pluck up the courage to phone Annett. It reassures me to hear her guttural accent and yes, of course, I'm invited. I forget to mention one small point: I've forgotten how to ski . . . I ruptured a ligament in my knee when I was twelve years old and never wanted to ski again after that. Plus, my mother has always regarded snow and winter sports with pure horror. She is an avid sun worshipper.

33

Elliot

I'm seeing the owl again today. I never thought she'd be able to help me, but I really do feel better each time we talk. I say "we" but I'm the one who does all the talking. Her job is to ask questions. If you can call that a job! I tell her about our trip to the cemetery, the snow that looked like a white page waiting to be written on, the carousel and the first time I held Morgan's hand. I tell her about my Tintin diary and how I write to my mum. She listens carefully, nodding every now and then, and says that all of this is very good and that she's proud of me.

That's weird. How can she be proud of me? We hardly even know each other. But it's been so long since anyone has said anything like that to me, that I feel all tingly inside. The last time was with Dad when I scored three goals in the school football tournament.

And then she goes quiet and looks at me with her huge eyes and sits up really straight in her chair. She does that a lot. It really annoys me. I finally pluck up courage and ask her THE question. "You know, the marbles I have at home . . . I was wondering . . . should I give them back?"

She says it's a good question and what did I think. I reply that they are not really mine, but the thing is, I can't just show up with them one morning and give them back. The other kids all hate me anyway and it'll only make it worse if they see how many I stole. She asks me if I ever feel tempted to do it again.

I don't. I mean I don't even know why I did it. At the start I just wanted to punish Alex, then it became a game. But now I can't stand seeing them in my room. They look ugly.

She asks me how I think I could give them back and sits there as still as a statue. I knew she wouldn't help me. I'll just have to figure it out on my own *again*. I really don't see the point of her sometimes. Suddenly I get an idea. "What if I give them to the headmistress? Then *she* can decide what to do with them."

The owl thinks it's a good idea and says that the headmistress will see it as a step in the right direction.

I have a feeling she is going to say our time is up. But I still have something really important to ask her. It's even more important than the rest and I can't keep it to myself for another whole week.

I grab the pile of letters I stole from Morgan out of my backpack. "I wanted to show these to you too."

"Very well. What are they, letters addressed to your aunt?"

"Yes."

"And how did you get them?"

"I just happened to find them in the drawer of her bedside table. There were so many that I figured she wouldn't notice," I mumble, feeling ashamed.

She keeps staring at me, so I look down. Then she repeats my words like a parrot, "You *just happened* to find them in the drawer of her bedside table."

I tell her that it was a long time ago in September or October and that I swear I haven't taken anything else. She continues, "Okay fine, so you want me to read your aunt's private letters?"

No, *I* want to read them to her as there are many things I can't stop wondering about. I explain that the letters are from a girl who lives halfway around the world who is grown up now, she is seventeen, and that I think Morgan went to

Vietnam the year she was born. And the girl writes to her all the time, and really likes Morgan.

The owl simply says, "So . . .?"

I tell her that I wonder if Morgan had a child out there she abandoned, and that I'm afraid she might do the same to me and Lea. I can feel the tears coming. It's true that this whole story really freaks me out.

She looks astonished. She puts her huge round glasses back on, takes the photo and starts reading one of the letters. Then she bursts out laughing. "But Elliot, it's just a sponsorship programme! For years, your aunt has been giving money to a child so she can go to school. She hasn't abandoned anyone! On the contrary, she has *saved* a child."

I feel like an utter idiot but at least it's a weight off my mind. She then tells me to read what it says at the bottom of the page, in tiny letters: *Save the Children Vietnam*. It's a pretty famous charity.

I can't think of anything to say. She just stares at me, absently, before adding, "Your aunt is a generous person, you see. Right, I'll see you next Friday at the same time. And promise me you won't take any more letters without her permission. And you need to stop worrying that you're going to be abandoned, Elliot . . . See you soon and have a good weekend!"

I leave her office, feeling as light as a feather. I chuckle to myself on the way back, happy to be walking alone. Of course, I did think it was a bit strange that Morgan would abandon a little girl on the other side of the world. Things like that only happen in fairy tales. But I'm relieved to hear it from the owl. Some people have bad luck all the time, and I would hate to be one of them. Take Tom Thumb for example. For a start, he's really small. Then his parents abandon him several times. And after that he enters a house where an ogre tries to eat him. That boy really is jinxed.

*   *   *

At home, Morgan has a surprise for us. She is taking us to the cinema tomorrow to see the latest Disney. Oh my God, is she ill? She's going to leave Snoopy alone for more than two hours?! Has she booked a dog sitter? Lea is leaping up and down in the living room with joy. Morgan also wants to talk about the school holidays. She has signed us up for the day camp during the first week, then the second week we will go skiing in Germany with Oma Annett and Opa Georg. And Morgan says she is coming too! Wow, I didn't know she could ski. She said she hasn't skied for ages but will soon get back into it. I ask her if we can go to Grandma Cat's the first week instead of camp.

Morgan's smile instantly disappears. "Look, Elliot, we can't do everything. I would prefer to go to Oma and Opa's this time. You haven't seen them for ages, and they need you."

We had a fab Saturday, the best one in months. We went to the cinema and had popcorn and Coke! When Grandma Cat called in the evening, I couldn't wait to tell her all about our day. She seemed a bit upset. I ended up telling her that she needn't worry about us as we are fine here, and that Morgan is even coming skiing with us at half term.

I hear my aunt's bedroom door creak. I've got a feeling she heard everything. Which just goes to show that grown-ups listen behind doors too.

34

Morgan

Poor Snoopy is limping more and more. If I didn't have to see that awful vet, I would take him straight back there. Unfortunately, he is the only one on duty on Saturdays. I half-heartedly make an appointment hoping that between now and then the arrogant idiot will have slipped on a banana skin and broken his leg.

So here we are again in Sir Lancelot's office. As usual, he isn't very friendly, and just smiles at the children and shakes my hand without looking at me. His full attention is on the dog. Lea won't leave her four-legged friend, even while the vet examines him. "You won't hurt him, mister, will you?" she asks.

"No, young lady, on the contrary, I'm going to make him better," he replies surprisingly gently.

Lea is still worried and hopes he won't have to have an injection.

He carries on examining Snoopy. "Clearly you're out of luck today. The sprain has healed well, but his paw pad has split. It's benign but painful, and it's bothering him a lot, look."

I crane my neck to see over Lea and Elliot's heads.

"Can't you see it?" he asks impatiently.

"Not clearly, no," I say.

"Really? Look, there, can you see it now?"

His expression irks me somewhat. I tell him that I'm sorry but it's not obvious to me as I'm not a veterinary surgeon.

There goes my pride and my unfulfilled dreams with it. He makes me feel so incompetent that I wonder how I could possibly have envisaged opening a boarding kennels. He continues to interrogate me, asking me how long ago I first noticed Snoopy was in pain. Two weeks ago, I reply, when he got his leg stuck in a snow hole. I said we didn't notice anything at first, then he started to limp again and I just assumed the sprain hadn't healed.

He tells me they are two different things and that normally a short walk in the snow shouldn't damage a paw pad, but that some dogs are more fragile than others. He writes a prescription for some ointment and tells us not to take Snoopy out in the snow for several weeks.

Lea squeals that we are going skiing. He says in that case Snoopy must wear doggie boots. Lea is delighted at the idea of dressing up my beagle. She covers him in kisses. "Don't worry, Snoopy, I'll look after you. You know what, mister? When I grow up, I want to be a vet like you. And my aunt's dream is to open a dog kennels!"

"Is it really? he replies. "When she grows up, you mean?"

His printer churns out the prescription, which he hands to me, adding that he thought I was a nurse and that caring for animals is not quite the same thing.

I may be blond but I'm not a total bimbo! Taken aback, I remember how humiliated I was on our first visit when he made me feel like the wicked stepmother who hadn't bothered to notice that her niece was running a fever. "I trained as a nurse, but I run a day nursery now. I've always dreamt of opening an exclusive boarding kennels. But dogs and kids are not the same thing, as you have just so kindly pointed out. So I might as well give up on the idea."

He doesn't pick up on my sarcasm but gives me a funny half smile, saying that he always wanted to open a boarding kennels himself but never had the nerve for such a tremendous undertaking. He goes on to say that living in the countryside surrounded by healthy animals is far more appealing than being stuck inside these four walls with sick ones. The momentary brightness in his eyes quickly fades as he gets back to business.

He hands me the prescription and asks me to settle up with his secretary. Then he advises me to make an appointment for a check-up after our holiday.

I go to reception. Through the open door, I can hear him talking to Elliot. "What about you, kiddo, you alright? You haven't said a word since you arrived."

I tense up. Is he checking in with Elliot to see if I'm looking after him properly? Maybe I'm paranoid. I really need to cut myself some slack. Elliot comes out of the consulting room.

"What did he want to know?" I ask him in a low voice.

Elliot snaps that the vet just wanted to know how he was and why am I asking anyway. We leave with a prescription as long as my arm and another appointment that I'm already dreading. To add insult to injury, Lea says that she thinks the vet looks like their dad. Elliot calls her a crackpot. Lea then says how handsome he is and what did I think.

I tell her in no uncertain terms that he is not my type.

That afternoon I receive a message from my mother, who accuses me of depriving her of her grandchildren during the school holidays. I reply tersely, saying that their other grandmother has the right to see them too. Her response is loud and clear:

Thanks for your empathy.

Fine. Let's just leave it at that. I then notice an email from the therapist, who wants to see me. It's just one pain in the neck after another today. She understands that my schedule is "extremely busy" but a meeting would be "most appreciated."

Elliot has made a lot of progress. However, he still has a lot of anxiety, so it would be good to discuss this.

I've been trying to avoid a one-on-one with her for too long now. I'll have to face the music sooner or later. I've always refused to see a therapist up to now. The shame I have been carrying all these years has left me mute; I just can't talk about it. She offers me a slot between noon and two o'clock the day before we go on holiday. I have no choice but to accept.

35

Elliot

Today is the big day. I even wrote it in my exercise book, like the owl told me to. Today I return the marbles to the headmistress.

I didn't tell Morgan, and she didn't ask me either. But I know she has an appointment with the owl soon, so I want to do it before then. This morning she spent at least twenty minutes in the bathroom plaiting Lea's hair. The result wasn't mind-blowing but my little sister was thrilled. In the meantime, I discreetly placed the pouch of marbles at the bottom of my schoolbag. It weighs a ton.

After lunch, I ask to go back into the classroom pretending I left my scarf there. The other kids are outside playing, so I should be able to take the marbles to the beanpole without being seen. On my way back up the stairs, I notice the paintings that frighten Lea. Tom Thumb is putting on his seven league boots. Not his boots, by the way, but the ogre's. When I think of all the fuss they made just because I stole a few marbles, while he stole the magic boots *and* lots of silver and gold, and everyone praised him. The other day I told the owl that in fairy tales the heroes do nothing but lie and steal. She told me that in their case it was to protect themselves. I don't agree: Tom Thumb didn't need the treasure to protect himself, the boots did that.

The headmistress's office is at the end of the corridor. The door is slightly open, and I hear a voice. Great, she is there. I quietly approach, clutching the pouch tightly. I hope I don't run into anyone, especially not Alex! He might get the wrong idea and think I'm stealing again, which would be a shame just as I'm trying to fix things.

The headmistress is on the phone. I'll wait outside until she hangs up, it's more polite. Through the window, I watch the children playing tag in the playground. I can see Alex with them. Lea is in the corner with her gang of friends. She's laughing, and her plaits are half undone, but she doesn't seem to care. All the children look like they're having fun without me.

Suddenly, my ears prick up when I hear our family's name. I promised the owl that there would be no more rummaging through drawers, but I never said I wouldn't listen at doors. I'm sure that Morgan was snooping during my conversation with Grandma Cat the other day. I go nearer, trying not to make a sound, and press my ear to the door.

"On what evidence are you basing this, Mr Mercier?"

Is she speaking to Grandpa Paul? Grandpa Paul is on the phone to the headmistress? Wow! And there was me thinking he didn't even know the name of our school. I listen carefully.

"Rest assured, Mr Mercier, we're keeping a close watch on Elliot and Lea."

So, it *is* us she's talking about.

"Of course, we see your daughter regularly, Mr Mercier I for one have never noticed the kind of behaviour you're talking about. You understand that I have to treat such allegations with caution. I guessed, how shall I put it . . . that there was some *tension* between your wife and daughter, which is not unusual given the situation. But I have to use my own judgement. In fact, I'm surprised that you're contacting me. If you are so sure of what you say, why don't you go through the proper legal channels?"

Of course, I can't hear what Grandpa Paul is saying, but it can't be anything good. The headmistress goes on. "Yes, I'm in regular contact with the children, I can see that they are slowly making progress. I would instantly spot a sudden change in their behaviour. However, I do understand your concern and I promise to keep a close eye on your grandchildren and your daughter, though I must reiterate that I have never had the slightest suspicion that your daughter is an alcoholic. Obviously, if it were true, protecting the children would be our absolute priority."

I almost drop the marbles in surprise. To be on the safe side, I place the pouch on the floor. Morgan, an *alcoholic*? Has Grandpa gone crazy or what? How can he think such a thing! Ah, I guess Grandma Cat told him. So, it's all my fault. Suddenly I go icy cold and start shaking. I see the empty bottle and the glass on the table from when Morgan's friend left all that mess. I remember it well now. I deliberately told my grandma all about it. Everything was weird that day, I felt so miserable, I wanted her to come back and get me. I can still hear Grandma Cat roaring "What did you say?" down the phone. But I never said Morgan had been drinking! I betrayed Morgan and now Grandma Cat and Grandpa Paul are going to do the same. Just as things were getting better and I was starting to feel a bit more at home and everyone is trying their best. Morgan never drinks! And why is the bean-pole poking her nose into this?

I want to scream. I kick the pouch of marbles. It splits open and the marbles roll off into the corridor, making a terrific noise. The headmistress's door opens wide.

She asks me if I have been standing there long. I must look really angry. I'm also scared. I scramble around on the floor desperately trying to pick them up. She helps me, then she takes me by the arm and closes the door behind us saying, "Right. I'm all ears."

That's not fair. I want to ask *her* stuff, not the other way round. But I can hardly admit to her that I was listening at the door. I show her the marbles, and instead of feeling proud of myself, I feel nothing. I dry the tears from my cheeks.

I hand her the marbles, saying I don't know what to do with them as I can't give them back. I daren't look her in the eye and fiddle with the drawstring on my hood instead.

She is delighted that I have returned them and says it's a step in the right direction. She says I have no reason to cry, it's good news. I tell her I don't know what we should do with them. Should we throw them away or give them back? If so, how? Or should we use them as prizes in the end of year tombola? She likes my last suggestion and I agree to help her with it.

I concentrate on my Harry Potter sweater that Grandma Cat sent me. My finger traces the outline of the magic wand. The headmistress puts her hand on my shoulder and gently lifts up my chin, looking me in the eye. "You know, Elliot, it was a good idea of yours to bring the marbles back. Everything will get back to normal now, you'll see—with the other children, I mean. I have faith in you."

It's funny, everyone is proud of me at the moment, except me. I hate myself for what I did to Morgan. I try to hold back my tears but can't. She asks me if there is anything else I would like to talk about. I shake my head. She asks me how things are with my aunt and I tell her that we are all doing our best and that Morgan is nice.

She goes a funny green colour. She has probably guessed I know everything. Or maybe she really is changing into a beanstalk. She takes her hand off my shoulder and says I must come and see her if ever there's anything I need to talk about. I thank her and leave.

I can hardly believe that Grandpa Paul bad-mouthed Morgan to the headmistress, and that Grandma Cat asked him to do it just to get us to live with her. And that she and Morgan can't stand each other any longer. Real families don't do that sort of thing. I run back to the playground as fast as I can and join in the game of tag. I can't concentrate and lose each time, but so what, at least I'm with the other kids. I've made up my mind: I'm never going to play marbles again.

36

Morgan

This woman is old enough to be my grandmother. I feel like a tiny little girl as I sink deeper and deeper into the huge green armchair. The frail, wrinkly lady places her unusual-looking spectacles on the desk and stares at me with her soft green eyes. I can see why Elliot likes her. He has never admitted liking her, but he always talks about "the owl lady with a million questions". But here in the softly lit alcove, I feel confident, which is a first for me, having spent my life avoiding shrinks and the like. Deep family analysis is not for me, thanks. I think "life's hardships teach us the art of silence"— Seneca's words not mine. I remember this from back when we studied him at secondary school. He really hits the nail on the head, which is probably why I never forgot this quote. My silence is the only thing that has never betrayed me.

"Ms Mercier, I'm delighted that you were able to come today." I let her lead the conversation, we're just here to talk about Elliot obviously. "Ms Mercier, how do you find Elliot, I mean, since we started his therapy?"

"Better. A definite improvement," I reply. "He's less angry and we even talk from time to time now. He respects me more too. He's made a lot of progress."

"I'm glad you can see the difference. I'm very pleased with your nephew's progress. He is a resilient child. That klepto-mania episode was just a cry for help, and we mustn't hold it against him. It's all behind him now. But he's going to have to get back on track, and this is where you come in."

"What do you mean?"

"Elliot needs to connect with the other children at school. He is very withdrawn. He needs to form a circle of friends. You can help him by letting him invite a couple of friends over from time to time, or by organizing a birthday party for him."

"Yes, of course," I reply, with relief.

Phew, that's all it was. No new dramas to deal with. I wait for her to continue, but she doesn't. I know it's a technique to get me to talk. Her silence starts to weigh on me but I resist and gaze around the room. My eyes roam from one trinket to another: a small bronze Labrador, dust covered books, some butterflies in frames, and several children's drawings. I'm entranced by a tiny statue of a very gentle-looking woman kneeling down; her body is naked and voluptuous, her belly is huge, her breasts are heavy, and her face is a picture of serenity. I think about my recent ultrasound scan, which, as I had anticipated, didn't pick up anything alarming. I try to imagine the joy of this woman who is clearly expecting a much longed-for child.

The therapist's polite cough startles me. She then resumes the conversation. I smile to myself. I can beat anyone at the silence game. I've kept it inside for twenty years, so I'm not going to let my guard down now.

She says that Elliot is feeling much better, but he nonetheless suffers from severe mental distress that is preventing him from rebuilding his life.

"Isn't that normal?" I ask.

"Of course, it's normal. But whereas one might have expected him to have a phobia of cars for example, as a result of his parents' accident, he is absolutely terrified of being abandoned."

I stiffen. "Is that what he said?"

"Not quite those words, he's only ten years old. But that's why I wanted to see you alone. Elliot is a bright child, very bright indeed. However, he has a vivid imagination that tends to get carried away with the misinterpretation of trivia."

I frown. Pure psychobabble, therapy in all its glory. She stares at me, then says that naturally she won't betray Elliot's trust, but to be perfectly frank with me, he appears convinced that I'm going to abandon him.

My heart sinks. "But why? Why would he say that?" I ask.

"It doesn't matter, what counts is what he's *feeling*. He's convinced that you've abandoned a child in the past. However ridiculous that may sound, he is deeply affected by it. These things aren't always rational, you know."

The sky comes crashing down on me. The black clouds had clearly not gone away for long. I desperately gaze at the wings of the boxed butterflies. Here I am, stuck like them, unable to fly away, frozen to my armchair, totally astounded by Elliot's extraordinary intuition, which has unwittingly unveiled my deepest secrets and fears. I clutch the handle of my bag tightly, lips quivering, grab my coat and jump up.

"That is indeed absurd," I say. "I'll try and get that idea out of his head."

The elderly lady gets up slowly and laboriously to see me out. Her hand rests on the door but she doesn't open it. She looks into my eyes once again. "Ms Mercier, your past is your business. No one is forcing you to talk about it. But as painful as it may be, something in our conversation obviously hit a nerve, and you must reassure Elliot. He has already lost his parents. Despite the tension between you, believe you me, he couldn't cope with losing you as well. He is very fond of you. Show him he has a place in your heart."

My eyes go blurry and my ears are ringing. I've never been this close to confiding in anyone before . . . And I don't want to. I can almost hear my mother's voice condemning me forever. I quickly wipe away a couple of tears that have the nerve to roll down my cheek. The therapist's hand is still on the doorknob. The words come tumbling out, against my will. "I couldn't. I just couldn't." It's worse than Niagara Falls. I'm in floods of tears. I bite my lips to stop myself from saying more.

She finally takes her hand off the doorknob and steps aside to let me through. "Don't remain a victim of your past. Come back and see me when you're ready. I'll be waiting for you. When silence has been exhausted, words must tell the tale."

I race down the stairs. *I couldn't. I just couldn't.* This phrase has been my lifeline for almost twenty years, I've clung to it so many times to stop myself from sinking: *I couldn't.* It's pouring outside but I don't care. I must get back to the nursery, but I can't in this state. I lose myself in the familiar streets of Batignolles. *I couldn't.* No, I couldn't because I didn't believe I could ever love you. I'm so sorry. *I couldn't.* Look at me, I've committed sacrilege by rejecting my maternal instincts, I'm a witch to be burned at the stake. What sort of monster rejects their own child, their own flesh and blood that they carried for nine months? But *I couldn't.* I would have seen my torturer every time I looked into your eyes. And what would I have told you? That you were the result of the shameful acts inflicted on me by that pervert? That you were unplanned and unwanted? Talk about a fairy tale! Best to give you to someone who would love you and let you believe you were delivered by a stork . . .

I look down at the rail tracks as a train honks on entering the station. *I couldn't.* No, I couldn't have loved you as I'm incapable of loving myself. Tears stream down my cheeks.

My mother knew everything. Yet, just as I expected, she let me down precisely when I needed her the most. All she could see was her own suffering because she wanted you. She wanted to raise you. All she could see was her own shame. The shame of having a slut of a daughter who got knocked up. I was too scared to tell her everything and was so afraid of what might happen to Emily. So I bore the brunt of her anger and her shame. And ever since the day I left the clinic without you, I ceased to exist for my mother. Although we got together for Christmas, Easter and the summer holidays, I had become transparent, a ghost. While Emily was larger than life. The perfect, beloved daughter. Protected from that predator thanks to me, though she would never know the truth.

I couldn't do it. I had to erase you from my mind, abandon you, forget you so I could start a new life. To forget is to be free, isn't it? When I ran away from that hospital just after you were born, I really believed I was finally going to start living.

My fingers clutch the fence, my hair is dripping wet, another train pulls into the station. As I tried to bury my shame, all I encountered along the way were regrets; to the point that I became obsessed with redeeming myself. I deliberately became a nursery nurse, deliberately run a nursery. I donate to umpteen children's aid associations, and I even sponsor a little girl on the other side of the world. She gives me the illusion of being loved. But nothing has really helped, you're still there inside me, my own flesh and blood, never letting me forget. I don't bother to wipe my tears, there's no point in all this rain. I just wanted to be socially acceptable. Yet, on the contrary, I've turned into a hateful human being. All because *I couldn't*. Do you know how many kids and then teenagers I've looked after over the years? Maybe one of them was you? I only had to see bright blue eyes and masses of blond hair, and my heart would start racing. Maybe one of them really was you?

As I walk along Legendre Street, I pass in front of the Sainte-Marie des Batignolles church. That big square church never inspired me before. In fact, I don't think I've ever set foot in it. I lost my faith when I was seventeen years old. But today I decide to go in. It's cold and dark inside. I'm soaked and shivering, but the silence is soothing. I wish I could hide my pain, slip it between two stones or offer it in prayer to someone. A side chapel catches my eye. Dozens of flames flicker in their little red pots. I walk closer. They are so pretty; each one a silent plea to the unknown, like secrets whispered to passers-by. It's very moving. I put a coin in the box and choose my candle. I light it and whisper, "Not a day goes by that I don't think of you. I just wanted to give you the chance to be loved. I'm so sorry."

Outside, a faint ray of sunshine dries my tears. It is still drizzling but now a rainbow paints the raindrops in multicolours. I slowly make my way back to the nursery. Deep inside my pocket, I find a whole bunch of little pebbles collected by Lea in the square last weekend that she stuffed into my pocket instead of hers. I scatter them, one by one, up to the underground entrance, thinking of that little red flame burning my grief in the darkness.

37

Elliot

Dear Mum,

Morgan is rubbish at skiing you know. Even Lea is better than her! Poor thing, she has us in hysterics. She keeps falling down, and then moans, saying it's our fault because we don't wait for her. You should've seen her sliding down the whole of the red slope on her arse! She was screaming so loud that Snoopy must've heard her from the apartment.

To get to Garmisch, we took the train to Munich, which took forever, and then we came here by car. I love it here. Oma Annett says she needed to hear the wind blowing in her head, and that the mountains really help. I know she thinks about you both all the time. Opa Georg is happy to see us too and tells us about the ski jumping championships. It's on TV of course, but there's a jump here, a real one! He took us to see it, wow, it's cool. He doesn't come with us on the slopes of course. It would be like putting a hippopotamus on skis; he could trigger an avalanche.

We're having a great holiday. Except for one thing: you're not here. We are trying our best though. The other night, Opa took out a board game with some sheep that have to be put in a field. You have to really think hard to win, it's not easy, but I won every time! It's the first time we've ever played a game with Morgan! We laughed so much that Oma whispered in my ear that she'd give one to Morgan for her birthday, so we could play it in Paris too. I panicked slightly when Oma winked at

*me saying it was Morgan's birthday on Friday; she had seen it
in her passport when Morgan gave her a copy this summer
when we travelled alone. I pretended I knew already.*

*Yesterday was the best day of skiing in my whole life. When I
found myself alone with Morgan on the chairlift, I was a bit
scared. I think it was the first time we were actually alone
together, strange, isn't it? I didn't really know what to say, but
then she started talking.* "I'm glad Annett invited me. It's great
to be here, isn't it?"

*I wasn't expecting her to say this. I mean the way she skis,
it's hard to believe she was having a good time. I ask her if she
was really having fun. She said yes, then added* "Elliot, I realize it wasn't easy for you at first, but things are getting better,
aren't they? I mean, with you and me?"

"Yes." *It's true that Morgan is nicer than she used to be. And
my head isn't as screwed up as it was.*

*She turned to face me. Her eyes were so clear that you could
almost see your face in them. She then said she was sorry she did
everything wrong at the start, and that it was very difficult for her
too, as she wasn't used to living with kids. She said we were getting
there, slowly, but that she would never be our mum, of course,
though we could still be happy together if we decided to be.*

*She then asked me if I knew the story of the Little Prince
who met a fox.*

I said of course, it was Mum's favourite book.

*She then said we were like the Little Prince and the fox.
And that we had to get to know each other.*

She said we should give it a go and asked what I think.

*She said we could promise to tell each other when things
were going well and when something was wrong. That it'd be a
good start anyway.*

"Deal?"

"Deal!"

We shook hands and it made me feel all tingly inside, as I figured she kind of liked me as well now, not just Lea.

Right behind us on the chairlift, Oma called out, "Elliot, wait for me, I'll race you down the red slope!"

I told her she wouldn't stand a chance of winning. I zoomed down like a rocket and almost took off!

It reminded me of when I was skiing with you last year. I thought my heart was going to explode, I was going faster than an eagle. If only you could have seen me! In the end I skied down so fast I was screaming with joy; it made my teeth chatter! Oma got down before me, but I didn't care, because I felt as light as a feather, as if I had won. We burst out laughing when we saw Morgan lying in the snow, her legs tangled up in her skis. She was in a filthy mood when she finally reached us, her helmet and mittens covered in snow. "Are you crazy or what? We almost lost Lea and I fell twice!"

Oma wiped the snow off her helmet with her glove and told her in her German accent, "It doesn't matter Morgan, that's how life is! You fall down, you get up and you start off again!"

In the evening, we walked around the old village and Oma let us each choose a souvenir. Lea spent hours deciding but I knew straight away which one I wanted. I chose a little snow globe with the town of Garmisch in it, because I know Dad liked it. After all, we are here in his house, in his country, and we have had a really great time with Morgan. And I thought that's what I could give her for her birthday. Lea chose a soft cuddly marmot with big teeth. I showed her the snow globe for Morgan. She thought it was a very good idea and said she'd draw her a picture to go with it.

Well, today was Friday, our last day ... And tomorrow, we take the car and the train. Lea has just fallen asleep with her marmot. I gave my snow globe to Morgan this morning for her birthday. She was really surprised. Oma didn't say anything when she recognized it, and just ran her fingers through my hair.

So you see, Mum, we're making progress. I think you'd be proud of me, too. Big kisses to you and Dad. I miss you both.

Elliot

38

Morgan

It's seven o'clock on Monday morning. My alarm goes off, sounding the death knell for the holidays. I grope for my phone in the dark. Despite being covered in bruises, I had the time of my life, surprisingly. I can't wait to see Viviane to thank her. It was the best advice she could have given me. And it gave Elliot and me the chance to get off on the right foot. His snow globe sits proudly on my bedside table. I was deeply touched by his present.

I wake the children, get their clothes out of the wardrobe and open their curtains. The sky may be a dull grey colour, but nothing can dampen my spirits today.

I give them a kiss before leaving them at the school gates. I turn to leave but Elliot calls out to me to wait. Lea has already gone in. He has something to tell me.

He stares down at his feet to avoid looking at me and twists the drawstring of his hoodie. He tells me how much he enjoyed our holiday, and how nice I was. He says again that he has something important to tell me. I reply that I'm all ears and bend down to his height to put him at ease.

"You're not going to like it but I think you should know . . . Before school broke up, I decided to return all the marbles to the headmistress. When I got to her office, the door was open and she was on the phone. I heard her say 'Mr Mercier'. I wondered why she would be talking to Grandpa. So I stood there listening at the door and I think he told her that you drank alcohol and that she should watch out for any signs. I didn't hear everything, but the headmistress said she'd keep an eye on you. I just thought you should know."

A shock wave goes right through my body. This can't be happening. My legs are shaking. Me, drink? Are they out of their minds? I only allow myself three glasses a year!

Elliot looks scared. I try to reassure him. "I don't drink. You know I don't. And how could Grandpa Paul even imagine such a thing? He's never been to ours."

Elliot's lips start to quiver. "I'm sure that's what she said, Morgan."

The bell rings. He kisses me on the cheek. "I have to go. See you tonight."

I feel dizzy. He wouldn't have made such a thing up. But why would my father do this? If there's a silver lining to all this it's that Elliot took my side. And that's huge progress. But still, it doesn't add up. Where does my father fit into this story? I wouldn't put it past my mother to come up with any number of mean tricks. We haven't spoken for two months. We've just sent a few essential texts here and there regarding the kids. And even these turned sour just before the holidays. But my father?

I get on the underground, racking my brain for the answer. The train stops without warning and I get thrown onto the lady in front.

Suddenly, I get a flashback.

That night, after Christmas . . . That night I almost put an end to things. I had been drinking. And given the state I was in I clearly didn't think to clean up the mess I left behind. That was so out of character for me. I never go out, and I never drink. Except that night I had one too many.

And the only person who could have seen the mess was Elliot . . .

A terrible vision worms its way inside my head: me, the bottle of vodka on the table, my day spent puking, Elliot startled by what he had seen, then Grandma Cat phoning. I can just hear her saying to my father, "You know, your daughter's not well. And she has started drinking. We must take the children off her."

I'm so pale when I get to the nursery that Viviane jokingly tells me I should ease off on the sunscreen. "You didn't get much of a tan, did you?! Was it nice?"

I nod, then apologize and rush to my office. I have to find out for sure. I dial the school's number and ask to speak to the headmistress.

After what seems like an eternity a voice says, "Ms Mercier? It's Carole Dubois. How are you?"

I tell her I'm fine and to excuse my candour, but did she receive a phone call from my father just before the holidays?

She doesn't reply, so I take her silence to mean yes. I have my answer and can't blame her for not wanting to say anything. She's caught between her professional ethics and her willingness to help us. "You don't need to say any more, I get it," I reassure her. "But please don't believe anything you've been told. I will clear this up. Have a nice day."

"Ho ... how did you find out?" I hear her stammering faintly.

I hang up. My hand is shaking. I'm seething with rage. My father ... I mean my father, who never sees anything or knows anything, chose to side with my mother! What on earth did she say to convince him to discredit me to a woman he doesn't even know? So, this is her way of making me pay for not handing my baby over to her? By taking Emily's kids away from me just as I'm growing to love them? These kids are my future, my chance to start afresh. I glance at the photos on my desk of Emily, Niko, Elliot, Lea and Snoopy and my father. Yep, he is right there, smiling. My father is an upstanding man, cold but fair, who always supported me, only too aware that Emily was my mother's favourite. But now she's got to him alright! She's managed to strike a nerve with that magic word: *alcohol*. My grandfather was a very heavy drinker. Consequently, my father has never touched a drop all his life and has an absolute horror of alcoholism. He even became a doctor specializing in the subject. He clearly acted on impulse when Grandma Cat fed him the details. "Paul, Elliot says your daughter drinks. We've got to do something about it, you know what *that* means. We can't leave the children with her any longer. No point in confronting her, she'll just deny it, you know what alcoholics are like. We need to investigate. This is what we'll do, Paul."

I take the photo of my father out of its frame, tear it up and throw it on the floor. I dry a tear. I won't give them the satisfaction of breaking me just when I'm finally getting back on track. Emily entrusted her kids to me and I shall keep them no matter what. They have given a whole new meaning to my life. It took a skiing holiday and a snow globe for me to finally open my eyes; I'm not going to leave them now. I have been a prisoner of the past for far too long. Elliot and Lea have freed me. I'm learning to seek out love, joy and tenderness in the most unlikely of places each day. And I will not hide away any longer.

There is a knock at the door. It's Jean-Michel. I didn't hear him arriving this morning, his CD player must have broken. He looks worried about something and fiddles with his hat. "Ms Mercier, I'm worried about Valerie Le Gall. I haven't seen her for a whole week."

Has Jean-Michel got the hots for her? I don't know what to say; she asked us to keep her illness to ourselves . . .

"Why are you so worried?" I reply, flustered. "As long as Lucas is here, that's all that matters, isn't it?"

Jean-Michel plants himself in front of me and puts his two large hands on my desk. He must be at least double my body weight. I fidget in my chair.

"Don't take me for an idiot," he says forcefully. "You and I both know she is seriously ill. It stands out a mile. She looks like death warmed up and believe me I know what that looks like! You weren't here last week, so you don't know that an older lady now brings Lucas to nursery and picks him up. She gets here early, she leaves late, we don't see her, and she doesn't say a word. I don't want to be intrusive, but let's just be good human beings and do the decent thing, check in on her. Can you give me her number?"

I tell him that for reasons of confidentiality, I'm not allowed to give out personal information. He glares at me and I feel wretched. I call Viviane and she joins us a few minutes later. I ask her if she has seen Ms Le Gall lately. She shakes her head and says Lucas's grandmother brought him to the nursery this morning. I can still hear Valerie refusing our offer to bring her son home at night, saying Lucas is the only thing that keeps her going. I panic; her child is still so young. I can feel Jean-Michel's angry eyes piercing me. I promise him I will call her.

He finally leaves.

Viviane comes up to me, looking pale. "She's got blood cancer," she whispers. "She told me one evening. I looked it up on the internet and apparently it can be treated and has a pretty good success rate. But I'm worried about her, you know . . . And afraid for Lucas."

I phone Valerie at least ten times but she doesn't answer. I finally decide to send her a bouquet of flowers with a get-well message from the whole team. Around five o'clock I see an unfamiliar lady arrive.

I call out to her, "Excuse me. Would you happen to be Lucas's grandmother?"

She says yes. I tell her that we are very worried about Valerie and would like to know how she is. She turns away and puts on her dark glasses mumbling something I can't hear. My optimism fades. I remember the little red candle I left at the church of Sainte-Marie des Batignolles before the holidays. What if I were to light another?

39

Elliot

Morgan got up in a foul mood. At first, I thought it was because of what I had said to her about Grandpa Paul on Monday, but watching her get Snoopy ready, I remembered she has the vet's appointment today. I don't know why she gets so uptight about that man. I think he's quite nice and Lea definitely has a crush on him.

On the way there, Morgan starts grumbling, saying that Snoopy is a lot better and she really doesn't see why he has to see the vet again.

He is waiting for us in the hall. "Ah, there you are! You're late. How are the plans for the boarding kennels coming along?"

I hide so as not to laugh when I see Morgan's eyes grow as big as saucers. She purses her lips and asks the vet how her dog is doing. She is not very polite even though he is taking an interest in her for once. He acts like nothing is wrong, looks at Snoopy's paw and pads and makes the dog walk as he watches. Lea squeals: she is afraid he'll hurt Snoopy.

"You're going to have to let me work a bit," he says, laughing. "I can't do anything while you're clinging to him like a leech. If you were my daughter, I'd have told you a while ago to go and admire the fish in the hallway . . ."

"Lea, stay here!" barks Morgan, not letting him finish. She is very tense. But Lea doesn't notice; she has a lot of questions.

"Have you got a daughter, mister? How old is she?" Lancelot looks taken aback.

"Well you said 'if you were my daughter', so I'm asking you how old your daughter is. Do you have one or not?"

Lancelot says he has a big daughter, who is sixteen years old. Lea asks her name and he says Laura. She then asks whether Laura wants to be a vet too. Suddenly Lancelot looks all sad. He pretends to be engrossed in Snoopy's paw, but I'm not fooled. Lea insists, even though it's obvious to me he doesn't want to talk about it. "I don't know . . . I don't see her much . . ." he says, eventually.

He examines Snoopy's pads. Morgan looks up, clearly waiting for him to continue, but Lea puts her foot in it again. "Really, so you don't live with her?"

"No."

"So you abandoned her then?" Morgan abruptly intervenes. She tells Lea to go and look at the pretty fish in the hallway.

Lancelot reassures her. "You read too many fairy tales, Lea. Laura lives with her mum. We are divorced. They live in Bordeaux."

"But if you don't see her, that's basically the same thing, isn't it?"

"Lea!" admonishes Morgan, bright red with embarrassment.

She is so red I want to laugh but it's not really the time. I pretend I didn't hear. Morgan apologizes to him and says that children often don't know what they're saying.

He says it doesn't matter and it's not a big deal.

Lancelot's a terrible liar, I can tell from his face. He goes quiet for a few seconds, then stands up straight. "Your dog is better now. No need to come back, unless he has an accident, which I sincerely hope he won't."

I step forward to put Snoopy's lead on, and Lea says bye. This time Morgan holds her hand out to the vet as we leave.

*　　*　　*

Once we're outside, Lea cheerfully frolics around, singing. I whisper to Morgan that it's sad he no longer sees his daughter. Morgan replies that she initially thought he was just obnoxious but it's more complicated than that. She says she even feels sorry for him.

"Yes, in life a lot of people wear disguises," I say.

She looks surprised. "You have no idea just how true that is . . ." she sighs.

Instead of going straight home, Morgan takes us on a detour to a big church standing right in the middle of the crossroads. I wait at the door with Lea because Snoopy can't go in and pray, but I see her take two small red candles and quickly place them down with the others.

"Why did you do that?" I ask when she comes out.

"I did it for two people who need help right now. There's the sick mother at the nursery. I want her to get better for her child's sake. The second is for someone I knew a long, long time ago . . . someone I'd like to hear from."

"And that's really going to make a difference?" I ask.

She says it might not *help* but it definitely won't *hurt*. And there's no harm in believing it might just work.

40

Morgan

I have an intake meeting this morning with some new parents. Their son is just over ten months old. His mother beams with joy as she holds him tightly against her, while his father chuckles at him. Their ethereal blond hair contrasts with the jet-black hair and smouldering gaze of their baby son.

"Little Tiago, what a lovely name. Are you of Portuguese descent?" I ask, as I show them into my office.

The mother bursts into sweet, infectious laughter. The father replies, "Not at all, we have Scandinavian roots, but our son is of Brazilian origin. He was born in France and came to us when he was four months old."

His words knock me out. I try to put on a brave smile. "Oh, you adopted him? How wonderful . . . He must be our first adopted child here. I . . . well tell me about him and your family. For us, it's vital that we know the background to ensure things go smoothly when you're apart."

The mother's pretty face tenses up and she clutches him even tighter. This is bound to be difficult for her and me. Nevertheless, I need to remain professional and do my best to reassure her. The father describes the long adoption process, the endless months spent waiting with no news, their dwindling hope, and their unspeakable joy when they finally held their baby son in their arms. "There are no words to describe our happiness, you know . . ."

I'm overwhelmed yet comforted by the joy I can see in their faces. I discreetly dab my eyes while he continues.

"Yes, it's moving isn't it! Adopting a child is a dream come true. We know practically nothing about his mother, except that she was Brazilian and very young. We wanted to give our son a name that would mean something to him."

I nod and desperately search for the right words, trying to hide the whirlwind of emotions this child's dark gaze has triggered in me. I pull myself together, telling myself to calm down, telling myself that this little baby is not here to judge me. "Still, it can't be easy all the time, I imagine? Your son must have moments of distress and anxiety?"

"No, why do you say that?" The mother stares at me in astonishment. "Tiago is our son. We will never hide the truth from him of course, but he is a very calm child. Besides, we love him so much, I'm sure we give him far more love than he would have ever received otherwise. Children sense these things you know."

She goes on to say how terrified she was at the idea of having to go back to work and didn't think they would get a nursery place so quickly. When Tiago joined them, she wanted to spend every minute of the day with him, they had waited so long. Yet they couldn't refuse the place they were offered as our nursery has such a good reputation and they only live two minutes away. I thank her and tell her that we do our best to ensure the well-being of all our children. Tiago's eyes torment me. I would never have imagined that a baby could wreak such havoc on my conscience.

I manage to snap back into my managerial role. "Given the situation and the fact that you are not returning to work right away, I would like to propose a very gradual settling in period. I will draw up a special programme for you. We may need you to stay with him longer than the average parent would—to help Tiago cope with his new situation and not rekindle any subconscious distress in him. He will have his own one on one carer whom he will get to know better than the others. Your son is already ten months old; it's important that he feels safe and secure."

Trying to conceal her gentle sobs, the mother thanks me and apologizes. Her husband takes her hand and I see them out.

Thanks to Viviane's gentleness and her magic way with children, Tiago's induction was a success. The only one suffering is me. I feel like I'm climbing up the Eiffel Tower without a safety harness. *Do not look down, do not turn back, do not hesitate.* It's a challenge, but I'm determined to make it. Thank goodness I have Lea's cheerful smile to greet me in the evenings because just seeing Tiago every day has opened up old wounds.

"What a delightful child! How lucky he was to find such loving parents. How could his mother have given him up? It's incomprehensible. Look how handsome he is!" The team is ecstatic and the girls delight in cuddling and pampering the new arrival. Meanwhile I can feel his sultry gaze pierce my soul. A constant reminder that my child is out there somewhere, happy, without me. Isn't that what I wanted? I wasn't even eighteen. What was the alternative, give him to my mother? No, I was scared to death, and she would have discovered the truth, so I chose to keep silent. Tiago's dark eyes revive my worst nightmares. I can't sleep, haunted by night terrors. What if my child is dead? Or worse still, condemned to a life of violence and misery? My mother would have looked after him. I wasn't even up to fighting to keep my own child.

The days go by. I'm at my wits' end. I've spent all these years waiting for the silence to heal my wounds. Now I realize that pieces of the jigsaw are still missing. And if I don't find them, I'll never come to terms with what I did.

41

Elliot

I love *The Blue Lotus*, it's my favourite Tintin. Especially the part where the crazy guy tries to cut off his head to help him find his way. I was so excited when I saw it in Morgan's book-case and I've already read it at least ten times this year. I'm just at the bit where he draws his sword when the phone rings. Eight o'clock on a Saturday morning. Who can it be? I pick it up quickly, so as not to wake Lea. Morgan is in the bathroom.

"Hello Elliot, it's Grandma Cat! How are you darling?"

"Great thanks, Grandma Cat."

"Really?" she asks. She always sounds surprised when I tell her we are still alive.

Why does she keep asking about Morgan? I told her she is fine and offer to put her on, but she refuses. She and Morgan are like in my history lesson on the battlefield, both of them in a trench shooting at each other, neither one daring to move forward . . . I ask her if she is okay, knowing she will give me a run-down of everything her neighbours have been up to for the last six months. But I like being nice to her.

Apparently, it's got colder there, it's only fifteen degrees and they can no longer eat outside, and the weather isn't like it used to be. And Mrs Maillard, their neighbour, won five thousand euros in the lottery. And something dreadful happened that she nearly forgot to mention. Their old neigh-bour, a real gentleman, who recently came back after many years away, got run over by a drunk driver. He was pronounced dead at the scene. She apologizes for telling me something so awful, but he was such a nice kind man. She says how dangerous alcohol is and to keep away from people who drink, and did I know anyone who drinks. Hmm, I'm not going to fall into *that* trap again! She wants to know if Lea and I would like to go and stay with them at Easter, as we didn't see them during the last holidays. Besides, Morgan will be too busy with work to do anything with us. I would love to go, but I don't dare ask Morgan because of the trench shooting thing.

The first week Lea and I will be staying with friends in Maisons-Laffitte. Morgan helped us track them down on the internet. It'll be fab, I can't wait. We'll then spend the Easter weekend in Paris with Morgan but have nothing planned for the second week, as far as I know.

"Would you like to come to Marseille so I can make a fuss of you?" she asks.

"I'd love to!"

"Okay, I'll send a quick message to Morgan, but you know what she's like. You'd better ask her yourself too, she never replies to me. Bye for now darling."

I hang up and I can already hear my aunt's phone vibrating. Morgan goes past with wet hair, just out of the shower. "Was that Grandma Cat?" she asks.

"Yes."

"What did she want?"

"She said she would send you a message about the Easter holidays."

"Ah, okay, do you want to go?" she asks. She sighs. I know she's making a huge effort. She'd rather we went to camp. I don't dare look at her but I summon up the courage to say yes.

"Okay, we'll see . . ." she says. "What else did she say?"

"You really want to know?" I ask. "It's only fifteen degrees, she can no longer eat outside, one of her neighbours won five thousand euros in the lottery and the other neighbour, who recently came back after a long time away, just got run over by a car."

Morgan drops her hairdryer and goes ghostly white; I think she is going to faint. When she asks me if he is dead, I say yes. She asks if I am sure, so I tell her to phone Grandma Cat if she doesn't believe me.

Morgan grabs her phone. Her hand is shaking so much she has to retype her password several times. That means she'll see the message about the holidays! I do hope she agrees. She types a brief message.

Grandma Cat replies instantly, she must be dying to see us. Suddenly Morgan breaks into hysterical laughter, laughing so much that she can't stop. It's like she's gone mad. This is worrying. When I ask her if she is okay, she replies she is on top of the world!

She makes such a commotion that Lea finally gets out of bed. She takes a record, grabs my sister by the hand and starts dancing, shouting, "It's Saturday, it's party time!"

Lea looks at me with big round eyes, as if to say, "Is she ill or what?" She really does seem to have gone crazy and now she is singing at the top of her voice and waving my sister's arms in the air. She finally stops dancing, dries the tears from her eyes, takes a deep breath and goes into the kitchen to get a glass of water. I overhear her ranting about "death" and "run over" and "finally living". She is in such a good mood that I seize the opportunity and ask once more if we can go to Grandma Cat's for the holidays. She says yes! Great, I was worrying for nothing.

"I'm so happy, we can play on the beach and hunt for shells!" cries Lea.

Morgan announces we are going out for lunch as we have some celebrating to do.

"Celebrate what?" I ask.

"That the sun is finally shining after six days of rain," she says. "Which just goes to show you should never lose hope."

I tell her the sun may be shining but it is still raining. But then lo and behold a rainbow appears! A rainbow has come to paint the raindrops in beautiful bright colours. Morgan and Lea start dancing again.

Morgan takes us to our favourite restaurant for lunch. We used to eat there with Mum and Dad. Lea is happy because there are balloons. I remember once, for my birthday, the waiters all lined up to bring me my cake with lots of flickering candles. It was so amazing that I tell Morgan about it while we read the menu. She gets up to go to the bathroom.

We are all in a really good mood, eating and talking. Morgan is even interested when I tell her about what I read in my latest wildlife magazine. Lea asks for ice cream for dessert, and then something incredible happens. Several waiters walk up to our table: the first one is carrying a huge cake with candles, and they are all singing, "Happy Birthday Elliot!"

Lea looks at me bewildered. "But it's not your birthday, Elliot!"

Morgan winks at me, clapping. I whisper to her that she is out of her mind. She then says why wait till June when we can celebrate it today!

I start laughing too, so much that I have trouble blowing out my fake birthday candles. Morgan may be a bit nuts, but I'm beginning to think she's quite cool. We finally leave holding three balloons each. Once we get outside, Lea tells us that we must all let go of one balloon. "It's for Mum and Dad, so they can join in the party too."

One, two, three! We watch the bright spots of colour float away, higher and higher, towards the sun and the sky.

42

Morgan

It's five o'clock. I need to fetch Elliot and Lea. Viviane said she would lock up. I have had a new lease of life these last few days. I have become super-efficient and am starting to discover real meaning in my job. I even found a few minutes to look up train tickets on the internet. I grudgingly accepted my mother's offer to come and pick up the kids on the pretext of a Parisian getaway with her friends over the Easter weekend. They will come back to Paris by themselves using the special rail service for children.

I leave my office to do the rounds. The hearse pulls up, music blaring. No hope of Jean-Michel changing! I don't know his daughter's mother, but I can imagine how annoying he must be to live with day to day. I greet the parents who are lingering in the hall and head towards the toddlers' room. They chirrup happily as they exchange building blocks covered in drool. Amara gently places a sleeping Tiago in a baby rocker and runs to save a child from the clutches of another, who won't let go of its leg. Tiago makes less of an impression on me when he's asleep, he looks so peaceful.

"Hello Ms Mercier! How are you?" Jean-Michel's loud voice startles me out of my reverie.

"Very well, thank you, Mr Rollin."

"Have you just seen a ghost? You look very pale," he says.

"No, you scared me. Discreet as always!" I retort. "We can hear you coming from all the way down the street."

He seems to think that his music adds a little spice to our day. I tell him that songs with lyrics like "I'm dying" are not exactly uplifting, nor are they appropriate, given that Valerie Le Gall could turn up any minute. He goes quiet then thanks me for sending her the flowers, saying how thoughtful it was. I ask him how he knows and he tells me that he has his spies. When I look intrigued, he admits it was Valerie's mother.

He bends down to pick up little Alice, who throws herself into his arms. I finish my rounds alone and then stumble across him once more in the lobby, trying to get his daughter to button up her coat.

The door opens and Tiago's father walks in, followed by a mere shadow of a figure. I hardly recognize Valerie who is now just skin and bone. Her mother is holding her arm. I'm speechless, and Viviane who has just joined me can't look her in the face. It's as if the real Valerie is hiding in that skeletal frame somewhere. She forces a smile, but it doesn't hide her weariness and exhaustion. Viviane invites her to wait in the hall and rushes to fetch Lucas. Valerie still finds the strength to unhook the little blue jacket and the dragon backpack from his peg. Her cheeks are sunken, her red scarf is stuck to her head. Even Jean-Michel is lost for words. Behind the door leading to the playrooms, I can see Amara's petrified face. Luckily, Lucas bursts through the door gleefully shouting, "Mummy!"

I wish I could find the right words to express my admiration for this female warrior. Words to applaud her for coming back here against all odds. Words to assuage her suffering, and words of praise for her will to keep going . . . but nothing comes out. Jean-Michel beats me to it. He crouches down in front of Lucas.

"You know, kid, your mother is like Spider Man, but better. She is stronger than any super-hero I know. You're too young to understand, but one day you will. And when you do, you'll respect her forever."

Then he turns to Valerie and gives her a genuine heartfelt smile. "I'm so happy to see you again, Valerie. I'm not going to lie to you, you don't look great, this rotten illness has worn you to a frazzle, but you're pulling through, and that's what counts. I can see the beauty of victory in your face. It's not about how much hair you have on your head. You are *beautiful*. Never let anyone tell you otherwise."

Valerie's eyes well up with tears and her lips quiver. The rest of us are stunned speechless by these breathtaking words. Valerie stammers a faint thank you and leans over to kiss her son. His grandmother puts the child in the pushchair and Valerie clutches the handles, using it like a walking frame. She turns around and shyly thanks me and all the nursery staff for the flowers, adding that they only lasted a few days, but kept her going for weeks.

Tiago's father lays his child down on one of the changing mats and puts his little coat on without waking him. You can see how much he loves him. He waves bye to us.

"That is a beautiful example of a father who found a son and a son who found a father: a match made in heaven," murmers Viviane.

Sometimes I wonder if Viviane is watching over me, like a guardian angel. A lot of the things she says resonate with me. I must be looking at her strangely because she laughs and reminds me of the time, saying I'll be late for school.

I look at the clock with surprise and then ask her for some Easter holiday tips for the kids. She says that there is nothing better than a good old Easter egg hunt, but that there are probably lots of good ideas online too.

43

Elliot

Dear Mum,

Today was Easter Day. Lea and I must have eaten at least three hundred chocolates each. Snoopy also had his share. We spent the first few days of the holiday at Victor and Margaux's house, our old friends in Maisons-Laffitte. Morgan helped us find them on the internet. We played football in the park like we used to, rolled around on the grass and went to see the horses. It was great fun.

While we were away Morgan worked hard getting Easter ready for us. She has changed so much you wouldn't recognize her. She even smiles now! This morning, she was the one who woke us up and told us to get dressed quickly before it gets too crowded.

We were still sleepy but followed her to the square with Snoopy trotting behind us. She was right; at this time in the morning there is no one around. Morgan told us to wait on a bench and not move. She ran off and I noticed that she was carrying a huge backpack. She looked so funny, like a giant turtle. A few minutes later she came running back, out of breath.

Lea asked what we were going to do next. She didn't really understand and thought we were here to play. Morgan then told her it was an Easter egg hunt!

I showed my sister the play area. Morgan gave each of us a small paper basket. I was convinced she had hidden everything under the slide. As I was running, I tripped over a bucket that was lying around and fell over, grazing my knee. I slid under the slide but there were no eggs there, just a badly taped paper rabbit, with the words "Look again!" Damn, they must be in the cabin then. Lea was already there and handed me a paper hen with "Not yet." written on it. It was so annoying, plus we had to hurry in case other kids got there first and found the eggs.

I asked Morgan if this was some kind of joke.

She didn't even turn around; she was too busy humming. All I could see was her big turtle shell. I scratched the dog's head and asked him to help, hoping he could sniff out the chocolate for us.

But all he did was jump up at Morgan, barking for joy. We continued searching everywhere, under the rocking motorbikes, in the tiny houses, but nothing . . . Only messages such as "Try harder!" or "Can't you guess?" All of a sudden, I saw a little painted egg between the branches of a tree and shouted to Lea to look up. But it was too high for us to get to.

This was the only egg we'd found so I had to reach it! I jumped, once, twice and on the third try, I managed to knock it down with a stick. Splat! I swear to you, Mum, Morgan had put a real egg in the tree! There was yolk all over the place, and she couldn't stop laughing. Lea just stood there, with her mouth open, not knowing whether to laugh or cry. She eventually started laughing when she saw Snoopy walking in the yolk and spreading it everywhere. I asked Morgan if she had really hidden eggs in the square.

"Who said I hid anything?" she replied.

"But you gave us paper baskets!" Lea piped up angrily.

"That's true but I never told you to search for anything."

I watched Snoopy circling Morgan, his tail wagging, nose in the air . . . and I figured it out! The joke was on us. There was nothing to find all along. I pounced on Morgan and pulled her backpack off. Here they were! Inside there were Kinder eggs, chocolate eggs, sweets; it was full to the brim. Lea just couldn't understand it.

"You made us look for nothing. Right from the start?"

"It wasn't for nothing Lea! The fun is in the hunt! Did you really think I would leave all those chocolate goodies in a public place where other people could have taken them?"

Morgan was crying with laughter. We split everything four ways: a big packet for Lea, the same for me, a small one for Morgan, and an even smaller one for Snoopy.

"Morgan, you're wearing a red dress! You look really pretty!" Lea suddenly cried out.

It's true that I hadn't noticed. Morgan's dress was brightly coloured, and so were her eyes and lips. Lea has already told her many times that she is pretty. We left the playground with our full baskets and then I had the urge to run along with Snoopy beside me. You'll never guess who we ran into, I mean literally, because I banged straight into him? Sir Lancelot, the vet!

He was out jogging. He said hello to us, and Morgan glared at me. I don't know if it was because I ran into him or because she didn't want to speak to him. I did need to apologize to him though.

"Hello sir, did I hurt you?"

"No, I'm fine Elliot, don't worry, hello Miss Lea, hello Ms Mercier! It's good to see Snoopy running about again! His paw looks as right as rain now."

"Yes, I think it is," replied Morgan politely.

Lea showed him her basket of chocolates. "Look what we found in Morgan's backpack!"

Sir Lancelot said that Morgan was better than Mary Poppins, which almost made her smile. She replied that she had merely organized an Easter egg hunt, and he said he was out jogging alone on Easter Day as he had nothing better to do.

Lea asked him to come with us, but he politely said no, saying he would just walk us back to the park entrance.

I'm not sure that Morgan was too happy about this and I was worried what we would talk about. But since I was wearing the Paris St Germain tee shirt that Dad bought me last year, the conversation naturally got round to football. He asked me if I was a football fan. I told him I would love to go back to the club I used to be in. He talked about the World Cup that was fast approaching and I whispered that I wasn't sure if Morgan would let me watch it as she hates football.

"Don't worry, I'm sure you'll think of something," he said. "It's only once every four years and I think this World Cup will be one to remember!"

When we got to the park gate, Lea showed him our building.

Morgan had hardly said a word. Lancelot reached his hand out to her, and she took it, and they looked at each other for a bit in silence. Even Lea didn't dare disturb them. I think they are friends now. Then Morgan stepped back and told us curtly that we needed to get back up to the apartment.

This evening we packed our cases. Grandma Cat is coming to get us tomorrow morning at eleven o'clock. Morgan was fidgety and nervous all evening. I can't wait to be in Marseille.

I love you both loads, big hugs.

Elliot

44

Morgan

I open the zipped pocket across the top of the suitcase. Good, their ID cards are there. I slip one hand into Elliot's backpack and can feel the return tickets and Child Plus rail cards. They also have their sunglasses, and a book each. Their pyjamas? I forgot the pyjamas! I never thought it would take so long to pack for just one week. I've been at it for hours. I can even anticipate my mother's snide remarks, "But you only packed them one thin jacket each . . . which won't be warm enough for April. What are these clothes?! I had to buy new polo shirts for Elliot. I couldn't let him wear those gaudy super-hero tee shirts in front of my friends, it was unthinkable . . ."

I couldn't make up my mind whether to make a list or not, then decided against it, as I don't want to turn into one of those neurotic mothers obsessing over an odd sock. It's ten o'clock. My mother doesn't arrive until eleven. Meanwhile the children are getting impatient and beg me to let them go and play in the square.

"Morgan, we'll stay in the playground, you'll see us by the window, we won't move, I swear."

Lea only has to look at me with those big brown eyes and I give in. They bound down the stairs happily while I put the kettle on.

Startled by the doorbell, I spill my tea. The water scalds me but I'm so nervous about seeing my mother that I don't notice the pain. I press the interphone to let her in. I'd recognize her slow, deliberate gait anywhere; she huffs and puffs as she climbs the stairs. She is early and the kids are outside, I'm trapped. I had hoped to avoid such a scenario at all costs. Her panting grows louder. I take a deep breath and pull myself together. Her last visit was particularly horrendous, so we'll just pretend it didn't happen, shall we? We are mature adults and we're not going to rip out each other's throats each time we meet. I calm down. I glimpse her shoulders in the stairwell. We'll just say the strict minimum to each other and then it'll be over. I can't fix the past, but I *can* fight for the present, which is exactly what I shall do.

"Hello Mum."

"Hello Morgan."

You could cut the atmosphere with a knife. We don't kiss, hug or even shake hands. Nothing. We avoid catching each other's eye. I tell her that the kids are playing out in the square.

"Really? By themselves?" she says, surprised.

"I can see them from the window and Elliot will soon be eleven years old. At his age I used to walk back from school alone." I open the window and call out to them to come back up.

They are playing on the rocking motorbikes, though Elliot is too tall for them now and has to fold his legs, which makes him look like a big grasshopper, but he is laughing and happy. They can't hear me calling. My mother gets herself a glass of water as I didn't think to offer her one, but she doesn't take her coat off. This should be quick.

"I left my suitcase at the bottom of the stairwell. I hope no one will steal it. Once the children are back, I'll call a taxi." Then she enquires how many bags I packed for them.

"Just one large suitcase for them both," I reply. I add that the return tickets and child reduction passes are in Elliot's backpack and I packed a book for each of them that they have to read for school. She listens and nods.

I know it is wishful thinking to ask her to make sure they do their homework. Becoming a grandmother has made her lose all notion of academic common sense. This is compounded by the fact that they are orphans, which gives her the greatest excuse in the world to spoil them rotten. For a whole week, they will be living the highlife with my mother. One long blur of carnivals, fun fairs, ice creams, restaurants, the beach . . . I steal a quick glance at her. For some reason, I feel extremely calm. We are alone, and now is the perfect time to set the record straight, without acrimony or anger. Now that I'm in charge of the children, I won't tolerate *anyone* trying to take them from me. I need to tell her this in no uncertain terms. She has to see that I'm no pushover.

"Mum, I have something important to tell you. I love Lea and Elliot very much. Something inside me has changed since I have been looking after them. I definitely want to live with them now."

She looks so shellshocked, anyone would think I had changed into Medusa with snakes for hair. "What did you just say?"

"I said I want to keep the children in accordance with Emily's wishes and I will fight you all the way, should you take the matter to court or try anything else."

"But . . . but you know you can't do it!" she cries in desperation.

For the first time in many years, I boldly walk up to her and face her, my blue eyes on hers. Blue against blue, the only thing we have in common. She flounders, taken by surprise. "I understand how much you love them," I continue, calmly. "I know that you would have given anything to look after them, and you would have done a good job, but Emily entrusted them to me. And I will not tolerate you using Dad to discredit me to the headmistress or anyone else for that matter. You know how he feels about alcohol and you also know perfectly well that I don't drink!"

"Elliot told me you had been drinking vodka!" she replies.

"What did he say exactly? That he saw a bottle of vodka on the table or that he saw me drinking? Go on, tell me, I'm interested, because it was Elliot himself who told me about Dad calling the headmistress. He overheard the whole thing from the corridor; he happened to be waiting to see her at the time."

My mother can no longer cope with my cold, steely, deliberate anger, which will not abate any time soon. She takes a step back. "You don't know how to love," she moans. "You just want to take them from me, like you did the other one. You played the part well alright, all these years pretending to be holier than thou, fawning over your sister to get in her good books, to make her adore you. And hey presto, she entrusts the most precious gift in my life to *you*."

She is sobbing so much she can't speak, but I don't flinch. This time *she'll* be the one who cracks, not me. I'll see this through to the end. It's high time my mother faces up to her responsibilities. Now that *he* is dead, I no longer live in fear. I take her arm, but she pulls away.

"Mum . . . It was the neighbour . . ."

"What?" she mumbles, looking perplexed and glassy-eyed.

"The baby . . . it was the neighbour," I repeat. "You thought you were sending me to a maths lesson, instead you were throwing me into the lions' den each time. I've been to hell and back!"

It's so hard, but I don't let my voice weaken. I can hardly believe my secret is out. Her face freezes with horror. She asks me if this is a sick joke, as it is extremely shameful to accuse a dead man.

"No! . . . My life has been ruined; do you really think I would joke about it? It went on for over a year. When I found out I was pregnant, I was already quite far along. I was so messed up and distraught that I told him everything. He said I had to get away, go to Paris . . ."

My mother looks devastated. Her expression oscillates between doubt and disbelief. Naturally, it was easier for her to cope with when I was the guilty party. Could she really have been so blind? Her eyes are panic stricken as she places her hand on her heart. "And . . . and why didn't you tell me at the time? Why tell him and not me? How am I expected to believe that?" she says desperately.

I explain how I had to promise not to breathe a word to anyone in return for him not touching Emily. I am so traumatized by the memory that I can't meet her gaze any longer. When I tell her how ashamed I was, and so afraid of her, she gives a haughty cackle and holds on to the sofa to keep her balance. A frightened Snoopy cowers behind me.

She asks me again why she should believe me. And if it were true, why did I keep quiet for so long? Was she such a loathsome mother that I couldn't bring myself to talk to her? I'm her daughter after all, she carried me for nine months, she would have seen it in my face, read it in my eyes . . .

She breaks down and can't speak. I hand her the glass of water. I have waited for this moment for eighteen long years. Tormented, she pushes the glass away, and starts hiccupping. "It's impossible, I'm not the blind monster you are making me out to be! And you think your father wouldn't have noticed anything either? What is your game, Morgan? Is this supposed to get you off the hook for giving your baby away? A child that I would have loved and raised?" Despair floods her voice. I take the blow she deals me. I have read enough on the subject to know that denial is often the initial reaction. Tears run down my cheeks. I can't even get angry; it's too painful.

"You wouldn't have believed me anyway," I whisper eventually. "No more so yesterday than today. I just wanted to protect my sister . . . because I loved her more than anything in the world."

I hear the sound of stampeding feet in the stairwell. My mother jumps up and rushes into the bathroom. The door opens and a flurry of joy engulfs the apartment, shattering the tension in one fell swoop. I forgot they have a set of keys. Grandma Cat reappears wearing her dark glasses. Elliot and Lea throw themselves at her for a hug. She struggles to put on a brave face and tells the children to hurry up otherwise they'll be late. The children reach out to kiss me goodbye and I feel a sense of overwhelming love when Lea puts her arms around my neck. I hold back my tears. The door slams behind them. I watch them leave from the window, taking my deepest secret with them. I don't care if my mother doesn't believe me, at least it's not gnawing away at me anymore. I take a deep breath. I am reborn.

45

Elliot

Hi Morgan,

We bought this postcard for you. We'll post it now, so you get it before we are back. This morning Grandpa Paul took us on the little train that goes all the way up to Notre-Dame-de-la-Garde basilica. We explained to Lea that the big golden statue at the top protects sailors. You should have seen the massive slope down; it was like being at Disneyland. The train went so fast we all started screaming!

The mistral wind was really strong this afternoon, so we took our kite to the beach. It was great, Snoopy would have loved it. The wind was so strong we broke the kite. We were scared to say anything, so we just folded it up and put it back in its case. Please don't tell Grandma Cat!

It's kind of weird, I'm really happy to be here, but I wish you were here too, and I can't wait to be back in my room with my own stuff.

I'm sending you big hugs and Lea says, "Me too, me too!"
We miss Snoopy loads. See you on Sunday,

Elliot

Hi Morgan, I hope Snoopy is well, big kisses!

Lea

46

Morgan

Once the children had gone, I decided to take up running. I have run every evening so far, which is so unlike me. I've always hated sport. I've run through the Batignolles area, around the square, and even up to the cemetery to say hi to Emily and Niko. I've run so much that I almost collapse with exhaustion. I've run in the rain, which is prettier than you'd think, I've run at sunset, and I've even run at night. When I received Elliot's postcard, I was thrilled and ran along bursting with joy, happiness and relief. No one has ever sent me such a sweet card before. I then managed to run headlong into a man who was jogging in the opposite direction, knocking him over. And of course, that man just happened to be Sir Lancelot.

"Oh, Dr Deprez, I'm so sorry . . . I hope I haven't injured you? You're going to think we do it on purpose, first Elliot and now me!"

"Call me Lancelot—we're not in the surgery now!" he says, smiling, as I help him up. "I know my name is a bit ridiculous but we are both named after characters from the King Arthur legend, you and I, so we'll just have to make the best of it."

I try to catch my breath. My hair is tied back, my cheeks are undoubtedly very red, and I'm wearing a black and fuchsia outfit I ordered online last week. He appears surprised by my new look.

"I wouldn't have recognized you. Do you run much?" he asks.

"This is my first time running regularly," I reply. "I decided to start once the kids were away, but I'm no good at it, and slow as a tortoise!"

"It doesn't matter. Do you enjoy it?"

"Yes and no. It does feel a bit like self-inflicted torture . . ."

He then asks me where I'm headed, so I explain that I went up to the cemetery and am on my way back now.

"That's a bit of a gloomy destination for a night jog. I hope you at least saw a will-o'-the-wisp? Can I run back with you?" he asks.

I accept, although I can't quite believe that I just said yes. At least he has slowed down to my pace, as I can't go any faster. He has the annoying habit of talking while running, which I'm incapable of doing. If I try, I end up purple-faced and gasping for breath like a carp. So I keep my mouth closed and listen to him without speaking.

"Running is addictive, you'll see. I run three times a week when I leave the clinic; I like Monceau and Martin-Luther-King park. I live on Boulevard Pereire so it's not far. Are Elliot and Lea back at the end of the week?"

I nod.

"It must be strange for you being on your own when the kids are away, though at least you have your dog. How long have you had Snoopy?"

"Seven years." It takes every breath in my body to utter these two words.

He looks surprised and apologizes if he appeared offhand with us at the surgery. Apparently, he is used to putting distance between himself and his patients and no longer realizes he is doing it. He often gets besieged by lonely old ladies who want to talk just to alleviate their boredom. They come to see him as soon as their darling pooches so much as break a claw. He says he is not a shrink and has to distance himself.

"I get it now. But you *do* do a rather good impersonation of a polar bear . . ." I say.

"I'll take that as a compliment." He chuckles.

But that sentence was already too long for me and now I have a stitch. I would rather die than admit it though, so thank goodness we are almost back. We leave the square at Place Charles-Fillion. I stop and go to shake his hand.

"What about your stretches?" he asks accusingly. "You won't be able to walk up your stairs tomorrow if you don't do them. They're even more important if you're not used to running . . . Here, watch me."

I perform them with as much grace as a small elephant. I was never any good at gymnastics. He says he is going running again tomorrow and that I'm welcome to join him. I laugh and refuse his kind offer; I won't be able to keep up—I get exhausted after twenty minutes.

He seems disappointed, though I don't know why. It can't be much fun running with someone as unfit as me. But then it hits me that we are spending the evening together and that I'm dressed in Lycra, which shows off my figure far more than my usual baggy skirts do. Maybe he sees more in me than just an awkward withdrawn adult still trapped in adolescent trauma. I guess what *he* sees is a woman in tight fuchsia coloured leggings. Little does he know I have been celibate since God knows when . . .

"I have to go, Doctor," I say, somewhat embarrassed as I twist the end of my long ponytail.

"Lancelot, please. Well, how about a drink if you don't want to go running?"

"I don't drink."

"Not even water?"

I give in.

He pins me down to eight o'clock on Saturday evening. He'll meet me in front of my apartment building.

He heads off, striding quickly. Once I get back to my apartment, I stare at my face in the bathroom mirror. Beneath my red and out of breath Sunday jogger face, I notice my bright blue eyes, milky white skin, and silvery blond hair. I had forgotten that I'm actually quite pretty. Anchored in my teenage trauma, not wanting to grow up and become a woman, I always hid my curves in the hope that men would leave me alone. I hated them all, every single one of them.

I obsess about meeting Lancelot all week. I should never have agreed to it. We'll have nothing to say to each other anyway. Besides, I have far too many secrets to get involved with someone. It's madness. Plus, he is divorced, his situation is complicated, and he is at least five years older than me, if not ten. There is just no way! I end up biting off all the fingernails on my right hand, and then the same on my left. I will have to buy myself a nail file and some nail varnish to mitigate the damage. I think about the kids all the time, but don't dare call them in case my mother picks up. As soon as my mobile rings, I grab it, whatever time it is, even during team meetings.

I stop off at the local department store to buy a sequined skirt for Lea and a sweater I spotted for Elliot. I wrap them up and place them on their beds. I tidy up, vacuum, and throw out some old forgotten drawings I find under the beds, pleased to see that the marbles are no longer there. I find Elliot's diary and put it back in its hiding place without opening it. But . . . what if I were to open it without reading it? I'm curious to see their Father Christmas list again, to see if I've improved in their eyes. It upset me so much last time. I avoid looking at the first wish, the one where Elliot wanted to go and live in Marseille. We have all moved on since then. I even have the nerve to believe he would prefer to stay with me now.

Pretty plaits starting from the top of her head (Lea)

Yes! I've managed this one, thanks to Viviane's eternal patience. And I'm sure that with practice I shall get even better at it . . .

Play football with Dad (Elliot)

I haven't come up trumps here, unfortunately . . . I suppose I could ask Lancelot, if I don't cancel our date. The thought of seeing him makes me feel like I'm suffocating. The World Cup is fast approaching though and Elliot talks about nothing else, so I'll have to think of something.

All of us dancing together in the living room (Lea)

Ah yes! Well, we danced like crazy the other day when I got the news about . . .

Hear Mum sing Twinkle twinkle my little star *(Lea and Elliot)*

This is actually my mother's song, handed down to Emily. My mind goes blank as I'm not my mother and I have absolutely no wish to be like her. I suddenly feel a pang of guilt about prying in Elliot's diary, and I quickly close it and put it back in its hiding place. I don't quite fit in here yet. I'm not ready. I also think it's best to cancel my drink with Lancelot. I'll tell him I have a bad case of cholera or tuberculosis . . . I pull out his business card from my wallet, take a deep breath and send him a cowardly text message telling him I have a temperature. I feel like a foolish blundering schoolgirl faking a doctor's note. When I try to close my wallet, the zip gets caught on my therapist's business card.

This is obviously a sign for me to contact her. I send her an email asking for an appointment. I can still hear her voice, "When silence has been exhausted, words must tell the tale." She may have a point.

47

Elliot

Morgan lets me take Snoopy out on my own now. She must really trust me as he means the world to her! Summer is on its way: the days are getting longer, there are lots of people sitting outside the street cafes laughing, there are people playing music, and others just strolling around. I like this neighbourhood, it's very different from where I used to live. School is getting better and I have made some new friends. The headmistress has been really nice to me. I don't know what she told the other kids, but since we went back after half term in February, they've started talking to me again and ask me to play with them. I even have a new best friend called Antoine, who invited me to his bowling party for his eleventh birthday. It was so cool! When I told Morgan about it, she said that for my birthday in June, she would bake a cake and that I could also have a big party at home.

"But it'll make a lot of mess, won't it?" I say. "What about your bonsai trees?"

She says she doesn't care, which strikes me as very odd. Something's not quite right there.

Tonight I walked around the whole square with Snoopy, then went down Cardinet Street and onto the bridge over the railway tracks. I really like it there. We stood for a while watching the trains coming and going, honking and generally making lots of noise. I wonder where all those people are going. I know that if you go that way you eventually get to Maisons-Laffitte. And further still, the sea.

"Hi Elliot!"

I nearly jump out of my skin.

"Oh, hello Doctor!" I say.

"Please, call me Lancelot."

"Are you out jogging?" I ask.

"No, I'm skiing, can't you tell?" he chuckles. "What are you up to?"

"Bungee jumping!" I reply. He laughs again.

He offers to walk back with me. He strokes Snoopy first and then we set off. He talks about the World Cup. I tell him that Lea and I are huge fans and that we are hoping our friends will invite us to watch it at their house as Morgan hates football. I tell him I have asked for the French team football shirt for my birthday and am counting on my grandma to send me one.

I tell him I'm going to be eleven on the 5th of June. He says it's his daughter's birthday on the 12th. And when I ask what present he is getting her he looks sad and says he has no idea what she wants. His wife and daughter have been living in Bordeaux for the last ten years. He agreed to let them move away but has lost touch with his daughter since.

I turn to look at him. "You should go; she's still your daughter. At least you *can* go. Even if I ask Mum and Dad to come, they can't."

He pats my back gently, just like Dad used to. "You're right young man, grown-ups question things too much, they complicate everything. What are you doing for your birthday?"

"We're having a party at home on the Saturday before, on the 2nd of June."

"Sounds good. What about your aunt, is she feeling any better?"

"Better from what?" I ask, surprised.

"I believe she was ill during the holidays?"

"No, she's doing great," I say.

"Oh, that's odd, I thought she had a temperature."

It's kind of him to worry about Morgan, but he must be confusing her with someone else. She was always in a good mood on the phone and was really happy when we got back.

She wasn't ill. I think something must have happened while we were in Marseille. I saw how they looked at each other on Easter Sunday. They reminded me of *Lady and the Tramp* eating spaghetti! And as for her pretending to be ill, that's what we do when there's a maths test. I feel sorry for him, Morgan obviously lied. We are almost home; we get to the edge of the square. I look up to the window and see Lea waving at me. She is waiting for me to go to bed. I have to go. Lancelot says bye and asks me to tell Morgan to call him as he has a friend who runs a boarding kennels just outside of Paris and that it might interest her. He must think I'm daft!

"Okay, but otherwise you could come to my birthday party on the 2nd and just tell her yourself. It's *my* birthday party so I can invite who I like."

"Don't you think I'm a bit too old?"

"It's up to you. It starts at three o'clock." I race Snoopy up the stairs back to the apartment. I win!

48

Morgan

I don't know why I made this appointment. I guess I was overcome with emotion that day. Now that I'm sat here, sinking deeper and deeper into the huge green armchair, I start to feel dizzy. The elderly lady smiles at me encouragingly, as she observes me from behind her portholes. They look just like aviator's goggles. She may be extremely short sighted, but she can read me like an open book.

"I'm glad you came back, Ms Mercier."

A heavy silence. I feel her green eyes dissecting me. She has tied the rope around my waist and now she's waiting for me to jump off the bridge. "So, what did you want to talk to me about?" she asks.

"Elliot of course," I mumble. "I wanted to update you on the situation." One step forward, three steps back, one step to the side, then back to square one . . .

"Really? Very well. Does he seem less distressed to you?" she enquires.

I tell her yes, that he has made huge progress. His school marks have improved, and he has made some new friends at school.

She says that she was *actually* referring to his fear of being abandoned. Okay, she is nudging me, so I move sideways. It's like a game of chess: she is the queen and I'm the bishop. I begin to regret coming.

I reply that he never mentioned anything about being abandoned to me. I'm aware that we got off to a rocky start, but things are gradually taking shape. We are certainly moving in the right direction. I then get a sudden urge, like I did the other day, to get the whole thing off my chest, to pour my heart out to someone who will finally listen and console me. I can't take the plunge though. If only she would ask me some more questions and not wait for me to make the first move.

Instead, she gets up and offers me her hand to shake.

"Since everything is progressing smoothly, I see no need to dig deeper. I suggest that Elliot comes once a fortnight up to the end of the school year. Then he can take a break until he goes back to school in September. Thank you, Ms Mercier."

Damn, I'm caught in my own trap. If I don't talk, then there's no need for me to stay. I freeze in my armchair and time stands still.

She sits back down and readjusts her oversized specs. "I'm guessing you came here because you had something to tell me. I wasn't born yesterday, you know. There's absolutely nothing, I mean, nothing you can't tell me. Whatever pain is eating away at you, you clearly can't bear it any longer. You want to talk about it. Have a little faith in yourself."

She puts down her glasses on the table. I finally see her face, her wrinkles of wisdom, her white hair, her gracious caring green eyes. I stare at her desk, the butterflies, the children's drawings, the subdued light. I bask in the warmth of her cosy cave. Maybe this *is* the right moment. I close my eyes and jump off that bridge. Somehow I know she will be waiting to catch me at the bottom.

I pour my heart out. I tell her every detail, every sordid little detail, the bare, hard truth, concealing nothing, exaggerating nothing. The neighbour, the maths lessons, the shame, the fear, the disgust. My pregnancy, the promise I made, the unwanted child growing inside me, gnawing at my sanity. The shame. My mother discovering me heavily pregnant, her wanting to keep the baby, while my heart rejected it. Giving birth anonymously. Running away from the hospital. My relief, my remorse, a lifetime of anguish and self-interrogation. The shame that still haunts me, extinguishing my heart's ability to feel anything else. My job in a nursery. My self-imposed solitude. My love for my sister, her wedding, the birth of Elliot and Lea, my bitterness in the face of her perfect family, and my pride at having protected her. Men, my desire to love, my fear of commitment, my disgust, my celibacy, the shame that never leaves me. The wastepaper basket overflows with my drenched tissues. My tears could irrigate a desert. She is the gardener watching the flowers grow. Her amazing green eyes sow seeds in me that heal the present and help the future blossom.

Silence descends again. Yet this silence is different. It is pure and soothing. It doesn't lie, it has no shame or anything to hide. I am too afraid to look up at her, dreading what she must think of me.

"You know, Ms Mercier, no one is obliged to love," she says gently. "Even one's own child. Life isn't like an advert for breakfast cereal, with the loving family sitting happily around the table. Maternal love is not innate, it is built and nurtured. You know this now, because you look after Elliot and Lea who are not your children, yet you want to love them as if they were. But you feel so much remorse over your own child that you don't allow yourself this love. It is high time you released yourself from these chains you're carrying." I stare at her, overwhelmed by her kindness, devoid of any judgement, and by the simplicity and truth of her words.

"Your child is not alone," she continues. "He has his own family now, but he will never be part of yours and you must accept this. You gave him the chance to be loved because you couldn't do it yourself. Given up for adoption on his first day in this world and taken in by loving parents, ready and waiting to devote their whole lives to him. That's quite a gift, don't you think? What greater gift is there to offer than life itself? At seventeen years old, you made an incredibly brave decision. And now it's time to rebuild your life. And you have been sent two lost children, so grab this chance!"

I step outside. I feel as light as the little white clouds above me. The sky has never looked so blue. The air carries the fragrance of spring. I head back to the nursery. The little ones are still napping. I tiptoe quietly through the dormitories. Tiago is fast asleep in his cot, sweetly aware of just how much he is loved.

Tonight, Valerie comes to pick up her son on her own. She walks slowly but surely down the hall, and straps Lucas into his pushchair, refusing Jean-Michel's offer of help as he ties his daughter's laces. He holds the door for her and stands back to let her pass. He even offers to drive her home, but a trip in the hearse—even a musical hearse like his—doesn't seem to appeal to her. As she leaves, she says a firm "goodbye" to me. I watch her wobble slowly away.

49

Elliot

Dear Mum,

Morgan threw me a really fab birthday party! She even asked Viviane, the nice lady from the nursery, to come and help. Morgan really did her best so I couldn't possibly have told her that Winnie the Pooh balloons were too babyish. Luckily Viviane arrived, shouting, "No, not those, this isn't the nursery!" She rushed off to exchange them for huge inflatable golden letters that read "Happy Birthday". I was so relieved. Can you imagine how embarrassing it would have been!

She even ordered me a cake in the shape of Darth Vader from the bakery. I was allowed to invite everyone in my class because Morgan thought it was important "after everything that happened". She's going to hate cleaning up tomorrow. There's even cake crushed into one of the cushions. We haven't told her yet, and just turned it over so as not to spoil the party. She is in such a good mood at the moment, so we're making the most of it.

Grandma Cat sent me a French team football shirt, which arrived just in time. Even Alex was jealous, which I liked. Morgan gave me a subscription to my science and nature magazine plus a box of Lego. I also got a gift from my mystery guest. Do you remember Lancelot? The vet that Morgan couldn't stand? I ran into him the other day while I was walking Snoopy and invited him. Morgan didn't know. And he actually turned up! He gave me a Panini World Cup 2018 album and loads of stickers to put inside! The boys in my class were so jealous. To tell the truth, I didn't think he would come. He must have been feeling sad because he'd wanted to tell Morgan about that boarding kennels and she never called him back. It wasn't very nice of her. I don't know why she is scared of him. When I talked to her about it, she pretended to ignore me. But now she had no choice. There he was, standing at the door with the album and a bouquet of flowers that he handed to Lea. I gave him an apple juice and a bag of sweets. Viviane turned the music up and we all started dancing. Everyone except Morgan that is, who insisted on tidying away all the wrapping paper that was lying around. After that we had our birthday tea, and then played the games that Viviane and Morgan had organized. When we put the music back on to dance again, I realized that Morgan was no longer there. Neither was Lancelot. The bedroom door was closed and I could hear them talking. I peeped through the lock, not to spy, but just to check if they were both there. And they were. They were sitting on the edge of the bed, smiling at each other. Except that Alex and Antoine came up behind me and pushed me out of the way. The bedroom door opened, and we all fell inside on top of each other. Morgan went bright red, got up and left the room. Lancelot shook my hand, thanked me very much and said he had to go. But I saw him whisper something to Morgan on the doorstep. It was a good idea of mine to invite him, don't you think? The party is over now, and I'm eleven years old for real. Morgan ordered pizzas for us and Viviane, then she told us to go to bed and that we would tidy up tomorrow. Lea is already asleep holding her marmot in her arms. You know, Mum, at first I didn't understand why you chose Morgan and I was really mad at you. But I'm glad now and I want to stay here. I love Marseille, Grandma and Grandpa. I know that they want us to live there, but this is where I feel at home, near you, and I can go and see you whenever I want. For my birthday, I still have one last wish, and maybe you can help me from heaven? I want Morgan and Grandma Cat to be friends. I'm fed up with being their go-between all the time. Why can't they just speak to each other normally? Grandma Cat isn't her usual self, I can tell. She still calls us a lot, but she doesn't tell us anything anymore. She always asks me if Morgan is there, and if she can speak to her. But Morgan never has time. I looked on her phone the other night while she was in the bath, and there was yet another missed call from Grandma Cat. She must have tried a hundred times this week! As for Morgan, she's nothing like she used to be; she is really cool now.

Goodnight, Mum, give Dad lots of kisses and hugs from me. I will really miss him during the World Cup. We were looking forward to it so much. I'll try and tell him all about it afterwards. I miss you both so much, all the time. So does Lea.

Elliot

50

Morgan

I recognized her writing immediately, that flashy garrulous way she has of doing huge round letters that devour the whole envelope. I put it inside my bedside table. I can't face my mother right now, even on paper.

After our last clash, I decided to cut her out of my life. I told her everything, she knows the whole story, and can take it or leave it. I'm finally free. In any case, she won't believe me now any more than she did eighteen years ago. So I may as well blot her out of my thoughts. The neighbour is dead, and I'm learning to love again. I'm rebuilding a new life with Elliot and Lea, and my mother will play no part in it if need be. After the Easter holidays, we maintained radio silence for several weeks. Then Elliot tried to pass her to me on the phone a few times. This took me by surprise, but I didn't have the courage to take her calls. At first, I thought she wanted to discuss arrangements for Elliot and Lea, but it then became routine. She would ask to speak to me every time she called the kids. I'm not ready yet, and, besides, if I must see her, it will just be the two of us. Elliot and Lea shouldn't be a part of this. She hasn't given up, however, and calls me non-stop on my mobile, even at the office. Now here I am, holding her letter, but terrified of opening it. The children are asleep, and the sun is setting. I can see its red, yellow and orange hues slowly sinking on the horizon. But I still can't muster up the courage to read my mother's words.

Sitting on my bed, I finally take the letter out of my bedside table. Other envelopes fall out of the overflowing drawer and flutter to the ground. A photo of Linh, the child I sponsored in Vietnam, smiles and encourages me. I have been sponsoring her for eight years now. This is my secret little sanctuary that no one knows about. Over the years, I have become very fond of Linh, her smile, her long plaits, and yet we have never met. I place the photo on my bedside table and put back the letters that are strewn across the floor. My heart pounds as I open my mother's letter. It is as if she is standing right there in front of me.

Sweetheart,

You're obviously avoiding me, so I have no choice but to put pen to paper. I sincerely hope you don't throw this letter in the bin without hearing me out.

I'm not sleeping, I've grown ten years older, and lost three kilos … The last few weeks have been the worst of my life, together with the weeks following Emily's death … I'm dealing with this all alone, I can't talk to your father … There is so much I want to say to you … First and foremost, I apologize. I'm so sorry that it took me all this time to see; all this time to realize the extent of the damage. It has taken me days to take it in, the shock of it all. You can't imagine how I blame myself. I keep remembering Monique, the neighbour from upstairs, the one who was rather hefty. She always told me to be wary of that neighbour who in her words was "too handsome to be true". As far as I was concerned, this was sheer spite on her part; she had a crush on him and, not being blessed with good looks, she didn't stand a chance. I even ended up telling her that more or less (probably more than less, you know me). Morgan, please forgive me for all those years I was blind and wanted to erase you from my life. I couldn't bear to look at you.

I hated you so much for what you did. Ironic isn't it, to see you throwing back at me my own incompetence as a mother. What kind of monster was I that you didn't dare talk to me? Did I terrify you that much? To the point where you preferred to give up your child rather than become a mother like me? How could I have not seen what was happening under my very nose and go on and on believing that I was right? When did this distance first come between us? I didn't want it, you know. Though I started it, it's not what I wanted. I believed it was the right thing to do. Now you're throwing it all back at me, and I truly deserve it. I'm so sorry ...

But there's something else you probably haven't thought of. I have also had my share of suffering, which has made my life very sad and bitter. Every day I have to bear the pain of being a grandmother who lost a grandchild. I wanted that child so much. As soon as I knew of his existence, I wanted him. You're surprised, aren't you? I was always so afraid of what the neighbours would say and think. Well, yes, I wanted that child more than anything else, my own flesh and blood, and I would have invented some story for the sake of appearances, but I would have raised him and loved him as my own. It certainly wouldn't have been the first time in Marseille! Remember Marcel Pagnol? When Panisse took Fanny's son in as his own? But I can see now that you didn't care about honour or keeping up appearances. I was your problem. You were entitled to do whatever you wanted, while I had no rights at all. I had nothing. When I discovered you had gone to the maternity clinic while I was shopping, without so much as leaving me a note telling me where you were, I went berserk. To think that I came to Paris specially, knowing you were due. I went to the nearest hospital and then to another, and another. Wherever I went, there was no trace of your name anywhere, nor that of the child. It was as if you had never existed. I lost track of you both.

Legally, there was nothing I could do; besides I had no proof. I came away broken, crushed, and riddled with shame, unable to admit to your father that I had let our grandchild slip away. I returned to Marseille, with an aching heart, and you ran off to the other side of the world. I couldn't face seeing you. Emily became my cure all. My heart turned to stone until Elliot and Lea came along. Those children, whom I love more than anything in the world, saved me. They pulled me out of my grief. Your sister's death finally finished me off. And I saw her last will and testament as the ultimate betrayal. Of course, she wasn't aware of what you had done, there was no malice intended. So you see, I had to get my grandchildren back at all costs and save them from your clutches. How could I trust you? You lived alone like a hermit all those years, and, given your track record, it was like a declaration of war. I didn't imagine for a second that you could possibly love them, I thought it was still all about you and me. Yes, I hated you. I'm ashamed to put this in writing, but there's no point in beating about the bush. You were the perpetrator and I was the victim. I should have seen what was going on, but I didn't. I should have been the one reaching out to you, but instead I withdrew. I should have been the one who comforted you, but instead I let you down. And I'm much poorer for it. I lost my grandchild. It's a heavy burden to bear. Every time I look in the mirror, I see a loathsome wicked mother. I'm not asking for your forgiveness. Don't ask me to forget. I'm so ashamed that I can't bring myself to tell your father, he would be so angry and hurt. It would break him. I have already lost so much; he is all I have left. I don't know if you will read this or if we will ever be able to face each other again. But I sincerely hope so from the bottom of my heart. Let's call a truce, Morgan; if not for us, then for Elliot and Lea …

Mum

I sit on my bed staring into space, the letter shaking in my hand. I wipe away my tears. I don't hear Elliot walking in. He sits down beside me and hugs me. "Don't cry. I used to argue with my mum too."

I run my hand through his hair, smiling at his naivety despite myself.

"It's a bit more serious than that," I say.

He pulls me close to him. "I don't care what happened between you, I don't want to know. But Grandma is sad and so are you, and I'm fed up with seeing you both like this. You're not going to be fighting forever, are you?"

He gets up and looks at the photo of Linh. "Who is this?" he asks.

"It's a child I've been sponsoring for several years now. It has been very rewarding. If you want, I can show you other photos of her later?" He nods. I take his hand. "Emily was right when she said she were a little treasure," I whisper.

I look at the letter beside me. I shan't read it again, it's too painful. I take it to the kitchen, grab a lighter and burn it over the kitchen sink. I wouldn't want Elliot and Lea to find it one day at the bottom of a drawer. I watch the flames lick my fingers until I can't stand the pain any longer. All those years of suffering gone up in smoke and only a few ashes to show for it. It's pretty ridiculous really.

51

Elliot

"Hey Elliot, do you know if Morgan read my letter?" asked Grandma Cat.

"How would I know Grandma Cat, I'm not the postman. Why don't you ask her yourself? The pair of you are getting on my nerves!"

I hang up on her. It's not kind to send your grandmother packing, but I'm fed up. She should go and see the owl if she wants to talk, it might do her good. I'm not going to waste my Saturday worrying about adult stuff, especially since there's a match on at eight o'clock tonight. Morgan has agreed to let me watch it at Antoine's house and Lea is desperate to go with me. It's going to be insane!

It's ten o'clock. I offer to take Snoopy out. Lea has just finished getting dressed and is hopping around like a kanga-roo. "Morgan, can I go as well, say yes, *pleeeeease*!" She makes her huge panda eyes and it does the trick.

"Elliot, can I trust you? Don't go too far and be careful when crossing the road . . . Do you have your watch?"

I nod.

"Okay, it's ten o'clock. I want you both back here by ten thirty at the latest."

"If not, you'll call the police?" I joke.

She gives me that look. She is *such* a scaredy cat, always worrying about what might happen.

We bound down the stairs. I put Snoopy's lead on and we set off for our first walk with no grown-ups! Morgan can't even see us from the window. Free at last! Lea is overexcited so I tell her to calm down. I'm in charge now. She asks if we can cross the bridge. I say we can. She wants us to pretend that the railway tracks are a big river and the trains are crocodiles. "Watch out there's a crocodile, watch out for the crocodile!" we yell, as soon as a train pulls into the station. People give us strange looks; they don't realize how dangerous the river is. Snoopy barks. We turn into the next street and end up right in front of Lancelot's clinic. Lea taps on the window.

"Are you crazy?" I hiss.

"I just want to say hi," she says. "He gave me some flowers remember, and he gave you a Panini album."

The window opens and Lancelot appears in a white coat. He asks us how we are. When we tell him we just wanted to say hi, he looks pleased and reminds us that Germany is playing Sweden tonight. I say that we can't wait and we'll be watching it at our friend Antoine's house. Even though I support France, I do hope Dad's team wins tonight. I mean, they *are* world champions, so it should be a safe bet!

He promises to cross his fingers for us but must go now as a patient has just arrived. "Elliott, I went to Bordeaux by the way. It was a good idea. Thank you," he says before closing the window.

Lea starts sulking. "I was the one who said hello first, but he only talked to you. What did he mean about 'Board-doe' anyway?"

I chuckle to myself as I know my answer will just set her off again. "It's our little secret," I reply. "You wouldn't understand, you're too young."

Then I race off with Snoopy pulling me along at breakneck speed. Lea chases me to the bridge, and, despite being out of breath, manages to scream at me to watch out for the crocodile ahead. Paris is one big jungle . . .

We are back home at ten thirty sharp. Morgan probably never left the window. She is a mega worrier that one. She was hiding behind the curtains when we got back to our building, but we could still see her. I told Lea not to mention the crocodiles otherwise she won't let us out on our own again.

The match was great. The Germans were feeling the heat but made a comeback at the last minute. Dad would have been proud of his team. Just thinking about it brings tears to my eyes. When Morgan comes to pick us up, I ask her if we can call Opa Georg, even though it's late. He is worn out from the game, as if he was the one running around for ninety minutes! We talk about the match for at least half an hour and I hear the beep of a second call trying to come in. When I hang up, it rings instantly. It's Grandpa Paul. What does *he* want at this time of night?

"Elliot, it's you I wanted to talk to. I figured that with the Germany game, you wouldn't be in bed yet. Can you keep a secret?"

"Yes," I say. "And by the way, *hello* Grandpa Paul."

Grandpa Paul gets straight to the point without even asking me how I am. To be honest, I'm surprised he even knows the World Cup is on. I don't suppose it features in his *Gardening Weekly*! "I suppose you've noticed that Grandma Cat and Morgan are not on speaking terms at the moment?" he asks.

"That's putting it mildly!" I reply. "It's outright war! Morgan goes all weird when she sees Grandma Cat's name on her phone. You'd have to be completely blind to not notice!"

"Alright," he says. "Then let's bang their heads together. I need your help. Do you have keys to your apartment?"

"Yes, I do."

"Could you let us in?" he asks. "We're going to come and see Morgan. Don't tell her though, or she won't agree to it, but this nonsense has to stop. We are a family."

I hesitate. I'm really not sure about letting them in when I know Morgan doesn't want to see them. But he says again that it's "really important", so I eventually agree. I make him promise that there won't be any arguments and that he will never again tell the headmistress that Morgan is an alcoholic. He chokes in surprise, then promises. They want to come round next Saturday.

I ask what time as France will probably be playing on Saturday. He says some time in the afternoon and suggests that Lea and I go to friends so they can be alone with Morgan.

I say okay and hang up. I don't like the sound of it though. I won't tell Lea, she repeats everything back to Morgan. Grown-up arguments seem to be way more complicated than ours.

52

Morgan

Itsi bitsi petit bikini already?! It's only three thirty. Jean-Michel is early today. I sigh and close my office door. I still have some pressing matters to deal with. The doorbell buzzes and he enters, humming cheerfully. Anyone would think he worked in a circus not a morgue; he's always as happy as a lark. But I just want silence. I need to concentrate.

I hear the doors opening and closing again. Then little footsteps rushing out and a mother trying in vain to put on her child's shoes. She asks him for the left foot, and he gives her the right foot. The child starts protesting so his mother threatens to leave him at the nursery, which upsets him even more. He doesn't like Delphine, or Viviane, as they are "not nice", and should be "put in the bin". My ears prick up on hearing my staff's names, but I don't pay any further attention once he says his own mother should go in the bin too. Just another one of those normal home time tantrums. It's understandable and a survival instinct; the children are finally reunited with their parents after having to put on a brave face all day in front of—possibly hostile—strangers. The cloakroom is a hub where children scream their heads off and exhausted parents, drained after a day of dealing with stressed bosses and neurotic colleagues, lose their rag. Quite frankly the last thing they want to hear is that their two-year-old wants to chuck them in the bin . . . It doesn't go down too well with this particular mother either.

"That's not a very nice thing to say," she protests. "Mummy hasn't done anything wrong and has even brought you a treat ..." I hear the door squeaking again and Jean-Michel's voice, as he puts his daughter's shoes on. At that very instant, the poor mother gets hit right in the face by her son's trainer.

"*NO CHOCOLATE ... NO WANT CHOCOLATE!!*" He rolls on the floor screaming as if he has been poisoned. He hiccups and cries, face down on the ground, while his mother stomps around impatiently looking at her watch.

"Tim, my darling, I came to collect you early today because we have an appointment with the paediatrician at four thirty. It's a long way from here and we don't have much time." The toddler just screams louder, and his mother loses her temper.

"That's enough, Tim. Now let me put your shoes on, we have to go!"

He resists, screaming and sobbing. His poor mother, who has clearly had a very trying day, shouts at him to shut up or she'll take his chocolate from him. The child doesn't stop. The whole nursery listens in. I prefer not to get involved. The parents don't like it when the manager intervenes.

Suddenly I hear a big sigh and, peering through the door, I see Jean-Michel's massive frame kneel down in front of the toddler, who is still on the floor. He strokes his hair and asks him if he is tired.

"NO!" screams the child.

"Yeah, I wish I could put my day in the bin too," says Jean-Michel.

"NO!" the toddler screams again.

"But the good news is, I was given this little plane, do you want to see it?"

The toddler stands up. Jean-Michel takes a metal plane out of his pocket and shows it to him. Captivated, the child calms down. Jean-Michel gets up and puts the plane back in his pocket.

"Thank you for showing me just how incompetent I am," says the mother, tight-lipped.

"Well, there was no need to get angry, or threaten to take his chocolate off him," he says. "After all he is only a kid."

She looks daggers at him and storms off, carrying her son.

I come out from behind my door. "You sure gave her a lesson . . ."

"Were you eavesdropping?" he asks, looking upset. "What a bitch!"

I don't get it. Does she really think her kid is going to calm down if she takes his snack off him? And when she tells him he has to travel across Paris on a crowded underground to see a doctor, what's he meant to say, *yippee*?

I tell him off for being too hard on the poor mother; we all have bad days. He then delights in telling me how bad *his* day was. How he had to bury the twenty-year-old victim of a motorcycle accident and how devastated and broken the family were. Nothing comes close to that, certainly not the failed meeting or that promotion you didn't get. To top it all, he says he never gets angry with his daughter, since it is our job as adults to put ourselves in their shoes.

"Maybe you are a truly exceptional person," I retort, "with a job that is a little . . . *unusual* shall we say, which helps you to put things into perspective. But I can assure you that this cloakroom is somewhere both children and parents can—and should—let off steam!"

"Well that's a shame!" he exclaims. "Because life is a gift, each and every moment is precious, and instead of shouting and telling ourselves that it's the end of the world if we're five minutes late for a doctor's appointment, we should be making the most of it. Believe me, I see corpses every day, so I know what I'm talking about. There's a lot of time for regrets when you're six feet under!"

I stand there astonished. He looks offended and says he isn't bluffing; his own life hasn't exactly been a bed of roses. And he can sympathize with the "one hell of a year" I have had too.

"But sorry, instead of gazing at my navel and crying into my tea, I decided to become an undertaker and live life to the full! Death is the ultimate destiny, no one escapes it. Plus I love helping people going through it. And since life is the only gift my mother ever gave me, I thank her for it every day, despite never knowing her."

Shocked, I ask him if he was abandoned. He hastily corrects me, saying he was *adopted*, not abandoned and that it is *not* the same thing. He goes on to say that Tom Thumb was *abandoned* in the woods by his dreadful parents, whereas adopted means you were taken on by parents who loved you even before they ever knew you. He adds that being abandoned conjures up gloomy and sinister thoughts, while being adopted is something magical. He tells himself time and time again to be grateful for all the love he has been given and may not have had.

"And if someone doesn't want you, they are making way for someone who does, you just have to find that person. The earth is round so even if you are both walking in opposite directions, you'll meet up again. You just have to be patient."

I'm dumbstruck, my mouth is agape. He gives me a gentle pat on the back and asks me if I'm okay, saying I look like I have just swallowed a fly!

I size up this bearded giant. Who would have thought that under his tough exterior of undertaker and grave digger, he has a heart of gold and embraces life, despite having had his own share of sorrow.

The doorbell buzzes. I open it. Valerie enters, still pale and emaciated, but looking a bit brighter under her big scarf. Jean-Paul rushes to hold the door for her. "Valerie, you look radiant today!" he says. "What brings you here at this hour? You normally get here at closing time!"

Valerie doesn't seem offended by anything anymore and replies in a crystal-clear voice that she wishes to take Lucas for a stroll in the park as the weather is so nice. "One of the advantages of being on sick leave," she adds.

"What, alone?!" he cries. "That is totally unreasonable, what if you were to feel unwell? Let me come with you, I promised Alice we would go for a short walk."

Valerie accepts and slips away to fetch her son. Jean-Michel gives me a contented smile. His hoarse voice resounds in my head. I have a crazy urge to go and get Elliot and Lea, right there and then, and be a bit spontaneous, like Valerie. The weather is perfect, it'll soon be the summer holidays and they will be leaving for Germany. I shall miss them. I hear Jean-Michel and Valerie cheerfully setting off with their two children.

Viviane appears. I tell her I need a favour and could she lock up as I have to leave right away. I reassure her nothing serious has happened and say it's just something *urgent* I have to do with the kids.

I dash off and head to the bakery where I buy a bag of little choux buns coated in sugar. It's four thirty. I stand in front of the school gates for the first time with all the mums who are always on time. Suddenly, I remember that Elliot and Lea won't be coming out throwing themselves into my arms and shouting, because they are enrolled in the after-school club. I go in and find them. We then head out into the June sunshine. Lea, her mouth full of choux bun, has sugar in her hair. I grab them both by the hand and we charge home crazily. Jean-Michel was right: there's always *someone* waiting for us. And, if we're very lucky, there's sometimes more than one.

53

Elliot

Dear Mum,

Morgan came to fetch us at four thirty today, for the first time ever. It was such a surprise! We had just gone into the after-school club when Lea saw her. She tripped over her shoelaces running, calling out to Morgan, asking her why she was there.

Morgan said she had a sudden urge to see us. We ran along the pavement, holding hands, not having the faintest idea what was going on, a bit like the day we had the fake birthday party at the restaurant. Sometimes Morgan is so happy she does weird things. I think it's because she used to be sad all the time and has a lot of catching up to do.

We didn't go home right away but went to the square instead and played on the slide. I say "we", because Morgan played on it too and she even tore her skirt. Lea and I chased away the ducks, screaming, and got told off by the security guard. Once home, we ran up the stairs, and when we got into the apartment, we began to dance. It was Lea's idea. She went to pick out one of Morgan's big black records from the pile, one that she really likes from that singer called Paf, or Piaf. She placed it over the hole, then put the needle thing on it and it went pffffftt. A croaky old voice began to sing. Morgan grabbed Lea and they started to twirl. The words are quite nice. They are written on the back of the record, so I have copied them out for you:

Bluer than the blue of your eyes,
I don't see anything better,
Even the blue of the skies,
Blonder than your golden hair,
One can't imagine,
Even the blond of wheat.

"Hey Morgan, blue and blond, like you!" cried Lea.

Stronger than my love for you,
The sea, even raging,
Doesn't come close.

I couldn't tell whether it was Morgan or Lea as they were joined together, spinning. You could just see a big torn skirt flying up, a mass of tangled blond and brown hair and four arms stuck together! I moved the furniture back because if they carried on like that, they would bang into the armchairs and break all of Morgan's bonsais. I'm turning fussy like her now, I told you it was contagious!

Lea shouted at me to join in. She tried to grab me, but they were going too fast. They were laughing so much and spinning around me so fast that I got caught up in it. We spun together like a spinning top until we all fell on the rug, all three of us. We looked at the ceiling that was spinning as fast as a carousel and laughed till we cried. Especially when Snoopy jumped on us and licked our faces.

We were out of breath, so we stayed on the floor, just lying there, looking up at the pretend stars. And we even made a wish when Lea saw a shooting star.

Well, it was a funny evening, Mum! You would have liked it. I'm just a bit scared because it's almost Saturday. Grandpa Paul and Grandma Cat will soon be here and I'm not sure

Morgan will be pleased. I wish you could help us. Aside from that, I don't have very good news for Dad ... Germany is out. He's going to be really upset. But France is pushing on, and we think they might make it to the finals.

Love you both lots, miss you too.

Elliot

54

Morgan

The summer holidays begin in one week's time, but practically everyone I know—kids, teenagers and adults alike—are acting as if they are on holiday already. Elliot and Lea are off to Antoine's house this afternoon for the France–Argentina match. After lunch, I took Lea on a small shopping spree. Saturdays are always a nightmare for shopping, but she has absolutely nothing to wear. We emerge laden like mules, but it's not our fault; there were so many lovely clothes. Plus the sales were on, and I can't resist a bargain. I would kill for a pair of the sandals I just found Lea. Unfortunately, they don't make them in size 7! When we get back, I see Elliot waving at me from the square. He was right to go out and get some fresh air, before being stuck in a room for two hours with a load of sweaty males! The game starts in forty-five minutes, but he tells Lea they must leave "right now" to get into the mood and put their red, white and blue make-up on.

"Do you realize this is France–*Argentina*, Lea?" says Elliot. "They're *really* good . . . I'm not sure how we're going to beat them."

Lea, always obedient, hands me her bags. I watch the two of them charge off and then I head home.

The door to the apartment building is open. I always tell Elliot to close it behind him, but he doesn't listen, it's infuriating. What's more, someone has had the nerve to stick pink tape on the doorbell right next to my name! A shiver goes down my spine. What if it were Lancelot? What if he stuck a cheeky little note there, on my doorbell, and then appeared on his white steed to whisk me and the kids off to the countryside to set up a boarding kennels? I'm getting carried away. Since Elliot's birthday, there has been no sight nor sound of Lancelot. He hasn't contacted me and I never see him out running, despite keeping an eye out for the evening joggers from my window. Following my pathetic fake illness episode, he's probably waiting for me to make the first move. I did send him a text, but he never replied. I remove the Post-it. I mustn't delude myself . . . But there is just one word written in capital letters: **SORRY**.

That's not Lancelot. Maybe it's for someone else?

I enter the building. In the hallway I see further traces of the joker. My mailbox is covered in yellow, blue, pink, and green Post-its. I unpeel them, one by one. It's a nice gesture, but I'm always the one who has to clean up afterwards I head upstairs, carrying my bags with me. On the stairs, I'm besieged again by a colourful mass of Post-it notes, each expressing their apologies! I don't get it. I stick my head over the railing to get a better look; they reach up to the ceiling, like rambling roses.

Sorry
Sorry
SORRY
Sorry
Sorry

This is ridiculous, I can't stop every two seconds to pull them off. I carry on up the stairs. I get to the second floor. The mysterious colourful mosaic continues. I then follow it all the way up to the fourth floor, where it stops right in front of my apartment. My heart sinks. My front door is ajar and drowning under multiple coloured stickers. I'm unsteady on my feet and my heart is pounding. Elliot is the only one who has the keys and he has just left. So who is it?

The door opens. Dad stands there, gazing at me fondly. I can see an unfamiliar sorrow in his grey eyes, a sorrow that I have only ever seen once before: on the day of Emily's funeral. He hugs me tightly.

"I know everything, Morgan," he whispers in my ear. "Your mother told me the whole story. Please forgive me. Forgive me for not seeing it. Forgive me for leaving you helpless and alone. Forgive me for being such a bad father. I'm so ashamed and sorry for what I did."

He leads me inside. My mother is sitting on the sofa, her dark glasses perched on her nose. She removes them.

Her eyes are bright red. She steps forward shyly and hugs me. I stiffen, my bags dangling at the end of my arms. Luckily, Dad thinks to take them from me. I have taken root, like a bonsai tree, I can't move. My mother is as speechless as I am. Even if I try to speak, nothing comes out. I'm frozen like a statue. It's Dad who starts talking, which is unusual because he is the most untalkative person I know. He obviously prepared his speech in advance; he hates ad-libbing. Apparently, after writing to me, Mum was so distraught that she ended up telling him the whole story. He describes how numb, appalled and angry he was.

"Your father was in such a state that he pulled up all his rose bushes!" my mother chips in.

Dad doesn't take his eyes off me. He continues to talk. He tells me how he felt so dazed, trying to make sense of it all. How could he have lost his daughter without realizing it? How could he have continued to laugh, smile and garden without realizing that I was sinking lower and lower into the abyss? How could his wife have lied to him all those years?

He gets lost in the details; he sobs and talks about Emily, our childhood, the pretty little blond girl I was, and his phone call to the headmistress.

"I have devoted my life to caring for others but failed to save my own daughter. You were utterly lost, and I didn't come looking for you . . ."

His voice wavers and then fades, washed away by his tears. This is not the unshakeable rock that I remember, but a humble white-haired little man. It suddenly hits me how much my father loves me. He is weak and fragile but not afraid to cry. He can't stop sobbing, like a small child.

I wish I could say something, but my throat is in knots. I hug him tightly and dry his tears with my fingertips.

"It's okay Dad," I whisper. "It's over now, it was all a long time ago. I'm better now. I'm sorry for not trusting you. I should have confided in you, but I was too afraid."

My mother gently hushes me and rather awkwardly hugs us both. We let the silence heal our wounds and dry our tears.

"We must never lose each other again," my mother whispers. "Do you hear me both of you?" She reaches for her dark glasses to hide her bloodshot eyes, but drops them instead. In my clumsy attempt to retrieve them, I end up standing on them. The arm splinters. She throws them straight in the bin without so much as a murmur.

Then we become aware of the afternoon sun, and the cries and shouts of our neighbours. People are singing, crying, screaming, as if the whole country is having one big massive party. France has just beaten Argentina!

"Why don't we all have dinner together with the children?" I suggest.

My father shakes his head. "I think there has been enough emotion for one day. I don't want the little ones to see us like this. Catherine's eyes are red and I don't feel so well. Elliot knows we're here; tell him we'll pick you up tomorrow for lunch. They mustn't know about all this. It's grown-up business."

They kiss me one last time. I watch them climb down the stairs adorned with Post-its, crushed by the weight of the years of unsaid family secrets. Now it's my turn to go down. One by one, I peel off the colourful petals of forgiveness. I stick them one on top of the other: ten, twenty, thirty, forty, one hundred. Once I'm back in my apartment, I arrange them into a bouquet and place them in the drawer of my bedside table. I shall treasure them forever. Outside, the clamour doesn't subside. "Vive la France" echoes from the windows of apartments near and far. I hear footsteps on the stairs, the door opens, Elliot and Lea burst in, their faces painted red, white and blue, shouting, "We won!"

My phone vibrates.

Dear Morgan, the last few weeks have been dreadfully busy. A veterinary conference last week, several trips back and forth to Bordeaux—I'll explain. July is approaching, please don't go on holiday without having dinner with me, even if you are ill or have a cold. Name the date. L

55

Elliot

I shall never forget the 15th of July 2018 as long as I live. We shouted, danced, had the fright of our lives, laughed, held hands, sang, and cried with joy. We were all at Antoine's house; me, my classmates, their parents, Morgan, and Lea. Mum would have said we were *packed in like sardines*. The heat was suffocating but we were so excited we didn't care. When we finally won, when we were absolutely sure that victory was ours, we all jumped up and screamed until we lost our voices. In the street people were waving flags, yelling and partying too. We turned the TV up full blast, so as not to miss any of it, and then proudly sang the national anthem. We had our arms around each other's shoulders and we were all wearing our team shirts, which are now missing a second star. Sat there with Alex and Antoine, I realized that life often works out; it's been nearly a year since we lost Mum and Dad, but, thanks to the World Cup, I almost managed not to think about it. I did cry of course, because Dad wasn't there to celebrate with us, but they were mixed tears of joy and sadness. Despite being German, he would have been so happy that France won! I began shouting, "Vive la France!" with the little bit of voice I had left, to stop having sad thoughts about Dad. Morgan was laughing with Lea, who was dancing like a wild thing, draped in a flag. My little sister didn't understand a thing about the match, just that we had won. I left my mates to go and dance with her, and we laughed till our sides split. We were sweating so much that all our make-up ran everywhere, but it didn't matter.

We all trooped downstairs. The atmosphere in the street was crazy. There was music playing and there were people everywhere, laughing and singing the national anthem. We were even allowed to throw some firecrackers and danced in the multicoloured ocean of colour, feeling like we could do anything we wanted. We ran around and danced, until Morgan wanted us to go home. But we could still hear the party from the apartment. It was like we were hovering high above it like when we fly our kite. It was magic. I'll remember it for the rest of my life.

Morgan defrosted a pizza, and we ate it around the small kitchen table. "So, did you like it at camp this week?" she asked.

"Oh yes, the dance class was fab," answered Lea. "What did you think of our show, Morgan?"

"You were wonderful, Lea, a real ballet dancer!"

Lea had a massive grin over her face.

Unbelievable, she wasn't *that* amazing! She really thinks she is a star, but all she did was dress up in ballet shoes and a pink frilly tutu and lift her leg up, while holding onto a bar. She twirled a bit and then everyone clapped.

I can see our suitcases ready in our room. Tomorrow we fly to Munich on our own to see our grandparents. Lea looks a bit sad. Just as she is about to go to bed, she finally spits it out.

"Morgan, what about you, what will you do when we are away?"

"I have no choice. I have to stay until the nursery closes."

"But you'll be bored!"

"I would have preferred to come of course, but I have so much work to finish before the holidays . . ." explains Morgan.

"So, we're not going to see you at all for two weeks?" whimpers Lea.

"No, but I'll call you. And you'll send me a postcard I hope?"

"I promise," says Lea. Calmer now, she adds, "Morgan, will you put flowers on Mummy and Daddy's grave too? It's nearly one year since . . ."

I didn't dare ask her myself. Morgan goes pale.

I close my eyes and see Mbappé scoring, Griezmann, Pogba, Pavard, Giroud, all my heroes holding up the Cup, and I feel a bit better. They spur me on. I open my eyes again. Morgan nods, then strokes Lea's hair, smiling. I wish she was coming with us. We would have shown her the lake, the house, the kayak and the diving board, and she would have loved it all. Morgan leans over Lea and starts singing:

Twinkle twinkle my little star
I wonder where the sweet dreams are.
Up above the world so high,
Time to close your big brown eyes.
Twinkle twinkle my little star,
Dream sweet dreams my pretty Lea.

That was Mum's song! Lea is beaming. She asks Morgan how she knows Mum's song.

Morgan laughs. "It's not actually your mum's song; it's Grandma Cat's," she tells us. "She used to sing her version of it to us when we were small."

"But I put it on my list to Father Christmas," protests Lea.

"Well maybe the list got sent to me instead."

"What about me? If Lea has her song, can I have a cuddle?" I chip in.

Morgan takes me in her arms and hugs me tightly. She ruffles my hair. "I'm going to miss you, you know," she whispers.

"Me too and I'm going to miss Snoopy."

"You'll probably miss Snoopy more than me!" she laughs as she leaves the room.

I sit there in the dark. I can still hear cries of joy ringing in my ears. I see flags waving; the cup being lifted and France as world champion. I drift away. I'm in a huge stadium, playing football with Opa Georg and Grandpa Paul. We're losing, then suddenly out of nowhere comes Dad and he passes the ball to me. I score and we win; it's the best day of my life! I throw myself into Dad's arms, but it's horrible, he's as cold as ice! I jump back and he is all black and white. His hair, his skin, his teeth, everything is a greyish colour. I'm scared, I want to leave, but he takes my hand and holds me tight. I'm cold, yet I stay there not daring to move until I start to warm up again and feel better. I huddle up against him, breathing in his smell, and give him a kiss. When I finally dare to take a look, his eyes are brown again and his hair is blond. He is back to normal again.

"Dad, you're there, you're back!"

I squeeze him with all my might, I never want to lose him again. I wish this moment would last forever.

"It'll be alright son, you've done the hardest part, I'm proud of you," he says, in his nice familiar accent.

He puts his arm around me and says, "I will always be there for you, I promise. Listen to the wind, it will talk to you about me. Look for me in the stars. I'm one of them now. Some have been dead for a long time, but they still light your way at night."

And he disappears. I wake up with a start. Through the window, I can see the wind shaking the trees and my dream comes back to me. If only I had a butterfly net to catch it with. Then I could put it in a jar and hide it under my pillow. And keep it forever.

56

Morgan

Today is really dragging . . . time seems to have stood still. I'm nervous as hell thinking about tonight and the minutes seem like hours. Suddenly a wave of panic sweeps over me. I don't want to go; my stomach is churning.

I'm having dinner with Lancelot tonight. What if I disappoint him? In fact I *know* I'll disappoint him. He'll see me as boring, meek, inexperienced, prudish, and uptight. He might just get up and leave. I need time, but what if he is not willing to wait? He might want to rush things. What if he were to discover my murky past, what then? Should I tell him everything? I went through my wardrobe at least ten times, searching for something to wear, but I have nothing suitable. All my clothes are too baggy, too dull, too long, too *me*. I ran to the department store last night in desperation. A kind sales assistant turned me into a princess with the help of a gorgeous floral print dress; it's not black and it's not long, but it's also not too fussy or too ridiculous. And it's not too "young girl in the flower of her youth" either, although that's actually how I feel right now. Timid, anxious, Cinderella finally ready for the ball . . . eighteen years later. And what if we take things further? I think about it day and night. I can't lie to him; I will have to tell him the truth. I have been a prisoner of my past for too long now. It took me eighteen years to release myself, I can't go through that again. Not telling Elliot and Lea is different, they're just kids. My duty is to protect them from the harshness of the adult world. I can't spare Lancelot though; I will have to tell him. Even if it means losing him. I've been sleeping alone for a hundred years, I'm prepared to wait for the right Prince Charming to wake me up. I won't broach the subject on our first date though. It's obviously still very delicate. When he says, "Now tell me about yourself, Morgan," I shan't jump right in with, "Glad you asked. When I was seventeen . . ." No, of course not. But it will be soon. And it will either make or break us.

I glance at my watch. It's 6 o'clock already! Time has suddenly speeded up. I do the rounds and check on each group; I greet the parents and hear the musical hearse pull up.

"Let's get him a new CD for Christmas," I whisper to Amara and Delphine. "I can't take this music every day all next year as well."

Delphine laughs but Amara is already singing along to Dalida's greatest hits in a fit of giggles. I walk towards my office, but as I'm about to open the door to the cloakroom, I overhear two people deep in discussion. I don't need to see them to know who it is. My hand remains on the door handle.

"You know that Alice often talks about the merry-go-round ride she had with Lucas!"

"Really?" says Valerie.

"Of course not, she can't speak! But if she could, she would . . . A great time was had by all!"

I hear Valerie chuckling, followed by one of those awkward silences that make you blush. One of those moments when you both look towards a window, neither one daring to make the first move.

"I'm delighted to see you looking so much better, I really am," Jean-Michel says.

Though I can't see them, I imagine Valerie smiling and starry-eyed, savouring the moment, dreaming of what might come next. Like all those who come within a hair's breadth of death, she is clearly grabbing the present with both hands.

"And I was wondering if you would be free for dinner sometime?" he adds, encouraged by her silence.

I can just see her blushing now. Lea would draw the scene to perfection: a giant in shining armour with "boom boom" written on his heart; a beaming princess, her hair hidden under a headdress, butterflies around her eyes, a black steed in place of the hearse and there you go! A piece of sticky tape here, another one there and now the lovers are stuck on her bedroom wall. My heart beats fast, I need to hear the rest. Please don't turn him down!

"Yes, I would love to," she replies. "My mother will be staying for a week. She can babysit Lucas. Is Friday evening okay for you?"

"Yes, perfect!" he beams.

And the knight in shining armour opens the door to let his beloved through, nearly crushing me in the process. The lovebirds look at me, giggling happily. I return to my office. Shortly afterwards I hear the hearse leaving. This time the voice of Johnny Hallyday bellows out of the speakers. Jean-Michel has changed his CD at last!

I promise you the savour of my kiss.

I laugh to myself as I pour my tea. Jean-Michel, who would have thought it? At least Valerie should get the message loud and clear . . . I hear a church bell ring seven times. My hand slips, scalding me. I'm playing Cinderella tonight, and have no desire to turn into a pumpkin at the twelfth stroke of midnight. In the cloakroom, I hear footsteps hurrying, doors slamming, and children shouting. Then the nursery is finally silent. I do a final check, turn off the lights and close up.

On my way home, I call Elliot and Lea who bombard me with kisses down the phone. Once I'm back at the apartment, my transformation into a princess can begin. I style my hair and do my make-up. I hardly recognize myself. Snoopy pokes his wet nose between my legs in encouragement. I decide to take him along too. After all, I do have an appointment with a vet. And holding his lead will give me confidence. When I arrive at the restaurant, I can just make out Lancelot sitting outdoors on the terrace. I walk up to him and he greets me with a big smile. The sparkle in his eyes tells me that I will never need to lie again.

ONE YEAR LATER

AFTERWORD

ELLIOT

Dear Mum,

It's been so long since I last wrote to you. I even left blank pages in my diary in case I got time to fill them in later. So much has happened, I don't know where to begin.

I'll be starting Year 6 on Monday and can't wait! I like my school, I like my friends. Last year I was in charge of the student journal. It's thanks to you that I love writing so much. I'm trying to do as much as I can now, because we might be moving soon. I like it here in Batignolles, it's my home now, but the place we are going to is amazing. It's a big house with dogs everywhere.

I'd better tell you what's happened.

You know Morgan's dream was to open a boarding kennels for dogs? Well, she's almost there. Do you remember the vet Lancelot? His friend who ran a dog kennels near Paris has just retired. Lancelot used to help her out a lot and take care of the dogs when they were sick. When he heard she was retiring, he told Morgan she should apply. And guess what, she got the job! She talked a lot about it to us. She was worried about uprooting us from Paris and taking us away from you and Dad again. I knew that she would refuse the job if me and Lea didn't want to go. We went to visit it and it reminded us a bit of our old house. By train it's no further than Maisons-Laffitte, so we can still see our old friends. You should have seen the massive smile on Morgan's face when we told her we liked it and could imagine living there. She hasn't given them her answer yet, but I think she will say yes.

She will be sad to leave the nursery, and especially Viviane, who she calls her guardian angel. But Viviane is leaving too. Her boyfriend Matthew has just got a grant to open a sports club for children in need. We met him. He is mega cool, you should see his muscles! Viviane is going to work with him. I hope it will work out okay for her as well as for Morgan, because she's the nicest lady I've ever met. I know we will see her again because she and Morgan have become really close friends.

You know what? Lancelot is going to work at the kennels too. He will take care of the dogs when they are sick. But that's not the only reason. He and Morgan are in love and they are going to get married! They just told us. Grandma Cat will be thrilled. Talking of lovebirds, remember that huge man with a beard at the nursery? He was there at your funeral. Well he is now in love with the mum who is late every evening. And the way she looks at him, I think she is too. He drops off the two kids in his hearse every morning.

Lea was thrilled when she heard about the wedding. She begged Morgan to let her be her bridesmaid. Morgan was delighted and said of course. She agreed to let Lea wear flowers in her hair and carry a bouquet too.

There was something else I wanted to ask them, but didn't dare. Luckily Lea came straight out with it.

"So does this mean you're going to have babies?" she asked all excited.

Morgan laughed, so did Lancelot.

"I don't think so," she said. "I already have two children in my life and I'm very happy as I am."

"What about Lancelot?" asked Lea.

"Lancelot has his daughter, so altogether we are a family of five."

"No, six!" said Lea indignantly. "You forgot Snoopy!"

I think Lea wanted them to have a baby, but I'm glad they're not. We're a family now. We may be stuck together with

Sellotape, but I love my family. Lancelot's daughter Laura has just turned eighteen, she is nice and often visits us during the holidays. When I think how Lancelot didn't even dare phone her before! Grown-ups are stupid sometimes. Look at me giving good advice. Maybe it's all thanks to the owl! Laura wants to become a vet too, so she might stay with us, as there will be a lot of work. Oma Annett and Opa Georg said they would come too. We haven't told Grandma Cat and Grandpa Paul yet because they have gone to Vietnam for six months to work in an orphanage. They got this sudden urge to pack their bags and go there. They send us photos by email. I wonder how Grandma Cat is coping because there are no geraniums, no roses, no balconies, no nail varnish, and no sea view. And worst of all there are huge cockroaches everywhere, day and night; they're even in the toilets. The thought of Grandma Cat in her flip flops amongst the cockroaches is very funny. But they look happy. They even sent a photo that really knocked Morgan for six. It was Linh. I recognized her instantly. Morgan has promised she will take us there one day too. When I think of all those awful things I imagined about Linh, when in fact it was all quite simple.

I don't want you to be sad, Mum. Morgan and Lancelot will never replace you and Dad. And Lea agrees. Lancelot even said it himself. His actual words were: "I'm not your father, kids, but I want you to know that I will always be there for you." I think it was a nice thing to say. Lea couldn't help but ask him if he would really stay with us forever. He replied that he and Morgan had been through enough to know that they would stay together for the rest of their lives. Morgan then squeezed his hand as if they were sharing a secret.

I'm not afraid of moving house again because this time we won't be losing anything like before, just building something better. Besides, wherever we go, you will always be in my heart.

Sometimes when I'm sad, I listen to the wind and I search for you both in the stars.

Mum, Dad, I love you so much. Please look after us from heaven.

Elliot

P.S: I'm putting one of Lea's drawings between the pages. You will recognize Morgan, Lancelot, Snoopy, and of course Lea and me. The tall girl is Laura. You are both stars, the ones that are smiling. It's raining and the sun is shining as well. The raindrops are all different colours. You see, Lea is just like you.

Acknowledgments

I can't begin to describe the emotion I felt when I finished writing this novel. I am particularly fond of it and it might never have seen the light of day without the help of the many wonderful people I met along the way. I would love to stick thousands of Post-it notes everywhere, saying THANK YOU to them all. So here they are.

THANK YOU first of all to François, for believing in me and giving me that push from the very start. Without you, none of my novels would have seen the light of day.

THANK YOU to Corentin, Clément and Martin, my three little treasures and my constant source of inspiration, who never hesitate to give me advice.

THANK YOU to my parents, my brother and my sister for being so supportive of me throughout this journey. You read, re-read, listened, and reworked many details, never letting your enthusiasm wane. THANK YOU.

THANK YOU to Marabout and to La Belle Étoile, especially Christine, my editor, for her kindness, her subtle and astute editing and her invaluable advice; Hélène, for choosing me, and Béatrice, for everything . . .

I would like to thank my very first readers for playing the role of editorial critic with such enthusiasm each time: Mum, Annabelle, Aurélie, Paul, Ségolène . . .

Thanks also to my talented brainstorming team: Lucie, Lucile, Sophie, Émilie, Isabelle and Marie-Odile in Athens. We finally came up with a great title!

I am very grateful to the people with whom I consulted regarding technical details: Sylvie, the incredible midwife who shared with me the emotional experience of a "secret" birth. Dad, for his obstetrical knowledge; Adeline, for relating her experiences in assisting teenage mothers; Diane and Marie, for questions relating to day nurseries.

Finally, I wish to extend my heartfelt thanks to all of the readers of my first novel who encouraged me to continue this fabulous adventure, and especially the bloggers who supported me when I was still an unknown author, and the French community in Munich who were a great help.

As I write these words, my thoughts go out to the mother in my neighbourhood suffering from cancer, whom I have never dared speak to. I was so happy to see that her hair is growing back. And to the pale-eyed girl, who came into my life and left it again just as quickly, who gave birth in France before leaving without a trace.

Please feel free to contact me on Instagram (aurelietramier_ auteur) or Facebook (@aurelietramier.auteur).

See you soon!
Aurélie

Credits